FREEDOM'S JUST ANOTHER WORD...

LEN JOY

PRAISE FOR LEN JOY'S FREEDOM'S JUST ANOTHER WORD

Chicago, all its energy and warts intact, is alive and well in Len Joy's new novel, Freedom's Just Another Word. It is perhaps his most ambitious work to date, teeming with Mr. Joy's familiar crowd of quirky, vividly drawn characters who revolve around the central figure of Jake Doyle, a once prominent and now faded star columnist for the Chicago Tribune, whose reputation is tarnished by an ill-fated affair. Mr. Joy skirts issues of closeness to contemporary themes and concerns and a possible recognition of character types with his usual mastery of description, dialogue and place.

He remains a master fiction writer, and I always look forward to seeing new work from him.

GARY D. WILSON, *AUTHOR OF THE NOVELS SING, RONNIE BLUE AND GETTING RIGHT.* HIS NEXT NOVEL, *THE NARROW WINDOW,* IS DUE OUT IN FEBRUARY 2024.

It's been a long time since I've read a novel in one sitting, but Freedom's Just Another Word would not let me go; it is simply a fascinating "page-turner" in the purest definition of the term. I'm usually not a big fan of first-person narrative, but author Len Joy uses the lead character Jake to tell a fascinating story that hits all the current societal hot spots in the United States today. Everything from gun control to racism to women's rights, the fickle justice system, and political intrigue is covered through Jake's eyes and experiences as he tries to juggle all the balls without dropping any.

The best book I've read this year.

Joy's outstanding latest novel takes readers on a columnist's journey as he struggles to survive in the newspaper world of the 21st century after his fall from grace years earlier. Jake Doyle was at the top of his career when he fell in love with his much younger intern, throwing his career into a downward spiral. Now years later, Jake is divorced and is struggling to make ends meet as Chicago Tribune columnist and part-time Uber driver.

Joy imbues the plot with a sense of urgency and he beautifully conjures nuanced characters who will stay in readers' minds for a long time, expertly weaving together their stories.

Although corruption and political intrigue make for a major part of the plot, it's family, friendship, love, human connection, and self-discovery that remain at the heart of the story. As the novel builds toward its heartwarming climax, it also delves into highly-charged issues of me-too moment and misogyny. Jammed with terrific characters, expert prose, and an overall feel-good wholesomeness, **this is a book to savor.**

Len Joy cultivates a gritty form of self-realization in his character which makes him both flawed and likeable from the beginning.

Joy's ability to traverse the social and political tides of Jake's environment brings readers directly into contact with its disparate forces, from boxing and exes to adult children who are also finding their way in their lives.

Readers who enter his life to absorb Jake's first-person revelations about his scattered relationships with job and life will find in Jake many of the components of their own psyches; especially in moments which teeter on the fine edge of failure or success.

Jake's return to his writing prowess in producing a column which is both enlightening and highly controversial opens new doors of opportunity he and his readers won't see coming.

Against the backdrops of boxing, fighting for identity, and confronting self and family lies the astute, vividly realistic story of a man who attempts to reveal and save others while making difficult choices to do the same for himself.

Freedom's Just Another Word is highly recommended for libraries and readers looking for powerfully compelling fiction about middle-aged characters who face real-world danger, the impossibility of fairy-tale endings, and the promise that tomorrow will be different. Maybe.

DIANE DONOVAN - *MIDWEST REVIEW*

Front cover design by Tim Barber, dissectdesigns.com

Interior Design by Danielle H Acee, authorsassistant.com

ISBN: 9798585924699

ONE

WEDNESDAY, 4:30 P.M. — FEBRUARY 14, 2018

Evanston Township High School

I used to be famous.

Not traffic-stopping, movie-star famous. Newspaper-famous. That's a lower bar. My column in the *Chicago Tribune*—"Jake's Corner"—used to be syndicated in 200 papers. Back in '98 I was nominated for a Pulitzer for my reports on corruption in the city council. But then the wheels came off.

When the *Trib* was sold last year, the new owners cut me back to two columns a week at a fraction of what I had been making. I'm driving for Uber just to pay the rent on the tired ranch house I moved into last year when Tawni and I split.

I had a deadline in eight hours, and I didn't know what to write about. I had hoped one of my customers would inspire me, but I had to pick up my daughter. Her car was in the shop because she rear-ended an Evanston cop and picked up her third DUI in two years. Girl's never had much luck. She teaches journalism at Evanston Township to kids who have never read a newspaper.

Inspiration is unlikely.

When I pulled up to the corner of Dodge and Church, Charlotte was waiting for me next to a mountain of snow the plows had deposited after last week's blizzard. She was so not like her mother.

By design.

They were both blonde, but that's where the resemblance ended. Tawni was statuesque and fashion-savvy, and she had a disarmingly beautiful smile. Charlotte was built like me—not statuesque—and she also had my fashion sense—our prime objective being comfort. She didn't smile much; her natural countenance resembled a scowl, which she called "resting bitch face."

And, of course, Tawni would have never been waiting for me— that would be a waste of her precious time. The queen waits for no one.

"So, how's the world of high school journalism today?" I asked as Charlotte slipped into the front seat.

Resting bitch face transitioned into a full-blown scowl. "For kids who grew up with Twitter and Snapchat, you'd think they'd be able to write a decent story in less than three hundred words." She buckled her seat belt and threw her bag in the back seat. "Can you drop me off at the garage? My car's ready."

"Sure. Dexter Auto, right?" I knew that. I was just stalling as I summoned the courage to ask the question I had to ask. "How's rehab?" I gripped the steering wheel a little tighter, anticipating an outburst. The court had sentenced Charlotte to a counseling program.

She surprised me with her mild response. "It's not rehab. It's more like an AA meeting with a driver safety theme. I've got four more weeks." She sighed. "I wasn't driving drunk, Dad. I'd had a couple of drinks, and I glanced down to turn on the radio when that cop stopped for no reason."

"I thought you'd given up the booze." I wasn't judging her. I love drinking. Giving up alcohol would be hard for me. Probably impossible.

"That was the first drink I had in almost two years." She laughed bitterly. "I was celebrating."

"Celebrating?"

She looked at me with an I've-got-a-secret look. "I was accepted at Stanford Law. I was so happy when I got the news, I bought a bottle of champagne. I had a couple glasses, then poured out the bottle. I knew I was being stupid."

"Stanford Law? That's fantastic! I didn't know you wanted to be a lawyer."

"I didn't tell anyone. Not even Greg. It was a long shot. There aren't many thirty-one-year-old first-year law students."

"What about Greg?"

She shrugged. "After the DUI, he dumped me. I don't blame him."

Greg, her erstwhile boyfriend, was a science teacher at the high school. They had been going out for two years but seemed to break up every other month.

"He'll be back," I said.

She shook her head. "Not this time. He quote unquote 'met a more compatible partner.' On Tinder." She laughed.

"Tinder?"

"It's a dating app. You should try it. Better than trolling the bars. Especially at your age."

I ignored the age jibe. "I'm not ready to date. Are you okay?"

She gave me her Tawni *are-you-crazy?* look. Okay, she got some things from her mother. "You mean about Greg? Yeah. I'm cool. We weren't right for each other. And he would never move to Palo Alto."

I agreed with that assessment, but I knew better than to say so because chances are next week they'd be back together.

As I headed up Green Bay Road, we passed the storefront my son Devante had moved his rib business into last year. A hand-painted sign —*Just Ribs*—was tacked up above the smudged windows.

My fall from grace had been all on me. I fell in love with someone I wasn't supposed to fall in love with. She was twenty-one; I was thirty-five and married. She was my intern. She had a baby. We named him Devante.

I'm supposed to say I was wrong. That I made a mistake and I'm sorry. But I loved Monique and I love my son. My heart wanted something it couldn't have. I don't think that makes it wrong, just impossible. I have no regrets.

Devante's twenty now and he's a good man. Better than I am. He has big plans just like his mother did. He's going to be one of those celebrity chefs someday. Even though I didn't raise him I've been a part of his life, and I'm grateful for that.

"Devante needs a better sign," I said.

"He's going for that 'hood' vibe," Charlotte said. "He's developing a real following. Everyone loves Antoinette's special Jamaican rub."

Antoinette, Monique's Jamaican mother, was Devante's legal guardian. Two summers ago, after his high school graduation, he started cooking Jamaican ribs in her kitchen and selling them from a food cart. A year ago, he rented that rundown storefront on Green Bay. The kid had ambition to burn.

We were stopped at the corner of Green Bay and Central. The 435 from the loop had just left the Central Street station, and passengers were streaming across the street even though the light had changed. Everyone anxious to get home. It didn't make me nostalgic for my commuter days.

"Hey, your mom is getting an award this weekend. One of those right-wing think tanks she works with—they're naming her 'Person of the Year.' A banquet at the Hyatt. She wants us to attend."

Charlotte looked terror-stricken. "You want me to have dinner with a bunch of right-wing, right-to-life Trumpsters? Are you out of your fucking mind?"

"It's for your mother. She wants you there."

That's sort of a lie. She didn't actually ask for Charlotte, but I'm sure she would be pleased if her daughter showed up.

"No way she wants me there. I'm a heathen who supports baby-killing. Besides, she's not talking to me. We had a huge fight on Sunday."

I could see that my family unity tactic wasn't working, so I adroitly shifted gears. "Come on. We liberal Democrats need to stick together. Don't make me go in there solo."

Now her terror face had been replaced by disgust. "You're a DINO, Dad."

"You mean like a dinosaur?"

"Democrat in Name Only. God, you probably voted for Trump."

That was hurtful—and untrue. I don't even know why I wanted her to go. Throughout her high school years all I did was referee fights between her and her mother, but I guess I clung to the illusion, or delusion, that we were a family. It was nostalgia for a past that didn't even exist.

"Okay, forget I asked." I pulled into the Dexter Auto parking lot. I stared straight ahead, pouting. It was my final card.

She threw up her hands.. "Okay. I'll go if you agree to talk with my journalism class."

"Great. I'd be delighted to talk to your class. Maybe I can convince them to pursue another profession. It's Sunday night at six. I'll text you the details."

TWO

Charcoal Oven

It was snowing hard when I pulled into the Skokie Hampton Inn. Fat, wet flakes that would be hell to shovel. Golf Road was a mess. The plows couldn't keep up. Huge banks of snow lined the edge of the hotel parking lot. I hate snow. It makes this part-time Uber gig a full-time pain in the ass. I swung around to the entrance and popped the trunk. A big investment banker conference was underway at the Orrington Hotel in Evanston, and I had been driving bankers to and from the hotel since I dropped off Charlotte.

My passenger—in her early thirties just like Charlotte—had been on her phone since I picked her up in front of the Orrington. She was still wearing her name tag: *Hi I'm Jennifer from Goldman Sachs.* Her nametag was a lot more friendly than she was. For the twenty minutes it took me to get from downtown Evanston to Skokie she chewed out the poor schmuck who had messed up her reservation. Apparently, there were no vacancies at any of the other hotels in the area, so she was stuck out in Skokie at a "goddamn tacky Hampton Inn."

I set her bag on the curb under the entrance awning. Couldn't have weighed ten pounds. Millennial women know how to pack. Not like my ex. We'd go on an overnight getaway, and Tawni would have two saddlebags stuffed with documents and a full suitcase. She's a pro-life activist, so she could never travel light. Too many souls to save.

Jennifer from Goldman Sachs pulled out the Rollaboard handle. "Thank you," she said, and gave me a smile that might have been sincere. When I was younger, a woman smiled at me, and I would think it meant something. Sometimes it did. But after Devante was born, I stopped fooling around. I guess he made me grow up. You could say that Monique and Devante saved my marriage because Tawni refused to let me go. She was stubborn like that.

Until last year.

It wasn't another woman or booze that broke us up. I had stopped trying, and Tawni found a better model. Someone who gave a damn. I'm fifty-five now and I know my limitations. I can't drink all day and then pound out a story in ninety minutes. With Monique gone and Tawni out of the picture, I might be tempted to indulge my weakness for younger women, but I know I'm invisible to ninety-nine percent of them. I'm okay with that. Invisible's better than the alternative.

When Tawni and I split up, we sold our house in Glenview. I rented a foreclosure special in Skokie, and Tawni moved in with her new boyfriend—a wealthy lawyer who had an impressive lakefront mansion in Evanston.

I warned her that the Evanston city council had declared it to be a nuclear-free zone, and most of the cars still had their Obama-Biden bumper stickers. They weren't going to welcome a right-to-life activist. But she didn't listen. No surprise there. Evanston had a squad of parking enforcement Nazis and cryptic parking rules. ("No parking on the second Tuesday of the month from October to March," and so on.) Tawni would have been buried in $100 parking violations, so she let me have the Chrysler.

It's not a bad car for Uber: charcoal gray so it resembles a limo and has plenty of leg room and comfortable seats. Not as posh as a Lexus, or as economical as a Prius—the car of choice for most drivers—but it works for me. The Uber app beeped. Jennifer rated me five stars and gave me a five-buck tip. God bless expense accounts. I brushed off the road slush that had accumulated on the windshield. My shoes were wet from wading through the snow at the hotel entrance, and my feet were getting cold.

It wasn't late, but my deadline was in less than four hours. That used to be more than enough time even if I was half-in-the-bag, but those days were gone. Everything took longer now. My brain was slowing down. I decided to head over to the Charcoal Oven for some inspiration. It's my favorite bar—only five blocks from my home, so if I get seriously shit-faced I can walk home. My buddy Enyart is the bartender.

The Charcoal Oven is an old-fashioned supper club, like from the '50s. Cozy little dining room with a no-frills bar for your serious drinker. No dining customers tonight, but there were two thirty-some-thing women at the end of the bar arguing. They were an odd couple. One Black, one White. The Black gal, who had a close-cropped Afro, was wearing baggy jeans and a flannel shirt and was built like a line-backer. Her friend was a slender redhead with what I would have called a Dorothy Hamill hairstyle, but I'm sure that just dates me. Whatever, she was cute and dressed very corporate.

The linebacker was angry. "I can't believe you, Amanda," she said, her voice a low hiss.

Enyart was hanging at the other end of the bar watching the televi-sion. I was surprised; it was tuned to CNN instead of ESPN.

I walked past the ladies, who didn't notice me, and sat down across from Enyart. "Bulls win?" I asked, knowing that would get a response.

Enyart stared at me, feigning disgust. "Who cares? They suck." He grabbed the Crown Royal from the top shelf and poured a shot for me. "If they armed those teachers, this wouldn't happen."

"What?" I looked up at the screen. A covered body was being wheeled out of a school. The ticker at the bottom of the screen read, *17 Killed in Florida High School Shooting.* "Damn. Another school shooting?"

"Another punk with a gun. I'm just waiting for the CNN douchebags to blame Trump for this too."

Every liberal columnist in America would be writing about gun control tomorrow. That's why I loved arguing with Enyart. His over-the-top observations often helped me find a fresh angle for a news story. I fired a shot that was bound to get a response.

"Maybe instead of more weapons, we try getting rid of all the guns. This doesn't happen in the U.K."

Enyart started wiping the bar down with a vengeance. "Jesus, Jake. When are you going to get your head out of your ass and drop that liberal bullshit? Married thirty years and you didn't learn a goddamn thing from that wife of yours?"

Enyart loved everything about Tawni: her hot bod, her take-no-prisoners attitude, and her right-wing, let-them-eat-cake philosophy. The feeling was not mutual. Enyart was too crude for my ex.

"Even Tawni would agree that if you make it harder to have a gun, maybe there would be fewer innocent bystanders killed."

Like Monique. Shot while waiting for the Damen bus. Wrong place. Wrong time. Instead of savoring the whiskey, I chugged it and pushed the glass back to Enyart for a refill. "You need to work on your bartender skills. I don't think you've grasped the concept of empathy."

"Gun control!?" His voice almost broke as he refilled my glass. "Like they have in Norway, right?"

I knew he was setting me up, but I played along.

"Yeah, Norway doesn't have much crime."

Enyart stared at me, bug-eyed. "Remember when that crazy Norwegian slaughtered sixty kids who were on an island retreat? Outlawing guns really helped them. I guess the shooter didn't get the memo telling him it was illegal to have an AK-47." He dared me to offer some defense. "Now that fucker's sitting in some country club prison complaining about his meal plan. Son-of-a-bitch will be out in five years!"

I had the feeling he was exaggerating, but Enyart read everything left- and right-wing, so I didn't challenge him. I vaguely remembered that massacre and made a mental note to check it out later. Could be something there I could use.

"How come you're not watching Fox?" Enyart was not hard-core right-wing like my ex. He could be even more profane about some of the bloviators on Fox than the ones on CNN. And he had some surprisingly liberal tendencies. He had a live-and-let-live attitude on all matters of personal choice, whether it be a woman's right to choose or gay marriage or drugs. He just believed if you chose to fuck up your life you should live with the consequences. His day job was running a gym in Uptown where he taught kids to box and tried to keep them off the streets and out of the gangs. He'd been a Marine—awarded a Silver Star during Desert Storm—and after that mini-war was over he spent a couple years boxing for the Marines. I met him in 1994 at the Chicago Golden Gloves Tournament in Cicero.

He leaned closer to me and attempted to whisper. "The lesbians asked me to turn it to CNN." He grinned slyly and stepped back, sizing me up. "You need to get back in the gym. You're getting an Uber gut."

"I know. I'm not in your weight class anymore. Guess we'll never get that rematch." Enyart was a fitness nut. Didn't drink or smoke; watched his diet. Still weighed 165 with probably less than ten percent body fat. Still had his Marine haircut and body. Whether he was bartending or working in his gym, he always wore a form-fitting white polo. He must have owned a dozen. He thought of himself as a ladies' man. I would say that assessment was at best a split decision. Most women considered him an outspoken blowhard, but there were some who saw that underneath all his bullshit was a decent guy who would literally give you the shirt off his back.

"I don't mind moving up a class," he said. "How much you weigh now, 190?"

One ninety? Who was he kidding? I gave him the fisheye. "I stopped weighing myself when I broke 200. I'll stick with training. Cornermen don't get hit."

When I was growing up I lived with my mom in an apartment over Flanigan's Bar on Halsted. It was my Uncle Ralph's bar. He ran a sports book on the side. After high school, while I was going to night school at DePaul, I ran the bar and would go along with Ralph if he had a challenging collection. In those days I was in shape. Lifted weights, sparred at Gold's Gym. I was a wannabe Rocky Balboa. I looked tough, but I wasn't. Fortunately looking tough was all that was required. Nowadays I've been helping Enyart train Devante for the Golden Gloves tournament coming up in March.

Enyart laughed. "You were good at not getting hit," he said, his voice gravelly. "Did you sign Devante up? I figure he's too busy with his damn hot dog stand to do it himself."

"Ribs, not hot dogs. He's busy, but he's game. He figures if he wins the tournament it will be good for business. You know, 'Local Rib Czar Packs Punch...' He signed up for Novice 168. It's a tough weight class."

Enyart waved his hand dismissively. "Brawlers, just like you. Devante's got some skills. He just has to remember to use them when he gets in the ring."

"As Mike Tyson said, 'Everyone has a plan till they get punched in the mouth.'"

I was one of Enyart's victims on the way to his Golden Gloves championship back in '94. I was thirty and had entered as part of a feature article I was writing for the *Trib* on weekend warriors. I hadn't done any boxing since I stopped working for Uncle Ralph, but I got myself in shape and figured, being a lefty—there's not that many southpaw boxers—I'd have an edge. If I got a lucky draw, I might win a bout or two. Unluckily, I drew Enyart in my first match. He was fresh out of the Marines, twenty-four years old, and it looked as if he had been chiseled out of granite. I knew I didn't have a prayer before I stepped into the ring.

It was three rounds, and I went the distance, but only because I tied him up every chance I got. I lost in a unanimous decision, but the feature was a hit. Helped me get my column.

There was a crash at the end of the bar as the linebacker gal stood up suddenly, toppling her barstool. "Fuck you, Amanda!" She grabbed her parka and stormed out of the restaurant.

Enyart shook his head. "Happens every other week," he whispered. He turned to the redhead. "Come on down, Mandy. Meet Jake."

The woman grinned at Enyart as she uprighted her girlfriend's barstool. Then she grabbed her backpack and her drink and joined us. The way she was dressed—classy navy-blue suit with two-inch heels—I figured her for a lawyer or one of those investment bankers, like smiling Jennifer from Goldman Sachs.

"Doesn't look like I'm staying with her tonight," she said. She didn't seem too upset about that.

"Mandy, this silver-haired fox is Jake Doyle, a real man of the people," Enyart said.

"The name's Amanda! I told you before, every time you call me Mandy you have to buy me a drink. I want a good whiskey, not that cheap shit Bianca was buying." She turned to me. "What do you recommend?"

"Give her the Crown, Enyart."

Enyart grinned and gave her half a shot. "Here's a taste, A-Man-Duh."

She settled onto the barstool. "You know, you're not an awful bartender, Enyart. You just need guidance." She smiled impishly at him and then turned to me. "Sorry for the scene. My girlfriend's high strung."

"High strung?" Enyart snorted. "Ditch that broad. Try a man. You need a change of pace." He winked again, which was his way of pretending he wasn't serious. But I knew he would be happy to volunteer his services.

She shrugged. "Men are too predictable." She downed the shot and licked her lips, making sure she got every drop. "You're right. I need a change."

"Now you're talking, Mandy!"

"Yes, sir. No more cheap whiskey for me. From now on I'm only drinking the good stuff. And you owe me another drink." She winked back at him.

Enyart grinned and reached for the bottle, but she waved him off.

"Rain check. I have to be in court tomorrow."

"Are you a lawyer?" I asked.

"No, I'm a stenographer. My girlfriend's a lawyer."

"Really?" I didn't want to say that she didn't look like a lawyer, but that's probably what my expression revealed.

"She's legal aid. They don't have much of a dress code."

"Oh, for the love of..." Enyart was glaring at the TV. "What'd I tell ya, Jake? Shithead reporter doesn't blame the shooter. Oh no. Don't blame the fuckhead with the gun. It's society's problem." He pointed his remote at the screen and muted Anderson Cooper.

"Oh my," Amanda said, looking at the scene being replayed for the hundredth time. Her hands cupped her face. "Not another shooting."

Enyart slammed his fist down on the bar. "Shoot a few of those cowards and this would stop. I guarantee it." Enyart's face had turned red. It always did when he got himself worked up.

Hah! I had my inspiration. I figured Amanda would have a strong reaction to Enyart's outburst. It would be a great debate: Gay, liberal, millennial debates a Desert Storm war vet with a Silver Star.

Amanda continued to stare at the screen as if she hadn't even heard Enyart. They were again showing the sheet-draped body being removed from the school on a gurney. "I agree. Kill them all," she said, sounding more sad than angry.

Damn. I didn't expect that. I had assumed Amanda would be totally on the gun control side. A good reporter shouldn't make assumptions like that. I needed a new angle.

"Really? Kill them all?" I asked. "You think arming Miss Grundy is a good idea?"

Amanda looked at me, surprised. "You watch Riverdale?"

"Uh, it was a reference to the Archie comics."

"I know. In the TV show they made Miss Grundy hot," she said, arching her eyebrows. "Do you read comic books?"

"That was a memory from forty years ago. These days the only comic I read is Dilbert."

She wrinkled her nose. Obviously not a Dilbert fan.

"So, you want to arm all the teachers?" I asked. How could anyone think that would be a good idea?

Enyart poked my forearm with his finger. "That's what you liberals are always doing. Creating some kind of straw man to make the idea sound stupid. That was Obama's trick."

"It was?" Enyart had a rough time with Obama. The dude was so smooth, no one could land a punch. It drove him crazy.

He leaned in again and spoke slowly, as if I were a child who just didn't get it. "They don't all have to be armed. Almost every school has some ex-military. If somebody is shooting back it changes the whole ballgame." He took another look over his shoulder at the TV screen. "Look at that chart."

The CNN reporter had finished his on-scene report, and they were back in the studio. A graphic up on the screen read: *Mass Shootings in the U.S.*

Amanda recited the numbers, "Twelve killed in Aurora, Colorado, at a movie theatre. July 2012. Twenty-seven shot at an elementary school in Newton, Connecticut. Sixty killed and 400 wounded in Las Vegas sniper attack. And 49 killed at the Pulse Club in Miami in June 2016." She swallowed hard. "Killed for being gay." She was close to tears.

In the old days I would have reached out and patted her arm or hand or made some kind of contact to show I felt her pain. But I couldn't do that anymore. I turned toward her with my hands clasped together, like our old parish priest. "I don't think more guns will make the situation better."

Enyart made a face. "Gun control won't stop any of those shooters. That's just unilateral disarmament."

Amanda sighed and glanced at her watch. "I need to call a cab." She pressed the phone to her ear and then glared at it and put it down on the bar. "Busy signal. I'll have to use Uber."

Enyart's eyes lit up and before I could stop him, he said, "Jake's an Uber driver. He can drive you. He's got a five-star rating."

Amanda swiveled on her chair and looked at me like I was Santa Claus. "Really? That's the first good thing that's happened to me today."

"Uh…where do you live?"

"South of Waukegan. Just beyond the naval base."

Fuck me. A thirty-mile drive in a blizzard. And a dead haul back. Two hours roundtrip if I'm lucky. That would leave me less than two hours to write my column. "Geez. You've got a long commute."

"I moved back in with my mother and stepfather." She looked down, embarrassed. "It's only temporary," she said softly. "How much will it cost?"

Something told me I should just say no, but if she were my daughter I'd want someone to look out for her. "If you order it through Uber, it will cost you over a hundred. They goose the rates when weather gets bad. I'll charge you fifty dollars cash. That okay?"

She nodded eagerly and gave me a hug. "Thank you so much."

I stood up and grabbed my jacket. "Let's go before the storm gets worse." I pulled out a ten and put it on the bar.

Enyart pushed the bill back to me. "Save your money for a Glock or a Sig Sauer. You need some protection in your line of work."

"Driving's not that dangerous," I said.

"I'm talking about your column-writing. You keep pissing people off."

Amanda stared at me. "Oh my god. You're Jake from 'Jake's Corner'? I love your column."

I know I was probably grinning like a schoolboy, but I couldn't help it. She was so spontaneous I was certain she was sincere.

"Thanks," I said. "I didn't think anyone under thirty read newspapers anymore."

She punched me in the arm. "It's online, dude. And I'm thirty-five."

I turned to Enyart. "I'll see you at the gym tomorrow? You got some time to spend with D?"

"Of course," he said. "We'll get him ready for his match."

THREE

Home

There were no windows in the Charcoal Oven, so when you entered you left the outside world behind. That world had become a raging blizzard. At least six inches of snow had fallen since I arrived. And the wind was roaring. There was no way anyone was driving to Waukegan.

"Oh my god," Amanda said. "Do you think I can get a room at that hotel?" She pointed down the street to the DoubleTree.

"All the hotels are sold out. Some bank conference. How about your girlfriend? Where does she live?"

"East Rogers Park. But she turns her phone off when she gets pissed at me."

I couldn't have made it to Rogers Park even if she could reach her girlfriend. "I live five blocks from here. You can stay in the spare bedroom."

She didn't argue. She was smart enough to know that there were no good options. And she probably figured a guy who was old enough to have read Archie comics was safe.

It took fifteen minutes to cover the five blocks to my place on Kedvale.

"Is this Evanston?" Amanda asked, squinting out the window at the 1950s ranch houses.

"Skokie," I said. "I couldn't afford Evanston."

Amanda didn't have boots, so I pulled all the way up the driveway to the garage. "Do you have a snowblower?" Amanda asked.

"No. I like to shovel." Not exactly the truth. I couldn't afford one.

"Me too. I'll help you shovel tomorrow."

"In those shoes? I don't think so."

She lifted up her backpack. "Running shoes. I'll skip my run. Shoveling is a good workout."

That was cool. I don't think Tawni or Charlotte ever offered to help me shovel. "Hope it stops soon, or you might be regretting that offer."

I guess it would be fair to say that I hadn't finished moving in yet. It's only been a year. My house has three bedrooms upstairs, same as our house in Glenview had. The downstairs has an open floor plan with the kitchen, den, and living room all part of one large L-shaped room with a separate dining room I didn't figure to ever use.

I moved last May. That first day I got the bedrooms squared away, the kitchen set up, arranged all my books on the bookshelves in the den, brought home a thirty-six-inch Sony flatscreen from the Best Buy at the mall, ordered a sectional sofa for the living room, and then…nothing.

I had plans to replace the furniture Tawni had taken, but I never got around to it. Didn't even unpack all the boxes. I should have been thinking of this as a new beginning—the first day of the rest of my life and all that. I hadn't tried very hard to make my marriage work, but I hadn't planned on it ending. I was comfortable living in Glenview, writing my column, sitting out on the patio with a beer and *The New Yorker*. It sounds dull, but it worked. For me, but not for Tawni.

I gave Amanda a quick tour, ignoring her quizzical looks, and then I sat down at the kitchen table with my laptop. Amanda went to the den to watch the news. She was about to turn on the TV when she noticed the only two photos I had managed to unpack and display.

One was a cheesy Olan Mills family portrait with six-year-old Charlotte, missing her front teeth and grinning maliciously on Tawni's lap while I stood behind them with a look of pure adoration. The other was Devante's high school graduation photo.

"Your wife is hot. Who's the Black dude?"

"Ex-wife. That's my son, Devante."

She nodded as she processed what I had just told her. "Must be a story there."

She waited expectantly. Millennials share way too much. No boundaries.

I looked at the wall clock. I had less than three hours to finish my column. "It's a long story. I don't have time tonight."

Her head tilted, trying to read me. "Okay. I can wait."

I still wanted to do my column on her and Enyart, but I needed something more. "I was surprised you agreed with Enyart," I said.

She scowled. "We agree on a lot of things."

"Really? Like what?"

"Bulls suck. Cubs are overrated. Ali was the greatest of all time."

"I was thinking more about politics and social issues."

She gave me that same wrinkled-nose look that she had when I told her I read Dilbert. "I thought you'd be more direct. You're acting like a pussy."

I had to smile at that. "How so?"

"You want to know why I said 'Kill them all.' You think it's because of the gays who were slaughtered at the Pulse. But you're wrong. My father was a Chicago cop. Pulled a guy over to let him know his taillight was out. Just helping out a citizen. Bastard shot him. He died two days later. So I say kill all those sons-of-bitches."

"You're right," I said. "Not about arming the teachers. I think that would get a lot of innocents killed. But I am guilty of assuming I knew what you believed."

"Some people want to save the world," she said.

"You don't?"

She shook her head slowly. Her jaw set. "No. I just want vengeance. That's why I like Enyart. He understands. And he has a simple world view."

MONIQUE

Monique?
I'm here, Jake.
I was hoping you'd show up tonight. I miss you.
I know.
Do you miss me?
I'm not real. You know that.
Your ass feels real.
Let's go swimming, Jake.
Where?
The Orrington Hotel.
They don't have a pool and you can't swim.
I'll hold on to you. Do my breasts feel real, too?
Not so tight, Monique. I can't breathe.
You don't need to breathe. Have a little faith…

Chicago Tribune

February 15, 2018

Jake's Corner
A Cabbie, a Lesbian, and a Boxer Walk into a Bar...

This was supposed to be a column on gun control. Another school shooting. So much senseless killing.

Last night, at the end of my Uber gig, I decided to stop at the Charcoal Oven for a quick one and a chance to get Enyart the Bartender's take on the world today. Most of you know Enyart—leans right, ex-Marine. Desert Storm vet and a Golden Glove champ who doesn't pull his punches.

I can tell right away that something's up. Enyart and Margie are at the end of the bar watching the news. Scenes of the carnage at Parkland High School. Seventeen dead. It's the fourth mass shooting in the last twelve months.

Margie is a sophisticated, smart professional. And gay. Enyart is Enyart. You couldn't find two people who have less in common. After watching the report, Enyart's prescription for this tragic and seemingly intractable problem was to arm the teachers.

"Don't leave those kids defenseless!" he says. "If someone starts shooting back, the next guy won't be so anxious to try his luck." I can appreciate the sentiment—no one wants to see children hurt—but I don't think giving every teacher a gun is the answer.

"Why not eliminate the guns?" I ask.

He looks at me like I'm a schoolkid. Tells me about the mass shooting in Norway back in 2011, when a gunman went to an island and shot and killed sixty kids. It's a horrific story. Norway has tough gun control laws, and it didn't help.

Margie is listening attentively. Nodding her head. She seems to be agreeing with him. Enyart's conclusion is to "Kill those SOBs!" (Only he doesn't say SOB). He pounds the bar and almost knocks over my beer.

I expect Margie to disagree. But she says, "My father was a Chicago cop, and he was shot by someone he was trying to help. So, I'm with Enyart. Kill them all." I didn't agree with her, but I could see why she believed what she believed. I probably would too if my father had been killed in the line of duty.

Okay. So, what's the deal here?

I thought this column would be one of ten thousand offered up this week on why we need gun control. We (the media) always come to that conclusion. We write our columns, pointing fingers and assessing blame and nothing changes. If I knew the answer, I wouldn't be writing a newspaper column.

What I do know is that we all label people. It's human nature.

I'm always writing about Enyart. He's the arch-conservative gun-loving law and order hard case. I use him as a foil. Did you know he reads news journals voraciously? Everything from *The New Yorker* and the *New York Times* to *National Review* and *The Wall Street Journal*. He knows both sides of all the hot-button issues, and that's what makes him a formidable debater. And would you believe he collects Tiffany lamps? I've never mentioned those things because they don't fit my narrative. Shame on me.

I labeled Margie, too. Gay. Young. Professional. I added up all those labels and assumed her politics would be liberal. Of course she would support tough gun control legislation. I was wrong. Those labels don't accurately capture Margie's story. She has understandable reasons for her position.

If we rely on the labels we assign folks instead of trying to discover why they believe what they believe, we are doing ourselves a disservice. We are being intellectually lazy.

Many folks on the right and the left want the same thing. For sure, nobody wants to put children at risk. We just disagree on how to achieve the goal.

Our country is polarized. Gun control. Abortion. Income inequality. Climate change. And of course, the issue no one can escape: the President's conduct. Those issues divide us. We need to have honest debate. But if we label ourselves as "The Resistance," and refuse to engage, that's like deciding everyone who doesn't agree with us is a traitor. Unworthy of consideration.

That mindset is myopic and dangerous. And it's tearing the country apart.

We need to do better.

FOUR

THURSDAY, 9:00 A.M. — FEBRUARY 15, 2018

Kennedy Expressway

Amanda slept in my never-used guest bedroom, and I banged out my column and sent it off for the metro edition. In the morning she helped me shovel out, and then I drove her to the Criminal Court Building at 26th and California. On the ride down she read the draft.

"That's not bad. You hardly sound at all like a pussy. Why'd you change my name?"

"The names have been changed to protect the innocent. Although I'm not sure you qualify."

She laughed. "Will you get a lot of comments on it?"

"There are a few diehard trolls who hate everything I write. Mostly right-wing nutjobs. But lately a fair number of crazy lefties too. I figure I'm doing something right when wackos from both sides hate me."

She smiled at that notion and then stared out her window as I took the express lanes on the Kennedy. I could tell she was thinking about something.

"You have a lot of room in your house. When did you move in?" she asked.

"Last May. Why?"

"Well, it looks as though you just moved in. Everything's still in boxes. As if you're not planning on staying."

"I guess it's taken me awhile to accept that my marriage is over."

She nodded. "I was just thinking…" She paused and stared out her window.

"What?"

"I hate living with my mother and her husband. Could I rent a room in your place? Just for a few months. 'Til I figure out the Bianca situation."

Another surprise. A crazy idea, but then I thought, why not? I could use some help with the rent. "How about $100 dollars a month? No lease. You can help with the cleaning. Not my strong suit."

The wrinkled-nose look again. "It's gay guys who are tidy. Women, not so much."

"I wasn't assuming you were. Really. I've learned my lesson." I gave her my most sincere look, but she knew I was spoofing her.

She clapped her hands together. "Great. I'll bring my stuff over on Saturday."

FIVE

THURSDAY, 11:00 A.M. — FEBRUARY 15, 2018

Italian Village

I had just dropped off my new roommate at the Criminal Court building when I got a call from the man who saved my career.

Back in '98 when the *Sun-Times* published a Sunday front-page story headlined, "Trib Columnist Jake Doyle Has Lovechild with Teenager," Hector Gonzales had just been promoted to Tempo editor. That made him my boss. The Tribune Syndication Services immediately dropped my column, and Hector was under intense pressure to fire me. Even the mayor's office and several aldermen jumped on the bandwagon. But Hector wouldn't do it. He was standup. We had worked together for ten years by then. That made us family. And in our world, family trumped everything.

Most folks can't understand that kind of loyalty. Hector had a real family. He had married his high school girlfriend, and they had five kids in eight years. He couldn't afford to lose his job. But he was cocky and confident and probably thought he was bulletproof. We played together for the paper's sixteen-inch softball team. That's a misleading statement. I stayed planted on third base, guarding it like I was afraid someone might steal it—a boxer out of his element. Hector was a smooth shortstop with the grace of a dancer and the reflexes of a cat. He weighed 130 soaking wet, but he was always front and center whenever there was a brawl—and there were plenty of them.

Last year, six months before the *Trib* was bought by billionaire golden boy Timmy O'Neill, Hector was named managing editor. O'Neill made his money in real estate but had become a newspaper baron. He owned papers all over the country.

Two months after O'Neill took over, most of the editors and two thirds of the reporters were gone. Those of us who survived had our salaries slashed. With all those editors eliminated, Hector was back to being my boss. I was still family, but I'm sure he wished I had grown up and moved out of the house.

O'Neill had appointed his personal attorney, James Sullivan, to be the point man for his slash-and-burn strategy. Sullivan was less than useless. Hector had to do all the dirty work of downsizing, and he could never be sure he wouldn't be the next head to roll. It had taken its toll. The high-energy shortstop had become a paunchy, nearly bald wreck.

His stress level was palpable. I could tell something was wrong. "Can you meet me for lunch, Jake?"

It was just after ten a.m. "I'm at Cermak. I can meet you at the office in thirty minutes."

"No. I'm meeting with Sullivan in five minutes. I made a reservation at Italian Village for eleven thirty."

He wasn't really asking. "Damn, Hector. I don't rate your club? I've got my sports jacket in the trunk." Hector had scored a membership at The University Club when he became managing editor. Couldn't get in there without a coat and tie.

"Sullivan cut all the club memberships."

"Oh. Sorry, man."

"That club wasn't my kind of place anyway," he said.

That was true enough, but I know he wanted that membership. It was well-deserved recognition, and it pissed me off that O'Neill and Sullivan had yanked it from him.

"I'll get us a booth on the lower level. I'll probably be there early."

"I gotta get to my meeting," Hector said. He was obviously not looking forward to it. "Don't eat too many breadsticks while you're waiting for me. And lay off the martinis."

"Hey. You know I never drink before eleven."

I made it to the restaurant just after eleven o'clock. It was empty but they seated me. The lower-level dining area was famously dark. A good place to eat if you didn't want to be seen. I settled into a corner booth in the back and checked my phone.

I'm not a social media guy. I have a Twitter account, but I never tweet. It's hard enough to trim my profundity to six hundred words. One hundred twenty-eight characters? Forget about it. I had a text from Charlotte:

> OMG! Check this out. It's gone viral. So unfair.

She posted a link to an article in the *Huffington Post* by Lucy Hall. Never heard of her, and I don't usually read the *HuffPost*. I clicked on the link:

The Trib's notorious sexual predator and not-so-liberal Jake Doyle has shown his true colors—calling the Resistance "Traitors."

Ever since the Harvey Weinstein story hit last year, sexual misconduct allegations were being reported every other week. Minnesota Senator Al Franken was the subject of a CNN expose, James Franco and Jeremy Piven were skewered in the *New York Times*, and last month *The New Yorker* devoted twenty pages to Woody Allen.

I know I shouldn't be surprised to be labeled a sexual predator. I had been a hotshot columnist—a rising star in the newspaper world— when I had an affair with my intern, a beautiful Black woman who was only twenty-one. That might not be smart, but the head doesn't rule the heart. It wasn't a crime. At least it wasn't twenty years ago.

But Lucy Hall didn't care so much about my notorious past. That was just a booster for the story she wanted to share: a so-called liberal columnist dared to suggest that those fine folks who called themselves The Resistance were not perfect. The fact that I never called them traitors as her lede suggested didn't matter. She wrote two thousand words about my six-hundred-word column, but most folks wouldn't read beyond her clumsy opening. The takeaway was summed up by the first of four hundred plus comments posted on the *HuffPost* website:

Creepy old white guy calls the Resistance traitors.

Her story was an unintentional parody with misquotes, misspellings, and tons of outrage. I had started skimming the comments hoping to find at least one intelligent response when I got a call from Tawni.

Calls from Tawni were never good news. Even when we were together.

"Damn good column this morning," she said.

Uh oh. Starting out with a compliment was absolutely not a good sign. She'd do that—like a skilled boxer—to get me off balance before coming in with a left hook.

"Uh…thanks." I braced myself.

"How'd those snowflakes at the *Trib* take it? Are they sending you for counseling?"

No way was I telling her that Charlotte had sent me the *HuffPost* article. Charlotte, liberal press, and my scandal: a perfect storm of Tawni hot-buttons.

"Haven't heard anything. I'm meeting Hector in five minutes." Closer to thirty, but I was hoping to discourage her from talking too long.

She laughed like only Tawni could laugh. An explosion. A laugh she reserved for stuff that wasn't funny. "Jesus, Jake. You think he's giving you a fucking medal?"

"Huh?" I could play dumb with the best of them.

"Tim O'Neill is a liberal darling. He has an agenda! He doesn't tolerate heresy."

"I'm not a heretic."

"That's what Robespierre said before they guillotined him."

"Well, geez, Tawni, thanks for checking in. I'll give Hector your best."

"Wait, Jake. I had a real reason for calling. Not just to bust your balls."

"Yeah?"

"You didn't RSVP to the award dinner. You're coming, right?"

I hate everything about banquets: the food, the speeches, the uncomfortable chairs, the meat locker a/c. But a banquet full of self-righteous conservatives—I don't have a word for how much I didn't want to go to her banquet.

"Wouldn't miss it for the world. I'm bringing Charlotte."

"Really?"

Charlotte was the only name that could leave Tawni speechless. Our daughter was a hardcore lefty, living out there next to the anarchists; and Tawni was a right-wing zealot, not quite as crazy as the conspiracy theorists who still believed Obama was born in Africa, but close.

Tawni was uncharacteristically quiet for a few seconds. I have no doubt she loved her daughter, but what had been a contentious relationship when Charlotte was a rebellious teenager had become a powder keg when Charlotte began to struggle with alcohol.

"She broke up with what's-his-name, you know."

"His name is Greg. You know that. He broke up with her this time," I said.

"Shut the front door!"

The only remaining signs of Tawni's matriculation at Bible-thumping Wheaton College was her collection of cursing euphemisms. "Don't get your hopes up. You know they break up all the time."

She sighed dramatically, and I could just imagine her look of motherly consternation. "Why don't you bring Devante along, too?" she said. "Charlotte is much better behaved when he's around."

When Monique was killed, I wanted custody of Devante, but I knew Monique didn't want that. Neither did Tawni. So Devante was raised by Antoinette, who had emigrated from Jamaica forty years ago. From her start as a house maid, she had built a thriving house-cleaning and handyman business, employing newly arrived Jamaicans.

When Devante was young, Antoinette often hired Charlotte to babysit him. Charlotte and Devante became great friends. It wasn't that Charlotte was better behaved when Devante was around, it was just that he made her want to be a better person. She was his big sister, and he looked up to her.

Having dinner with my two kids in the back of a banquet hall with an open bar where we could make snarky comments all night—this award thing was starting to sound much better. "Okay. I'll try to get Devante."

"We're sitting with Gordon LaPlante and his wife, Cookie," Tawni said. "You remember Gordon. He's the head of the Society."

Damn. I thought Tawni would be at some kind of head table, like at a wedding. I had no clue who Gordon is, and I'm sure I would have remembered a woman named Cookie. "Uh...if there's not room for us, we can sit in the back—"

"There's room, Jake."

"Oh." Sharing a table with conservative zealots was going to make for a really tense dinner if those folks tried to engage Charlotte in a political discussion.

"I have to say I'm surprised. Charlotte doesn't enjoy these kinds of things," Tawni said.

"You're her mother. She's excited for you." I don't know why, but I often find myself articulating things I wish were true about my family and its complicated relationships, even though I know they're not. I could see Hector making his way across the restaurant to our booth. "Hector's here. I gotta go."

"Good luck, Jake. See you Sunday night." She sounded sincere. I wasn't sure I needed luck, but I never turn it down.

Hector slowly wove his way through the tables. I tried to find some vestige of that graceful shortstop, but I couldn't. His face was grim and his step heavy. He didn't really want to be here. I stood up as he got to the booth. "Good to see you, Hector."

He struggled to produce a smile and clasped my hand limply. Distracted. "Hello, Jake."

"You don't look happy to see me, Hec."

He rubbed his temples. "This fucking job is killing me."

The waiter walked over and handed us menus. The Village wasn't one of those restaurants where the waitperson tries to be your friend. It was old school, like Berghoff's, where the waiter is there to take your order, not answer a half-dozen questions on food preparation. "Anything to drink, gentlemen?"

"Tea with lemon," Hector said.

I tried not to look disappointed. I really wanted Hector to have a drink. He needed one. The Village makes a generous martini, but I couldn't enjoy a mart while Hector was sipping his fucking tea. "I'll have a Moretti," I said.

I sat back in the booth, hands folded. I could tell Hector wasn't interested in any small talk, so I waited. He took a deep breath and was about to start his speech when the waiter returned with our beverages.

"Have you decided?" he asked.

I ordered the veal marsala, and Hector, who never met a steak he didn't like, ordered a pathetic house salad.

"You on a goddamn diet?"

He pressed his lips tight. "I have to get back to the office. Sullivan's not done chewing on me."

"Sorry, man. That sucks."

He waved me off. "Be careful what you wish for, right? We need to talk about today's column."

"Okay."

"Sullivan said Mr. O'Neill didn't care for it. He thought it was politically insensitive."

It was a very poorly kept secret that O'Neill was planning to run for president in 2020.

"Sorry to hear that." I wasn't. If everyone likes your column, you're doing something wrong. Or just preaching to the choir, like the prima donnas at the *New York Times*.

Hector sighed. "Did you see Lucy Hall's piece in the *HuffPost*?"

"I skimmed it. Is that what's bugging Timmy? She called me a sexual predator."

Hector waved his hand in front of his face. "Sullivan said O'Neill knew all about that. That's not the issue. It's the Resistance angle. Her story has a lot of traction."

"Traction?" I knew what he meant, but sometimes I have to be an asshole.

"Look at the reaction, Jake." He pulled out his phone. "Six hundred forty-nine comments. The damn article has been shared over two hundred times. We should get that kind of readership."

31

"So, the way to get..." I air-quoted, "...traction, is to write an article with a dozen mistakes and lead with an event that happened twenty years ago?"

Hector looked grim. I felt bad for torturing him. He was only doing his job. But his job sucked.

"Sullivan wants you to clarify your position. Explain that you don't think the Resistance are traitors."

"Jesus, Hector. I didn't say they were traitors. Did you read the column?" I took a gulp of the beer and was wishing I had a real drink.

"I know. I know. That's the point. Just explain that you didn't call them traitors. Say something positive about the movement. You know, how they're the true patriots. We need to get this story behind us before you get lumped in with Harvey Weinstein and Woody Allen."

"So that's what you want in my next column?"

"Sullivan doesn't want to wait until Monday. He wants you to tweet the, uh...clarification."

"Come on, Hector. I don't do tweets. What good would it do? I don't even have a hundred followers."

"We would see that it got retweeted. Mary and Eric and Connie. They have over fifty thousand followers."

Mary, Eric, and Connie were the other local columnists. Mary focused on working women; Eric was a snarky, millennial curmudgeon; and Connie did lightweight puff pieces but had won a Pulitzer twenty years ago, so she was bulletproof.

"Fifty thousand followers? Those dudes are popular."

Hector gave me a look, like I wasn't taking this issue seriously enough. "This could be good for you, Jake. Build your social media presence. Solidify your liberal base."

"You mean like Robespierre?"

"Huh?"

"Nothing. Just a Tawni joke. I don't see Mary Belton retweeting anything of mine." Belton had been on one of those panel discussions a few years back where everyone usually agrees with one another. Someone didn't get that memo and invited Tawni. Belton made the mistake of trying to engage Tawni in debate. It was like me taking on

Enyart. Except Belton didn't go the distance. Tawni got her so flustered she ran off in tears. She hasn't talked to me since.

"Mary Belton will do her job. We all have to pitch in. Can I count on you, Jake?"

I wasn't the only one who had to dine on a shit sandwich.

I was pissed, but I felt bad for Hector. Those assholes were literally killing him. I wanted to tell him that no job was worth that much agony, but I didn't have five kids to take care of. The guy was in a bind.

"Okay. I'll come up with something tonight. It won't be easy to reduce my brilliance to one hundred twenty-eight characters."

Hector finally smiled for real. "You need to keep up with social media. You get two hundred eighty characters now."

SIX

THURSDAY, 3 P.M. — FEBRUARY 15, 2018

Devon Boxing Club

I told Devante I would pick him up after his shift at Topo Gio's—a popular Italian restaurant in the Old Town neighborhood—and take him to Enyart's gym, the Devon Boxing Club, for his workout. Devante worked for the sous chef at Topo four days a week from nine in the morning to three in the afternoon. He lived rent-free with Antoinette and poured most of the money he earned into his rib business.

As I turned south off Clybourn onto Wells Street, I could see him standing in front of the restaurant in a black hoodie and jeans, workout bag slung over his shoulder, clutching his planner. He didn't go anywhere without that damn planner. He used it to keep track of his work schedule, business plan, and workouts. It was also his diary; he was always writing notes to himself. The kid had big plans.

Two blonde ladies laden with boutique shopping bags gave him sidelong glances as they headed into the Irish pub next to Topo. Devante looked both imposing and graceful even though he was simply standing at the curb.

"Damn, it's cold out there." He rubbed his hands together as he uncoiled into the passenger seat.

"You might want to consider gloves. And a hat."

"Yeah." He studied me. "You're not working out today?"

"No. I'm checking in with Enyart, then I need to get home." I wanted a chance to clean up the kitchen before Amanda got there. I'd been a little neglectful on my housekeeping. I sniffed the air. "You work with fish today?"

He grinned. "Had to sort dozens of scallops. The chef only wanted jumbo scallops. I can't smell them anymore. Stinks, huh?" He opened his planner and pulled out a flyer from the pocket in the back.

"Eh, it's not that bad. But glad I'm not sparring with you. What's that?"

"Apartment listings. I need to move out. Can't keep living with Grandma."

"Free rent is hard to beat," I said. I had argued against his renting that storefront, and so far that had turned out okay. I was worried he was stretching himself too thin, but he had his mother's stubbornness, and it was not easy to turn him when he got his mind made up.

"I know. I didn't want to move out for another year, but Aunt Kalise is coming for another visit."

Oh.

That was grim news. Antoinette was a devout Christian. Her sister Kalise made her look like a pagan. "How long she here for?" Last time Kalise came up from Jamaica she stayed for two years.

"Too long." He exhaled sharply. "Hey. Could I stay at your place? Just until she moves out."

All of a sudden I'm in demand. At least my house is. "Sure. You're always welcome. You know that. I just got a roommate, but I have plenty of room."

"A roommate? Who?"

"Her name's Amanda. She needed a place to stay while she sorts things out with her girlfriend. She just moved in today."

"Damn. You sure it will be okay? I don't want to mess things up with you and your lady."

I couldn't tell if he was serious or just busting my balls. "She's a tenant, not a girlfriend. She pays rent."

He nodded his head, not really believing me. "Got it. Want me to pay rent?"

"Only if you keep being a smartass. But if you do that, I'll just send you back to Aunt Kalise. She'll straighten you out."

Devante grinned. "Roommate. Rent. I got it. I can have Mr. Enyart drop me off tonight after our workout, when he goes to bartend."

I pulled into the parking lot across from the Devon Boxing Club. "Don't you have to pack?"

"I'm all packed. I knew you'd be cool with it."

The Devon Boxing Club had been a storefront dance studio on Devon Avenue before Enyart bought it back in '98. Unlike the old-time gyms, Enyart's place had good lighting and a hardwood floor. He maintained it like it was a Marine Corps barracks. Spit and polish clean, with a place for everything and everything in its place. The front walk was always shoveled and free of litter. He lived in the studio apartment above the gym, and with his afterschool programs and his neighborhood-watch mindset, he'd become a well-known figure in the neighborhood.

In the front section, two heavy bags hung from the ceiling, and along the walls were four speed bags, a leg press machine, a bench press, jump ropes, and exercise mats. One wall was mirrored—another inheritance from the dance studio. In the back, a sixteen-foot square section was roped off for sparring.

Enyart was in the front, instructing the kids in his latest afterschool program. There were six of them today: two skinny Black boys; a Black girl who was bigger and stronger than both of them; a stocky Indian or Pakistani; a Hispanic, probably Mexican given the neighborhood; and a scrawny Appalachian White boy. A rainbow coalition if there ever was one. The kids were in a circle with Enyart in the middle, an Everlast punching mitt on each of his hands. He pivoted and then lunged toward the girl, calling out punch combinations. "One, three,

four, five, come on Ruby, hit it like you mean it, don't think, react."
Then he pivoted and faced another kid. "Three, three, four, six! That's
it, Sanjay. Good pop!" He kept at it for fifteen minutes. You could tell
the kids loved the drill.

There was a collective, good-natured groan when he dropped his
mitts and yelled, "Okay, time to wrap it up with five minutes of core
work!" I didn't blame them for groaning. Enyart's core routines were
excruciating: planks, crunches, burpees, leg raises, flutter kicks. He did
the exercises right along with the kids, exhorting them not to drop
their feet or cheat on the crunch. He was relentless, and impervious to
suffering. At the end of the five minutes all the kids were sprawled on
the floor, moaning.

"That's a wrap for today. Get all your stuff before you leave. I'll see
you back here on Monday. Don't forget to do your homework."

Devante had changed into his workout gear and had started his
warmup routine. He had done five minutes of jump rope and was
shadowboxing when Enyart spotted him. Enyart marched across the
floor, his face serious as a heart attack. "Hey! Is that the hardest punch
you can throw?"

Devante stopped and grinned. "I'm just warming up."

"So your answer's, 'No?'"

Devante lowered his gloves and dropped his head. "I can punch
harder."

"What have I told you about these warmups?"

"They don't do any good if I don't follow the plan."

"Okay, then. Never take any punches off. You can't coast in the
ring. Do the drills the right way, or don't do them at all." Enyart
stormed off, acting and looking genuinely angry. That was Enyart.
Boxing was a perfect sport for him. No diplomacy required.

Devante resumed his shadowboxing with a marked difference in
the crispness and the power of his punches. He was a natural athlete,
and, while I was far from an expert, it was clear he had legitimate
skills.

After the warmup, Enyart drilled Devante on his punch combinations. Over and over again. "Okay, right uppercut. You're strong, D.
Don't load up. Bring it from here." He demonstrated an uppercut,

firing from his hip, not drawing his fist behind his butt as Devante had been doing. "You load up and you've lost the surprise and you've opened up your defenses. Defense. Defense. Defense. That was the one thing your old man was good at. Avoiding contact. Try it again."

Devante fired three uppercut combinations in succession. He knocked Enyart back on his heels on the third one. That didn't happen much.

"Okay, that's it. You ready to do some sparring?"

Devante stared at him, eyes wide. "For real, man?"

Enyart turned toward the ring where a trainer was working with a fighter on his footwork. "Hey Carlos, your boy ready?"

The trainer, a husky Hispanic with a full head of curly black hair, held up his hand and the boxer stopped circling. "Yes, sir. We're ready here."

"Come on D. Get your head gear."

We walked back to the ring, and Enyart introduced Devante to the trainer, Carlos, and his fighter. Jamal was light-skinned and had a compact muscular frame. His head was shaved, and his arms were covered with prison tats. He barely acknowledged Devante and stared off into space, projecting a don't-fuck-with-me attitude.

"You wearing that sweat?" Enyart asked. Jamal was wearing a loose-fitting gray sweatshirt with the sleeves cut off.

Jamal glowered at him. "It's fuckin' cold in here."

Carlos wheeled around and got in Jamal's face. "We're guests here. You show some respect." He didn't break his stare until Jamal finally looked at him. "You hear me, Jamal?"

"Yeah," he said. "Let's go."

"Okay," Enyart said. "Three rounds. Boxers to your corners."

I checked Devante's gloves. I wanted to give him some advice, but I had no clue who he was up against. Before I could embarrass myself, Enyart stepped over.

"Jamal was a gangbanger. He's been at Danville Correctional for the last two years. Carlos works with these kids when they get out, trying to keep them from going back to the gang. This boy's a brawler. Keep your guard up and remember your basic combinations. Nothing fancy."

Enyart tapped the digital clock outside the ring, which counted down three minutes. "Okay, gentlemen, let's go."

Devante circled cautiously as Jamal charged at him, firing haymakers, trying to end the fight with one punch. Devante bobbed and weaved, easily avoiding Jamal's wild punches. He returned fire with jabs and hooks. He didn't do any damage, but he was clearly frustrating Jamal. If we were scoring the round, D would have won on points.

The second round started out the same way, with Jamal charging wildly and Devante ducking the headshots and blocking the body shots. With a minute to go in the round, Jamal loaded up for an uppercut, just the way Enyart had cautioned Devante not to do. Devante leaned back, avoiding the wild punch, and then hit Jamal with a straight left hand followed by a quick right hook, knocking him to the canvas. Jamal slowly got to one knee and then pushed himself back up. Enyart stepped in front of him, holding him by the wrists.

"Okay, that's enough for today, son."

Jamal yanked his arms, trying to free himself from Enyart's grip. "Fuck this. I ain't done. Lemme go, motherfucker."

Carlos slipped through the ropes of the ring and bearhugged Jamal from behind. "Jamal, you ain't inside now. Mr. Enyart is lookin' out for you. Don't disrespect him." He pulled him back to the corner. "Get your gear. We're leaving."

As Jamal tugged off his gloves, he glowered at Devante. "Next time, nigger, I'll kick your ass." Carlos grabbed his shoulder. "There ain't going to be a next time if you don't fix your attitude."

Devante had retreated to his corner and was taking off his gloves. He frowned at Jamal's threat but didn't react. He kept his cool.

After Carlos and Jamal left, Enyart put Devante to work on the heavy bag.

"He moved pretty good today," I said.

"Yeah. Good thing he's not trying to make boxing his career."

I agreed, but it was an odd thing to say. "What do you mean?"

"He's a smart kid. Very trainable. And he's got the physical tools, but he doesn't have that killer instinct. Just like his old man."

I think there was a compliment in there someplace. "Can you drop him off at my place? I gotta get home and clean up."

"You having a party?"

With great reluctance, I told him about the arrangement I had made with Amanda.

"Damn. The Silver Fox is back in the game. Way to go, Jake."

He gave me that stupid wink.

"Fuck you very much. You and Devante."

SEVEN

THURSDAY, 5 P.M. — FEBRUARY 15, 2018

Home

I thought I'd have at least an hour to tidy up, but when I walked into the kitchen, Amanda, in black tights and a baggy sweatshirt, was furiously scrubbing the stove top. Bags of groceries were lined up on the counter.

She looked up from her work and smiled. "Hi, Jake!"

"You're cleaning the stove?" I asked, using my well-honed observation skills.

She gave me a look. "And your refrigerator. And the sink. They were all disgusting."

"Disgusting's a little harsh."

"Those appliances aren't self-cleaning. I'll bet you haven't cleaned them since you moved in." She paused. "Or maybe I should say, 'taken occupancy.'" She glanced in the living room at the unopened boxes of stuff I hadn't dealt with yet.

"You bought groceries?" I asked, making another shrewd observation.

"Yep. You are really close to the Jewel. It's a great store."

I pulled out my wallet. "How much?"

"Don't worry about it. If you're only charging me a hundred dollars for rent, I'm happy to take care of our dinners. From the looks of your refrigerator, you live on frozen pizzas."

"Not true. I often get fresh pizza delivered from La Rosa's. They make an excellent deep dish. But things are about to change because my son's moving in for a few weeks. And he's an aspiring chef. He should be here in a couple hours."

Her eyes lit up at the news, but her smile morphed into a look of concern. "Will he be okay with me living here? Will you?"

"Not a problem. I told him you were renting a room. He's a good kid. You'll like him."

"I was going to prepare dinner tonight, but maybe he'll want to cook?"

"No. He'll welcome the opportunity not to cook."

"Okay. I thought I'd grill fresh salmon. With rice and steamed broccoli."

I tried not to grimace. "Sounds awfully healthy. How about dessert?"

"Fresh strawberries!" She was actually excited.

"No ice cream?"

"Too much fat. If you want, next time I go for groceries I'll buy you some frozen yogurt."

"You're some kind of health nut, aren't you?"

"I'm a triathlete," she said. "And I turned thirty-five this year, so now I'm the youngest in my age group instead of the oldest. This is my year to kick ass." She blushed and her freckles seemed to glow. "I almost forgot. A special treat." She grabbed a paper bag from the grocery pile. "Crown Royal!"

"That's almost as good as fresh strawberries. Stop the cleaning and join me for happy hour."

She checked the clock. "Okay, happy half-hour."

We settled down on the beige leather sofa I had ordered on moving-in day. I had positioned it in front of the fireplace. I had planned to enjoy that fireplace all winter, but I never got around to buying firewood.

"I could bring up a video of a fireplace on my laptop, and we could pretend to have a fire," Amanda said. "Fireplaces don't really generate much heat anyway."

I swirled the whiskey and ice. "This is okay. I have a great imagination. I need to think about my tweet."

"You tweet?" She didn't believe me.

"Not if I can avoid it. But the boss asked me to. He didn't really ask."

"Why? Did you upset somebody?" She shifted on the couch and was staring at me. She didn't want another short-form answer.

I picked up my phone and clicked on the link Charlotte had sent me. "This is why." I handed her the phone. Lucy Hall had rehashed every detail of the affair, so letting Amanda read about it saved me having to try and explain. Maybe after she read it she wouldn't be so interested in sharing my house.

Unlike Tawni, who would provide nonstop commentary while she read, Amanda read the story without a word. Her face implacable. She was probably a great poker player. When she finished reading she handed the phone back to me.

"Lucy Hall is a fucking cunt." She stared at me as though daring me to refute her conclusion. Then she added, "And she can't write for shit."

"So—"

"And she can't fucking read either. You never called them traitors!"

I had a sudden insight. Tawni's ongoing commentary was a way to keep herself under control. Amanda was a pressure cooker—she kept it all together for as long as she could, then she exploded.

"It was twenty years ago. I know it makes me look creepy. I was thirty-five, Monique was twenty-one, and she worked for me. That's all most people had to know." I cleared my throat. My voice had turned husky. I wasn't used to talking about Monique.

Amanda took hold of my hand in both of her hands. "I'm sorry you lost her."

I looked at her surprised. Not sure what to say.

"You loved her, didn't you?"

I swallowed hard. "Yes," I said. "I loved her." I took a deep breath and tried to regain my footing. No one besides Devante ever asked me about Monique. Everyone wanted to believe it was a fling—a huge mistake—that wrecked my career. Not a love story.

"Why did you stay with your wife?"

"Tawni wouldn't give me a divorce, and Monique said she didn't want to marry me. I thought she would come around if I gave her some time, but turns out we didn't have any time."

"That article said she was shot?"

"Standing at the bus stop, two years after Devante was born. The kid was supposed to shoot the gangbanger standing next to her, but he missed."

"I'm sorry, Jake."

I sighed. This whole discussion was exhausting. I never talked about Monique and what happened with Devante. I couldn't talk about it.

Ever.

I picked up a pad of paper and my pen. "I need to write this damn apology."

"You're apologizing?" Amanda frowned. "I thought you believed what you wrote."

"They want me to correct the impression that I called the Resistance traitors."

"That's stupid. That bitch Lucy Hall should apologize."

I had the feeling I could add Amanda to the list of women I know who leave no opinion unexpressed.

"I think the goal is to put out the fire, not blow it up."

"Why? You're a columnist. Aren't you supposed to express your opinions? Would Mike Royko tweet some phony apology?"

"Royko? Jesus Christ. He's been dead twenty years."

"My father would read his column to me at the kitchen table. He loved the guy."

She wanted to shame me, but I was shame-proof.

"Royko was awesome. He didn't take shit from anyone. But he was A-list. Bulletproof. And there were three dailies in Chicago back then. If he wasn't treated right, he could pick up and leave. And he did. I'm not in his league."

"Don't sell yourself short. I love your stories."

"I appreciate that, but I bet you haven't bought a newspaper in the last five years. I'm grateful for my loyal readers, but if the newspaper fired me tomorrow most of them wouldn't even notice. The newspaper business is dying. Guys like me and Hector are dinosaurs. If I can help Hector hang on for a few more years I'm going to do that. I learned twenty years ago that I don't have many friends. Hector stood by me when no one else did. I'm not trying to save the world either. Fuck the world."

Amanda smiled. "When you do that tweet, I think you should add the hashtag fucktheworld."

"Oh. Hashtags. I've never figured those out."

"Draft your tweet and I'll add them for you." She raised her glass. "Fuck the world!"

Devante arrived just as I was putting the dishes in the dishwasher. Amanda had saved a portion for him, and after the introductions he wolfed down his meal, praising it between mouthfuls.

"This is really good, Amanda. Jake doesn't usually eat healthy. I mean like never. He's mostly a pizza guy."

"I know. He has a serious inventory of frozen pizzas."

Devante looked at me with alarm. "Frozen pizzas, Jake? Why don't you just eat cardboard? Probably has more nutrients."

"You're both food snobs. And health nuts. Amanda's a triathlete," I said, moving the conversation to something more interesting than my food habits.

Devante stopped eating and stared at her. "Wow. Do you do that Ironman thing?"

"I'm training for Wisconsin in the fall. Qualifying for the World Championship in Kona is on my bucket list. It won't happen this year, but someday." She blushed. Despite her millennial nosiness, I don't think she liked to talk about herself. "Jake told me you're a chef…and a boxer?"

Devante grinned. "The boxing's just for fun. But hey…" he turned to me, "…your paper is doing me a solid."

"How so?"

"That food critic—Darryl something?"

"You mean Dwayne Smith?" Smitty had been the *Trib* food critic for the last ten years. He'd be crushed that D didn't know his name.

"Yeah, that's it. Just after you left I got a call from his assistant. She said he did a taste test on ribs, and Just Ribs' BBQ ribs made the top five. He wants to interview me for the *Tribune* "Top Five" feature. The story's coming out next month."

"Oh. My. God," Amanda said, instantly grasping the import. "That's huge. They'll be busting down your doors. Uh…do you have doors?"

"Really? Is that true, Jake?"

"You heard of Giordano's Pizza?" I asked.

"Everyone's heard of them."

"That's right. They're nationwide. Have over a hundred locations. They were named Best Pizza in *Chicago Magazine* in 1976, two years after they opened their doors."

Amanda giggled. "Damn, you are a pizza expert, aren't you?"

"I wrote a follow-up column on the fortieth anniversary of that article."

Devante started making notes in his planner. He frowned and put the planner down. "She said Mr. Smith wanted to interview me in my kitchen on Saturday morning. He wants to see me in action. The two girls who help me have SAT tests Saturday morning." He chewed on his lip. "I guess I can do it on my own."

Amanda clapped her hands together. "Bianca and I can be your kitchen help for the interview."

"Bianca?"

"My girlfriend. She's a hot Latin. You'll be a rainbow of diversity."

"Really? You wouldn't mind?"

"Of course not. We love ribs."

"Thanks." He looked over at me. "You really think this *Trib* thing is a big deal?"

"Absolutely. It will put you on the map."

MONIQUE

I like that girl. She's cute. She reminds me of me.
Uh…no. She's a redheaded lesbian with no boobs.
Don't be superficial. She has attitude.
Not much of an ass either.
You should sleep with her.
A lesbian, remember. And I'm twenty years older than she is.
So…your cutoff is fifteen years?
You were different.
Why?
Because I loved you.

Jake Doyle @Jakescorner 6h

Peaceful opposition to views, policies, persons we don't agree with—call it Resistance—is our right as Americans. Those who resist the policies of the Administration are not Traitors. And neither are those who oppose the Resistance.
#Tribune #Huffpost #FTW

EIGHT

FRIDAY, 4 P.M. — FEBRUARY 16, 2018

Devon Boxing Club

D evante had been so pumped about the *Tribune* award that I
forgot to ask him about accompanying Charlotte and me to
Tawni's award thing. I gave him the pitch as soon as I
picked him up at Topo.

"Really? Miss Carter invited me?"

Devante was in awe of Tawni, and she genuinely liked him. Tawni
built a successful and lucrative practice as a right-to-life advocate, but
in the early years when she was just getting started and I was struggling
to hang on at the *Trib*, money was tight. But she never complained or
resented the support I provided to Antoinette for Devante's care.
Never blamed Devante for the sins of his father, I guess.

"Absolutely." I didn't think I needed to tell D that she was hoping
he would have a mollifying influence on his half-sister. "She'll be
thrilled that you can make it. Charlotte will pick you up at six."

I had worked Uber all day, so I decided to go offline for an hour and
catch Devante's workout. The Golden Gloves tournament was a

month away, and I was getting nervous even if Devante wasn't. Enyart was right, he didn't have that killer mindset. He had a sweet disposition, but he was athletically gifted, and that could take him a long way in this kind of tournament. Especially if he had better luck on his draw than I had.

He was an hour into his workout when the door to the gym slammed open with a bang. Jamal and a kid who couldn't have been more than fourteen stood in the doorway surveying the scene. Enyart had gone next door for a cup of coffee. Jamal strode across the gym to where Devante was working combinations on the heavy bag. He was locked in and hadn't heard the noisy entrance.

"Time for your rematch, nigger," Jamal said.

Devante stopped punching. "What you talking about?"

"You and me. Out in the street. I don't need no sissy gloves. I'm gonna fuck you up good."

I stepped in front of Jamal. "You need to leave."

Jamal put his hands on my chest and tried to shove me out of the way, but it's not easy to shove 200 hundred pounds. Okay, maybe 220. "Get out of my face, you fat fuck."

Devante threw down his gloves and stepped across the ring. He lifted Jamal off the ground and slammed him to the floor. "You want a piece of me, asshole? Come on." He was on his toes, ready for Jamal to make a move.

With a wounded animal growl, Jamal charged. He fired an overhand right, but Devante avoided the wild punch and grabbed Jamal's arm and whipped him to the floor again.

Jamal slowly pushed himself to his feet, rubbing his shoulder. He turned around, and I thought he was about to leave. But no such luck. He grabbed the kid and pushed him toward Devante and me. "Initiation time, Mo Mo. Cap this Kung Fu motherfucker."

The kid got wide-eyed. "Here? Now?" He pulled a handgun from his hoodie and waved it shakily at Devante and me. He was only three feet away, and I could see his lips trembling. That scared me as much as the gun.

"Fuck yes! What you waiting for? Do it!"

"Put the gun down." Enyart had returned. He marched across the gym floor and stopped when the kid turned and waved the gun at him. He was ten feet from the boy. "Maurice, right?" Enyart smiled and put his hands on his hips, all relaxed, as though the kid were pointing a water pistol at him. He turned to me. "Maurice here was the star of my afterschool class. Fast hands and powerful. Maurice packed a punch, let me tell you."

"It's Mo Mo. Maurice was a pussy name. And I don't need that boxing shit, I got this." He waved the gun, as if maybe Enyart hadn't noticed it.

"Waste the old fart, too. And the fat one," Jamal said. He had moved to the entrance, planning to make a quick escape.

Maurice turned the gun sideways like he'd probably seen those gangbangers on TV do. His head swiveled between Jamal and Enyart. His macho talk couldn't conceal that he was terrified.

Enyart took his hands off his hips and raised them slightly in a calming gesture. "That's not how you hold a sidearm, son. You got no stability with that sideways bullshit. Did you chamber a round?"

Enyart looked at me and winked.

"Cause if you didn't, when you pull that trigger the only thing that's happening is that I'm taking that gun away from you and shooting that piece of shit who put you up to this." Enyart glared at Jamal, like he was a Marine recruit who had fucked up.

Maurice looked quizzically at the gun. He didn't know what Enyart was talking about. "Uh…"

He turned back to Jamal for guidance. I took two quick steps, grabbed the kid's wrist, and wrapped my hand around the gun. I pointed the gun at the floor and pried it from him.

Enyart took over, forcing the kid to his knees. "Face down and don't fucking move, Maurice."

I handed Enyart the gun.

I didn't believe Enyart would shoot Jamal, but Jamal clearly did. He bolted out the door.

My stomach was churning. I had never even held a handgun, let alone had one pointed at me.

"Holy shit. Good move, Jake," Devante said.

My throat was tight. I couldn't speak. I was as scared as that kid had been. Enyart squeezed my neck. "You'll be okay in a minute. Just breathe. That was Marine-quality work, partner." He looked down at the kid. "Jesus, Maurice. Why did you have to get mixed up with that shithead?"

Maurice was whimpering, his face pressed into the floor. "I'm sorry, Mr. Enyart. Jamal took me in when my mom got busted."

"You should have called me," Enyart said. He turned to me. "Call 911."

"Please don't call the cops," Maurice said, his voiced squeaky with desperation. "They'll send me to juvie. I can't take that, man. They lock you up all day. I can't breathe in there."

I had my phone out, but the kid was so frightened I didn't know what to do. "What's he talking about?"

Enyart's hard-ass Marine demeanor softened. "They keep the kids locked up about eighteen hours a day. It's a no-win situation. If they let them all mingle, it just becomes a fucking gladiator training school for the gangs."

Maurice wailed and started to sob. "Please, Mr. Enyart."

"Any other options?" I asked. He had just threatened to kill me and Devante, but I didn't want to send him to jail.

Enyart exhaled slowly. "I can call Carlos. He'll put him up in one of those homes for kids trying to escape the gang life. And he can alert Jamal's parole officer and have his parole revoked." He clicked his tongue. "Maurice pointed that gun at you and D, so it's your call."

Maurice was sobbing quietly.

"It's okay with me," Devante said. "Jamal's the badass."

"Okay," I said. "I agree. Let's get Jamal off the streets."

Enyart called Carlos, and ten minutes later he arrived. He sighed wearily as he walked over to Maurice. "Get up, Maurice. I've got a safe place for you to stay."

Maurice got to his feet. He had wet his pants.

Enyart handed him a pair of DePaul sweatpants from his lost and found bin. "Here. Put these on."

That kid was as terrified as I was, but what if Jamal had done a better job of brainwashing him? Devante and I—his fat father—would have been dead. After Carlos and Maurice left, Devante and I packed up our gear. We were ready to leave when Enyart handed me a paper bag.

"What's this?"

"It's the kid's gun. A Sig Sauer," he whispered. "Keep it in your car when you're driving, just in case."

I didn't want a gun, but something told me this wasn't one of those times that I should argue with him. I took the Sig and stuffed it in my gear bag.

MONIQUE

Were you scared, Jake?
Nah. I was angry. He called me fat.
You can't lie to me. I'm omniscient. Like a god.
You mean Goddess. Okay. I was scared, but not for myself.
Devante?
I can't lose him too.
Is that why you took the gun?
No. I just didn't want to argue with Enyart.
Really?
I will never shoot anyone.
Never say never.
And Jake…
What?
You're not fat. You're husky.

NINE

SATURDAY, 6 A.M. — FEBRUARY 17, 2018

Home

I took a couple shots of Crown before I went to bed. I told myself it was to celebrate Devante's good news on that *Tribune* designation, but it was really just to calm my nerves so I could sleep.

It didn't work.

I couldn't take my mind out of gear. Nobody had ever pointed a gun at me before. I'd always imagined how I'd act if some mugger accosted me, but reality is always so much different from fantasy. I had been incredibly lucky. If the kid hadn't been as terrified as I was, he could have shot Devante. I could have lost my son.

I tossed and turned all night replaying those few moments. At 6 a.m. I gave up, made a pot of coffee, and picked up the *Trib* from the driveway. The top local story was about a Chicago Police commander who was shot and killed yesterday afternoon while trying to apprehend an "active shooter" in a stairwell at the Thompson Center. A thirty-one-year veteran shot multiple times by a four-time felon with an arrest record dating back to 1994.

Everyone had a gun it seemed. Now I did too.

The newspaper was thin. There were no *Tribune* national correspondents anymore; all the world news was coming from the wire services. Local reporting had been shredded as well. The paper was a shadow of what it had been ten years ago. I don't blame the owners. Young folks aren't buying newspapers. Something's got to give.

Amanda came down the stairs as I was finishing my coffee. She was wearing running shorts and a long-sleeved spandex top. "You're running in that? It's ten degrees out."

She grinned. "I have a hat and gloves. I'm doing a fast ten miles; I'll get warm quick. I asked Devante if he wanted to join me—boxers need to do a lot of road work—but he wants to get over to his place to get ready for the big interview."

She picked up the newspaper I had left on the table. The cop shooting was the headline story. She sighed. "Damn," she said softly.

There was nothing I could say to that. I had brought the Sig downstairs with me. I didn't know if I wanted to take it with me or not. I showed her the bag. "This is the gun we took away from that kid yesterday."

Amanda opened the bag and pulled out the gun. She checked the magazine and worked the action like a pro.

"You seem to know what you're doing."

"I do," she said. She went into a shooting pose, aiming at the television. "The muzzle velocity on a Sig Sauer P220 is twelve hundred feet per second. Serious stopping power."

Amanda picked up the magazine and clicked it into the handle.

"Jesus, Amanda. What are you doing?"

She ejected the magazine. "Relax, Jake. This is a good gun. It has a manual safety. I prefer a decocker. Get a shot off quicker."

"No fucking clue what you're talking about."

"Manual safety's probably better for you. The decocker action is a little more difficult for a lefty. We can go to the range. I'll get you checked out."

That damn woman was nothing but surprises. "Sure. I'll check my calendar and get back to you."

"I'm serious, Jake. There's a good range out in Des Plaines. I'll give you a lesson so you don't shoot your foot off. Or worse."

"I don't believe in guns. There has to be a better way."

She gave me a look that reminded me of Enyart.

I took the gun from her and held it as though it might explode. "What do I do with this?"

"Keep it in that paper bag, and put it under the driver's seat. There's been a lot of carjackings. If someone looks suspicious you can get at it quickly. Don't put it in the console. That's too easy to find."

I put the gun back in the bag and grabbed my coat.

Amanda was stretching, getting ready for her run. "Tonight, I want to make a special dinner for Bianca so she can meet you."

I suspected the reason was to allay any concerns Amanda's girlfriend might have about me.

"You want to show her that I'm not a notorious sexual predator?"

"I told her about the article. She said she'd be happy to kick that bitch's ass if you want her to."

"Probably not a good idea right now, but I'll take it under advisement. Have a great run."

As I sat in the driveway and signed into Uber, I kept thinking about that veteran cop who was killed. Enyart was right; gun control wouldn't have kept a gun out of the killer's hands, but the cop had a gun, and it didn't help him. I decided that my Sunday column would be about that officer.

Writing about the dangers of being a cop was not something the new *Trib* owners would like. Hector said I was lucky O'Neill was busy with his secret project to secure the Democratic nomination for president because he hadn't been satisfied with my clarification tweet.

As often happens after a blizzard, an arctic freeze had descended on Chicago. It was a clear, cloudless sky, and the temperature was barely above zero. A good Uber day. I called Enyart. I knew he'd be up. We met for lunch most Saturdays; lately we'd been rotating between Meier's Tavern in Glenview and Walker Pancake House in Evanston. As usual, Enyart skipped the opening pleasantries.

"You got the gun with you?" he asked.

"Yeah. Burgers or pancakes today?" I asked.

"No burgers. Rhonda's pissed at me."

"You need to stop dating the waitresses. We're running out of places to eat."

He made a dismissive huffing sound. "Meet you at Walkers' at noon."

I had a steady stream of fares until almost twelve. I checked out of Uber and made it to the pancake house by five after. Enyart was in the corner booth chatting up the waitress, a good-natured Polish lady who was used to his bullshit.

"Here comes the silver fox now. Fashionably late as always," he said. "Kinga recommends the pecan waffle. She thinks you need to cut down on the calories."

Kinga shook her head and stepped aside so I could slide into the booth. "You know I didn't say that, Mr. Doyle."

"It's a good choice, Kinga. I'll take it."

Enyart ordered a three-egg western omelet, and they brought us our meals in less than ten minutes. That's why the place was so popular with drivers—good food, good coffee, and quick service.

Enyart attacked his omelet as if he hadn't eaten in a week.

"Slow down, buddy. I won't steal your food," I said.

"Busy morning. I was driving around with Carlos. He was checking out places that Jamal hangs out. He was hoping he could find him and persuade him to turn himself into his parole officer. But no luck."

For someone who was supposed to be a knuckle-dragging right-winger, Enyart had a lot of do-gooder tendencies. That's why labels suck.

"Sounds like good luck to me," I said. "I don't want to run into that son-of-a-bitch ever."

As I was finishing my waffle, I got a text from Amanda:

> Devante's interview went great. Can you bring home a twelve-pack of Old Style?

Old Style? Nobody drinks Old Style.

I hate texting. I don't get it. My fingers are too fat. I could type seventy words a minute on a keyboard, but give me a damn phone and I'm useless. It's so inefficient. I called her.

She picked up immediately. "Did you get my text?" she asked.

"That's why I'm calling. Why do you want Old Style?"

"It's for Bianca. She's a Cubs fan."

"Cubs fans drink Budweiser too."

"She won't drink Bud. She's got a thing about St. Louis."

"Okay. What's for dinner?"

"Grilled, skinless chicken breasts with brown rice and a vegetable medley of asparagus, cauliflower, and carrots."

"What? No broccoli?" I asked. "I'll stop at Schaefer's and get a couple bottles of Chardonnay too."

"Hey. I bought some frozen yogurt for dessert."

"It still sounds too healthy."

When I got home there was an impressive fire in the fireplace, and Amanda and her friend were sitting on the couch talking animatedly.

"Jake!" Amanda jumped up, almost spilling the drink she was holding. "Join us. We're having highballs!"

"Where's Devante?"

"At his grandmother's for a special dinner. With his aunt, I think he said."

"Ah—a command performance with Kalise. The interview went okay?"

"It was great. Dwayne Smith was really impressed with Devante. I could tell. Have a highball!"

Amanda looked and sounded liked she'd had more than one. "Don't tell me you used the Crown Royal for that sissy drink."

"I told you, Bianca." They laughed. "Jake, this is my girlfriend, Bianca Pujols. Bianca, this is my landlord, Jake Doyle." She laughed again. She was half-in-the-bag. Maybe more.

Bianca stood up and shook my hand. She had a firm handshake and calluses. She was wearing a checkered flannel shirt and pressed jeans with cuffs and a wide black leather belt with a chain hooked to it like she was a night watchman. "Pleased to meet you, Mr. Doyle."

She had an accent. "Pujols? Are you Dominican? And please call me Jake. I don't need any additional reminders that I'm old."

"*Sí*. Dominican. How did you know, Jake?"

"As a faithful Cubs fan, I was tormented by Albert Pujols for many years. I was happy to see him go to the Angels."

Bianca nodded her head enthusiastically. "When I was a kid whenever the Cardinals came to town, my *papi* and his brothers would close down their shop, and all the families—wives, kids, cousins, girlfriends —would go to the game."

"That's where I met her," Amanda said.

"You met at a Cubs game?"

"No. She works weekends at her dad's garage. She gave me a lube job!" Amanda said and then laughed hysterically.

Bianca shook her head. "Girlfriend, you need to slow down." She smiled at me. "I remember on my fourteenth birthday I didn't want to go to the game—I wanted to hang out with my friends, but *Papi* insisted. That was the day Albert had five hits and hit three homeruns!"

"I remember that game. So why are you down on St. Louis?"

"They let Albert leave. No loyalty."

"Bianca brought you a housewarming gift!" Amanda said.

"I think his hearing's okay, Manny. You don't need to shout," Bianca said.

Amanda covered her mouth. "Oops. Sorry. Firewood. She brought firewood."

"Thank you. It's the first fire in the new house."

Bianca hitched her shoulders. "I just picked up a couple bags from 7-11. Amanda told me you didn't have any. Sorry we used up your special whiskey. I made her add the 7-Up. I have a sweet tooth."

"Ah. I brought beer. It's in the kitchen. Can I get you one?"

Amanda jumped up. "Oh god. I have to start the dinner." She took an unsteady step and fell back on to the sofa. "I'm a little dizzy."

"Let's take a break from your super healthy meals and order a deep-dish from LaRosa's," I said.

"I second that," Bianca said. "Come here, Manny. No cooking for you tonight."

Amanda scooched closer to Bianca as I went out to the kitchen to order the pizza and grab beers for Bianca and me. The Crown Royal bottle was empty. I brought Amanda a highball glass of ice and 7-Up. She didn't notice the difference.

An hour later I had just grabbed my second wedge of deep-dish when Devante returned.

"How is sister Kalise?" I asked.

Devante plopped down on the couch. "That woman said grace for five minutes. I almost fell asleep. She even said a blessing for you. Did the ladies tell you about the interview?"

Amanda was glassy-eyed with a shit-eating grin on her face.

"I have the feeling I didn't get the whole story."

"We didn't want to bogart your story," Amanda said loudly. "So tell him already!"

"You're shouting, Manny," Bianca said.

"Sorry," she said. She whispered loudly to Devante. "Tell him, please, before I explode."

Devante beamed. "Mr. Smith—I mean Dwayne (he wants me to call him that)—said they're picking one of the top five as 'Best in Chicagoland.' He told me I had a good chance. There're two other judges, but he's the only food guy, so his vote's pretty important."

"Who are the other judges?" Having Dwayne voting for him would be a big deal.

"Some lady columnist and Rod something from WGN."

"You're not too good with names, are you? Was it Mary Belton and Rod Dunphy?" Rod was a sky-is-falling liberal bloviator for Channel 9, and Mary was famous for holding grudges. I couldn't see her voting for anyone even remotely connected to Tawni.

"Yeah, that sounds right. Do you know them?"

"Not really."

Amanda whooped with delight. "Number fucking one, Jake! Can you believe it?"

"A little premature to crown him rib king. But it's a great development." I didn't want to get him too excited, but the way these "contests" usually worked, the winner was almost always the food critic's choice.

D was making notes in his planner. "If the demand takes off, I'll need more cash."

"More help too," Amanda said.

"Do you think Antoinette would loan me ten grand?" Devante asked. "She has that partner thing."

Antoinette and three of her friends had an arrangement where every two weeks they would put $500 in a kitty and one of them would take it. So, every other month she got an extra $2,000. It was really just a safer version of stuffing the money under the mattress. "You don't want to mess with that," I said.

Bianca nodded. "We had something like that too. But when my *papi* bought another garage, he got an SBA loan. I think he got fifty thousand."

"Great idea, Bianca," Amanda said. "The SBA is supposed to be helping guys like Devante."

Devante grinned. "Guys like me?"

"Yeah. Smart young entrepreneurs," she said without missing a beat. "What did you think I meant?"

"That's what I thought," Devante said.

"Where did he get the loan, Bianca?" I asked.

"Evanston Community Bank and Trust. Right next to the YMCA."

I looked at Devante. "Why don't we stop by there Monday morning before you go to work? You can fill out an application and maybe get a chance to talk with someone."

MONIQUE

Can I sit in the front seat?
That's a violation of Uber policy, but for you I'll make an exception.
You can kiss me.
Your lips are soft. You still taste like Juicy Fruit.
You're such a romantic. Where are we going?
The Hyatt. For Tawni's award.
Oh, Jake.
What?
You're like an uncaged bird who's afraid to fly away.

Chicago Tribune

Jake's Corner
Sunday, February 18, 2018
No Easy Answers

Yesterday, Commander Peter Brewer was shot and killed while attempting to arrest a man who had just run from other police officers near the Thompson Center. Brewer, who was in the area for a meeting, saw the man enter the building and attempted to stop him in a stairwell. The commander, a 31-year veteran of the Chicago Police Department, was killed by Ronald Davies, a four-time felon who had spent half his life in prison.

Davies grew up in the projects. His father was serving a life sentence for murder, his mother was a crack addict. He joined a gang when he was eight. He turned 21 in prison. The odds were against him from the day he was born. It would have taken an extraordinary human being to overcome the lousy hand he was dealt.

Alas, Davies was far from extraordinary.

We can all agree that this is a tragedy. We can't agree on much else.

We won't solve this problem by trying to ban guns. And we won't solve it by turning our country into the wild west, with every law-abiding citizen packing heat, ready to protect their homes and family with lethal force.

There is no policy genius in Washington or Chicago or New York or L.A. who is going to come up with a plan that stops gun violence. Maybe we need to think smaller. Figure out what each of us can do to help. Stop spending all our time *resisting* and try doing something positive.

Volunteer at a neighborhood food drive.

Become a Big Brother or Sister.

Join Habitat for Humanity.

There is no shortage of opportunities to help our community.

Want an example? Look at my friend, Enyart.

Right-wing, NRA member. Clearly a knuckle-dragging Neanderthal to many of my liberal friends. But on Friday I was at his gym —the Devon Boxing Club in Uptown. He was teaching a class of kids the fundamentals of boxing. Black. White. Hispanic. Asian. Boys and girls. Those kids spend most afternoons after school at his place. They get exercise, they learn defensive skills, they even do their homework. A dozen kids kept off the streets. Out of the gangs.

Enyart's making a difference.

Who knows what those kids will do with this opportunity?

Maybe save the world.

Postscript: Last week in my column on labeling people I suggested that those folks who call themselves The Resistance would do well to not label those who don't agree with their position as traitors. That apparently upset some people and inspired a few incredibly ignorant responses: one woman wrote in an online magazine that I had called The Resistance traitors. I did not, but I refuse to continue explaining myself. If you are not smart enough to understand what I write, my recommendation is that you stop reading my column.

TEN

SUNDAY, 6 P.M. — FEBRUARY 18, 2018

Hyatt Regency, Chicago

Tawni was being named "Person of the Year" by the Thomas More Society. They were a right-wing activist law firm mostly focused on fighting abortion clinics and lobbying against legislation that would make abortion more available. The open bar started at six and the dinner an hour later. I made it to the reception table at six o' five.

The only thing that made these banquets endurable was the open bar, and I intended to take full advantage. It's been my experience that conservatives are a lot less chintzy with their open bar selection than liberals. Not sure why. Enyart claimed it was because liberals would rather give away other people's money instead of their own. But I have to say that Thomas More was not starting off well. No Crown Royal, not even Canadian Club. My whiskey choices were either Jim Beam— not my favorite—or some house brand I never heard of. I took the Beam.

The cocktail reception area was set up in the hallway outside the banquet hall with a bar at each end. I sipped the whiskey as I strolled from one end of the reception to the other, weaving through the two dozen cocktail tables and the smattering of folks who had so far arrived. By the time I made it to the other end of the hall, I'd finished the whiskey. I handed my glass to the bartender for a refill and dropped a five-spot in his tip jar. I always carry plenty of cash to these events. I want to make sure the bartenders are taken care of; too many of these fat-cat types think that free booze means free service too. The bartender nodded appreciatively and gave me a generous pour.

I was halfway back across the room when Tawni made her entrance. She swept up to the reception table with the guy she had dumped me for trailing behind her. He was tall and blonde. They were almost too perfect a match. Barbie's Ken doll was dark-haired for a reason.

Tawni waved at me and handed her coat to her guy to check. She was wearing a shimmering royal blue gown that accentuated her figure and her blondness. It felt odd seeing her with someone else. The pieces in my world were being rearranged, and I still didn't have a place. I feared I never would.

I started to walk toward her and she met me halfway. "Thanks for coming." She leaned in slightly—with her heels she was taller than I am—and gave me a chaste hug.

"You're looking great, Tawni. Congratulations."

She stepped back, looking at me as though there was something written on my forehead.

"I talked to Charlotte this morning."

I sighed. Not a good start. I pressed my lips together. It took all my willpower not to ask why she had to do that.

"Don't give me that look. I have a right to talk to my own daughter."

"Of course," I said. "I hope you had a nice chat."

"I just wanted to remind her not to wear that polka-dot dress that she wore last year to the Christmas party."

I had nothing to say to that.

"It just wouldn't be appropriate for this crowd. That's all."

"I'm sure she appreciated the heads-up."

"Sarcasm doesn't become you, Jake Doyle." She punctuated that observation with her classic Tawni-pout. "Charlotte told me Devante opened a restaurant."

I could tell from her expression that she thought it was a bad idea and I should have done everything in my power to prevent it. Okay, I read a lot between the lines when Tawni speaks. But I am an expert.

"Not a sit-down restaurant. It's a storefront where he cooks. His barbeque ribs are very popular. He has a great takeout business." I wasn't about to tell her that I might be co-signing on an SBA loan soon. I could just hear that Tawni-lecture.

I couldn't be sure what Charlotte actually told her mother. I wouldn't have shared anything with Tawni, but that was Charlotte. Another millennial with no boundaries. "Devante's staying with me for a few weeks. Kalise is visiting, again."

"Oh yes. Antoinette's bossy sister." Kalise was as outspoken and strong-willed as Tawni, so they never got along. But before she could say anything more about Kalise, we were joined by her boyfriend, and she became political Tawni again. "Jake, I want you to meet Justin Reynolds. Justin's a lawyer at Meyer Waite and has been doing wonderful pro bono work for the Society. Justin—Jake Doyle."

Reynolds had blazingly white teeth and bright blue eyes. I knew I wouldn't like him. "Great to meet you, Jake. Loved your column today." He was obviously a suck-up, and to add to his list of defects he had an annoyingly firm, dry handshake. He made intense eye contact as if he were trying to hypnotize me. I almost forgot to thank him.

Tawni grasped my arm. "That was a great piece. You managed to make your friend sound admirable." She gave me that look again, which told me what she really thought of Enyart. "Have you had any pushback from the liberal darlings at the *Tribune*? How did it play on Twitter?"

I scanned the room looking for an escape, but of course I knew no one here. "I don't follow Twitter. Nothing from the paper." I swirled the ice and downed the rest of my whiskey. "I'm getting another drink." I was starting to remember why I made Tawni's life miserable. She deserved it.

Tawni was ready to work the crowd. She gave me her charm smile as she headed across the room with Mr. White Teeth following in her wake. "We'll see you in there," she said, looking back over her shoulder. "We've got the table right in front."

I had just finished my fourth whiskey when Charlotte and Devante walked in. Charlotte was wearing the simple black dress that at least half of the younger women were wearing. She was approachably attractive whereas her mother was striking. Beauty queen material. But the big difference was in attitude. Tawni embraced these kinds of events. She was always perfectly groomed and expertly accessorized. Charlotte looked more like the girl who is forced to dress up for her brother's graduation. Her dress was snug. I'm guessing she'd gained a few pounds since the Christmas party where she wore that infamous polka-dot dress. Of course, she could say the same about me.

Devante could have walked out of the pages of GQ. Black slacks, black shirt, black sports jacket. He wasn't the only Black man here, but probably the only one from the hood.

Charlotte hugged me tight, like she didn't want to let go.

"Hi, honey. You're looking great."

She shuddered and stepped back. "No. I'm not. I'm fat and blotchy. I hate this dress and my hair looks like shit." Her blonde hair was thin—lank, according to Tawni—and straight. She didn't work at it like Tawni, but I thought she looked good. I knew my opinion didn't count, so I didn't say anything more.

"You look great too, D," I said.

"God, he looks like a male model. And he doesn't even try. It's so unfair," Charlotte said. She hooked her arm through his.

The room was filling up. A waitress came up to us with a tray of stuffed mushrooms, and we cleaned her out. The bartender I had given all my business to stepped over. "Would you folks care for a drink before we close the bar?" he asked.

Devante shook his head. He wasn't old enough to drink, but they would have served him without question. Charlotte also declined, to my relief. I decided four whiskeys was probably enough, so we made our way to the table and what I hoped wouldn't be a disaster.

I surveyed the banquet hall and saw Tawni beckoning to us from a table that was directly in front of the elevated speaker's podium which was, at the moment, empty. Tawni was standing behind her chair with

Reynolds to her right. Across from them, an older couple, late seventies. The man was wearing a tux he probably bought when Kennedy was president. He was trim and it still fit him. Wish I could say the same. My closet in Glenview had resembled a Macy's suit rack. I had a matching collection of forty-four, forty-six and forty-eight regular navy blazers and blue suits. When I moved to my house in Skokie, I donated the forty-fours (that ship had definitely sailed), but I held on to the forty-sixes. One of these days I'm getting serious about my weight again.

The man was mostly bald, save a few wisps of gray hair. His wife, with hair whiter than Justin's teeth, had an unnaturally smooth, unlined face. She wore an expensive-looking crème-colored shift with a jeweled pendant that might have been opals. I imagined she was what Tawni would look like in twenty years.

As we headed toward the table, Tawni whispered something to Reynolds and then quick-stepped over to us, with her face frozen in her society smile. "Charlotte, honey, so glad you could make it." She held her at arm's length, studying Charlotte's face. I could tell she was about to give Charlotte one of her Tawni-critiques, and I steeled myself for the fireworks. But Charlotte beat her to the punch.

"I know, Mom. My hair looks like shit and I'm fat. And I didn't use any makeup."

Tawni's smile tightened into a painful-looking grin. "No, honey. Don't say that. You look lovely. I do have a compact if you want to take that shine off." She released her grip. "Nice to see you again, Devante. Let me introduce you to our hosts."

We dutifully followed her to her table. The Tawni Show had begun.

"Gordon, Cookie, I want you to meet my daughter, Charlotte, and her half-brother, Devante Baptiste." It was obvious that Gordon and Cookie had been briefed on Devante. "And I think you know my ex, Jake Doyle." Also on me.

Cookie smiled tightly, probably afraid her face would crack, and nodded at Charlotte and Devante. Gordon clasped Charlotte's hand in both of his hands with one of those preacher handshakes, "Very nice to meet you, Charlotte." And then he released her hand and shook

Devante's hand vigorously. "Welcome, Devante. Please sit down here." He guided Devante to the seat next to him as he turned to me and said, "Good to see you again, Jake."

I didn't remember ever having met him, but Tawni had dragged me to dozens of these soirées, and I used to hit the open bar harder in the old days, so it's possible. Lots of destroyed brain cells over the years. He didn't act like I'd done anything stupid, but he was a pro, so that's not a guarantee.

Charlotte took the seat between Devante and Reynolds, so I had to sit next to Tawni and Cookie. I had hoped to be positioned where I could head off any serious conflict between mother and daughter, but Gordon's move with Devante had messed up that plan. Reynolds was now the only human barrier separating the two women. I doubted he was up to the task.

"Gordon is the chairman emeritus of the Society," Tawni said, directing her comments to Charlotte and Devante. "And Cookie has been president of the Kenilworth Garden Club for..." she paused as if she were counting the years. "Decades. It's a marvelous organization. They do such great work there."

I doubted that Cookie was thrilled with the "decades" reference. Having introduced Gordon and Cookie, I was certain Tawni would now offer up Tawni-bios on Charlotte and Devante. That could be a disaster. I scanned the nearby tables. Two tables away, I spotted Judy Moy, the anchorwoman for channel 5. She was standing behind her chair, checking out the room. We had some history. I caught her eye and nodded my head toward Tawni. I was confident she would know the play.

Just as Tawni was about to speak, I leaned over and whispered, "Judy Moy wants to talk to you, if you could spare a few minutes. She's at the next table."

Tawni never turned down a chance to talk to the press. Especially the TV press. She spotted Judy and gave her a friendly wave and smile. "Excuse me, I'll just be a minute." She walked over to Judy, and they greeted each other like they were sorority sisters even though they didn't like each other. One of those skills Charlotte had never developed.

Having averted a disaster, I was now left with Tawni's vacant seat on my right and Cookie on my left. Gordon, engaged in conversation with Devante, had his fists up and was sort of shadowboxing in his seat. I heard him say, "Ali...", but the rest was lost to me. Devante appeared interested.

I turned to Cookie. "Do you go to many of these shindigs?" I asked, affecting my folksy, blue-collar manner.

She smiled, sort of. "Oh, yes. More than a few. I could probably recite Gordon's speech for you, verbatim."

"Oh, don't do that. Let me be surprised."

She smiled again and dabbed her lips with her napkin as she pushed the salad to the side. "That was an excellent piece in today's paper."

Wow. I wasn't expecting that. "Thank you." I was temporarily at a loss for words, which doesn't happen much, but was rescued by the servers who descended on our table, plucking away the salad plates and giving us all a small filet and salmon dinner. With some kind of mashed vegetable that wasn't potatoes. I looked quizzically at Cookie.

"Leeks," she said. She took a minuscule bite. "They're not awful."

She was clearly a woman of profoundly good taste.

Tawni rejoined us halfway through the meal. Judy Moy must have given her some hot gossip because Tawni had a look like she would burst if she couldn't share.

Immediately.

"Devante," she said, almost breathless. "Judy Moy loves loves loves your ribs."

Gordon, Cookie, and Reynolds all stared at Devante. "Ribs?" Gordon asked.

"I have a rib joint in Evanston. It's called Just Ribs," Devante said.

"His ribs are really popular," Charlotte said, surprising me with her enthusiasm.

"That's impressive, young man," Gordon said. "A boxer and restauranteur. Very impressive."

"Is that the Old Grecian Kitchen location?" Reynolds asked.

"That's right," I said. "They closed a couple years ago."

"Your business must be booming," Reynolds said. "I've seen lines outside your store every weekend."

Tawni was beaming. The restaurant was no longer such a bad idea. "Judy said," and she leaned forward and pretended to whisper, "that the *Tribune* is about to name Just Ribs the Best Ribs in Chicago." So much for the *Trib's* confidentiality.

"That's fantastic news, Devante," Reynolds said.

Devante had a deer-in-the-headlights look. I gave him a slight negative nod.

"I don't know about that," he said. "It would be cool if they did, I guess."

The kid had professional dissembling skills. I think I can take credit for that.

Of course, Tawni was an expert at bullshit detection. "I think you're being coy, but I understand. That will be huge for your business." She turned to Mr. White Teeth. "Justin, doesn't your council have programs to help small businesses?"

"Absolutely," he said. "Devante, I'm on the Evanston Development Council. We are actively seeking opportunities to help small business in the Evanston community. We have a ten-million-dollar grant from the federal government to support minority businesses. You could qualify for an entrepreneurship grant."

Devante was looking slightly shell-shocked. "Qualify for what?"

Justin put down his forkful of leeks. "A grant to help you grow your business."

"So, I borrow this grant?"

"No. It's an outright disbursement. Typically, five thousand, but with your story I think we could make it ten. You benefit. The community benefits. It's a win-win. I'll give you the link to the application. Fill it out and email it to me. I'll shepherd it through the process."

Devante looked at me. Antoinette had instilled in him a not unreasonable distrust of White people offering help. "It's a good idea, D," I said.

"Wonderful!" Tawni said. "Do you really think you can get it approved by the council?" She placed her hand gently on Justin's forearm and smiled at him with faux adoration.

Reynolds beamed. He was clearly bewitched by Tawni. "We'll make it happen."

As servers were bringing us dessert and asking if we wanted coffee, Gordon got up from the table. "Time to get this show on the road." He walked around the table and stopped at my chair. With his hands on my shoulders, he leaned over. "That column was first-rate. You're on to something. Keep it up."

Tawni gave me a look as Gordon stepped up to the podium. "Well, you're Mr. Popular today." She didn't sound pissed, but she didn't sound happy either.

Gordon kept his welcome remarks brief, and then he offered an effusive bio of Tawni, the Thomas More Society's Person of the Year. The award was a hunk of crystal from a place called Swarovski. I had never heard of them, but they must be famous as the crowd murmured its approval. Gordon invited Tawni up to the stage for a photo op. I hadn't thought about taking any photos, but Devante had his phone out. The kid was no dummy.

Tawni gave a short, effective speech. Gracious as hell. Diplomatic and open-minded. Hard to believe she was the same woman who was so tone-deaf with her own daughter. When she had finished and received a sincere and reasonable-length standing ovation, Gordon walked back to the podium.

"I want to recognize some of the dignitaries we have with us tonight." This is always the most painful part of the night for me. The finish line is within sight, and the coach calls a timeout and we have to wait. He recognized a judge, a real estate baron, a right-wing bloviator on talk radio, and then he said, "And seated at my table, we are honored to have the esteemed newspaper columnist for the *Chicago Tribune*, Mr. Jake Doyle! Jake, stand up and take a bow."

Fuck me. I didn't need this. I could feel my face burning. Possibly it was on fire from the eye-lasers Tawni was drilling me with. One of my cardinal rules: never, never, never upstage Tawni.

I half rose out of my seat, gave a quick wave, and sat back down. But Gordon wasn't done with me yet.

"Now many of you know that Jake tends to write more for the other team." He smiled and got a few nervous laughs. "But if you have read his columns lately, then you know he is on to something. There is a sickness in this society, and it's not a right or a left issue. It's an American issue. Jake Doyle has seen that, and he's doing something about it."

He pulled out a section of newspaper he had stuffed in his pocket and read my paragraph on Enyart's afterschool program. When he finished there was a thunder of applause. I'm afraid it was probably louder than the ovation for Tawni. Not probably. I had definitely won Queen for a Day. Which I knew would be a very pyrrhic victory.

As we were getting ready to leave, Gordon came over to me and shook my hand again. "Have you seen my show, *The Chicago Way?*"

That show had been a Sunday morning staple for local political junkies, but I thought it had gone off the air years ago. "Uh…I used to, I thought…"

"I moved off broadcast television five years ago. We livestream. No more mainstream media censorship, you know."

I didn't have anything to say to that. I had never actually watched the show. Sunday mornings were for sleeping late. "I didn't know that," I said. When glibness fails, the truth is always an option.

"My partner-in-crime is Rod Dunphy. He provides the liberal viewpoint; we try to be balanced politically, you know. His grand-daughter is getting married—on that liberal colony, Martha's Vineyard, of course. Would you be willing to fill in? There's a $500 honorarium, not that that's important. We broadcast live on Wednesday at noon in our offices at Willis Tower."

A month ago, I probably would have said no. But I guess that Lucy Hall story and the new *Tribune* owner's insistence on an apology bothered me more than I had been willing to admit. And I could use the money. "Sure thing, Gordon. Happy to help out. See you Wednesday."

ELEVEN

SUNDAY, 10 P.M. — FEBRUARY 18, 2018

Lake Shore Drive

Charlotte and Devante had taken a cab to the banquet, so Devante and I dropped her off at her apartment in Old Town then headed north on Lake Shore Drive. Devante was quiet, staring blankly out his window. "How did you like the banquet?" I asked.

"It was cool. Mr. Reynolds gave me the link to the grant application. It's pretty simple. I told him we were applying for an SBA loan. He thought that was a good idea. He said having the grant would make getting the loan easier."

"Just remember you can't mention the *Tribune* award. It could queer the whole deal."

"How did that reporter find out?"

"Had to be Dwayne Smith. He's lusted after Judy Moy for years."

He shrugged. "I won't say anything about it. Hey, that Gordon guy did you a solid, telling everyone about your column. You got a real fan there."

"I don't need that kind of publicity. I'm already in hot water with my bosses, and Tawni wasn't happy. That was her thing tonight."

He gave me a perplexed look. "That ain't your fault. She can't hold that against you."

"Can and will," I said. I tried not to laugh. The kid had a lot to learn about relationships. "Don't try to be logical."

"Damn," Devante said, more to himself than to me.

Traffic on the Drive started thinning out as we crossed Irving Park Road. We were approaching my old neighborhood. The soccer fields along the lakefront were dark and empty, and the lake was inky black. A lone runner was braving the winter cold and jogging on the trail that bordered the Montrose Dog Beach.

Devante was sitting forward in his seat, looking intently at the lakefront scene. "That's the dog beach," he said. "I was there."

"You remember that?"

"A dog licked my face, and then a lady put me on the dog's back."

"That was your mom," I whispered, more to myself than to Devante.

Monique was talented and ambitious, and she wanted to see the world beyond Chicago. She had applied for positions at the *New York Times* and the *Washington Post* with the goal of becoming a foreign correspondent. Having Devante changed all that. She let me see Devante every Saturday, but only because Antoinette insisted. I wanted to see him more, and I wanted to be with Monique, but she wanted to "move on," and I never pressured her. I didn't want to drive her away. I thought I was playing the long game. That day I had brought Bosco with me when I came by to pick up Devante. Monique loved Bosco.

She didn't seem angry at me anymore, so I decided to take a shot. "Why don't you come with us to the dog beach?" I asked. My hands were sweating. I was afraid to breathe.

But Monique smiled at me the same way she used to before everything went to hell. "Why Mr. Doyle, are you shamelessly using this precious dog to break down my resistance?"

"Is it working?"

She knelt down and hugged Bosco. "You are such a sweetheart. I need to be back by ten. I have an assignment."

"On Saturday morning?" After Devante was born, Monique landed a job as a theater critic for the *Chicago Reader*. They tried to cover all the storefront theatres the *Trib* didn't have time to cover.

"It's theater in the park. Over at Edgewater."

"We could come along," I said. I knew I was pushing my luck.

She fake-frowned and picked up Devante. "Not a good idea. Your son is a very vocal critic, and he would rather spend the afternoon with his father at the zoo."

We drove over to the beach, and I let Bosco off his leash to romp with all the other dogs. I pushed D in his stroller, and Monique and I walked hand-in-hand just like every other young couple with a baby and a dog. It felt so heartbreakingly normal. Why hadn't I tried harder to be with her? The long game was bullshit.

"That was your mom," I said again. My voice husky.

"You okay, Jake?"

I squeezed the steering wheel and tried to get a grip on my emotions. "That was Saturday, July 18. Monique was shot two days later."

Devante sat back in his seat. "Grandma said she was a happy person. Said she always had a smile on her face." He bit down on his lip. "I don't remember her." His voice was soft. Then he smacked his forehead with his hand, like a boxer trying to recover from a punch. "White people are weird."

"How so?"

"They got a whole beach just for their dogs. Damn."

I thought about pointing out that it wasn't a beach just for White folks and their dogs, but I knew how that conversation would go. "I don't think White folks have a monopoly on weirdness."

He tilted his head as he considered that possibility. "Maybe not a monopoly, but y'all got a serious lead."

MONIQUE

Why are all those people screaming at us?
A girl was shot.
Charlotte's gained weight.
It's just that dress. It didn't fit her.
They're rocking the car, Jake.
A girl was shot.
She's pregnant, Jake. The car's on fire.
You're crazy, Mon. I don't like this dream. I'm waking up now.

TWELVE

MONDAY, 9 A.M. — FEBRUARY 19, 2018

Evanston City Hall

Our bank trip started out great. The loan officer at ECB&T, a plump Asian woman named Kathy Wong, was a huge fan. "I love your ribs," she said. "I always promise myself that I will eat just half a slab, and I'll always break that promise." She pulled out a glossy folder with at least ten pages of documents. "Your business is exactly what the SBA is designed for."

"I'm applying for an Evanston entrepreneur grant."

Ms. Wong nodded her head enthusiastically. "That's an excellent idea. I can include a copy of that application with your loan application."

Devante looked over at me, uncertain of what he was supposed to say.

"He submitted the application to Justin Reynolds," I said. "He said he would submit it to the committee."

"Oh, my. That makes it a sure thing. Mr. Reynolds is very well-respected on the committee. That grant will enhance your prospects for getting this loan."

She took him through the comprehensive application. It would be a daunting experience for most small businesses, but Devante wasn't fazed. Business plan, references, market projections, he could provide everything they wanted. Even a co-signer.

He gathered all the materials. "I can have this back to you tomorrow. How long will it take to get the loan?" He had decided that fifty thousand dollars was what he needed.

She smiled, amused and impressed with his confident enthusiasm. "We do have a backlog," she said, checking her laptop, "but if everything checks out, we can probably have a commitment to you in sixty days."

Devante's face tightened, but he kept his cool. I was fearful that would be the case. The wheels of bureaucracy don't usually move fast unless you're connected. We were definitely not connected.

At least not yet.

Devante didn't say much on the short ride back to my house. More notes in his planner. Amanda hadn't left yet for work. She acted more disappointed than Devante.

"What are you going to do?" she asked.

"I don't know. It was such a cool opportunity. She was even a customer."

"When will they give you that grant?" Amanda asked.

"Mr. Reynolds said that it usually takes ninety days. I need the cash before then." He bit down on his lip and made another note in his planner.

"I could loan you a thousand," Amanda said. "And I'll bet Bianca would help. She has tons of money saved. Those Dominicans are super cheap."

"Thrifty, Amanda. Not cheap," I said. "And that's very cool of you to offer. You are definitely the best tenant ever." I turned to Devante. "It is a good opportunity. You need to complete that application."

Devante shook his head. "But they're announcing the winner of that contest soon. Maybe two weeks. Three weeks tops."

"First of all, you haven't won yet. And you might not. But the loan will still make sense. You'll get a boost from being identified as a top five rib joint."

"I'm going to win, Jake. I can feel it."

"You hand in that application tomorrow, and I'll loan you $25,000 from my 401(k)." Okay, that was an impulsive gesture, but it felt right.

Devante looked surprised. I guess he couldn't imagine me having that kind of money. "What's a 401(k)?" he asked.

"It's my retirement plan. I can borrow against it. No penalty. Just have to repay it before I retire. Which won't be any time soon…I hope."

"Wow. Thanks, Jake." Impulsively, he hugged me. He was not a hugger. I don't think we had been that close since he was a baby. It felt good. Like he really was my son.

MONIQUE

Proud of yourself?
He hugged me.
And they say money can't buy love.
I wanted to be a part of his life.
Do you blame me for that?
Yes.
Be careful what you wish for, darling.

THIRTEEN

TUESDAY, 5:30 PM. — FEBRUARY 20, 2018

Home

My next column wasn't due until Friday, so I got up early and signed into Uber. I was busy all morning. I had just dropped off an elderly Black man at Evanston Hospital when Devante called to let me know that he had submitted his SBA application. I signed off Uber and headed to the *Tribune* offices to take care of the loan.

The 401(k) was administered by the HR department. I never had much use for HR. I thought the department sucked up a lot of resources with useless programs that had nothing to do with putting out a newspaper.

I was not one of the department's favorites.

When the scandal broke, the head of HR, an old fossil named Harvey Judd, had wanted me tossed, but Hector had refused, which I'm sure cost him. Harvey was long gone, and O'Neill and his minions had gutted the department, which was the only cost-saving action they took that I supported. The department was now run by an officious functionary named Gail Leone.

When I told Yolanda at the front desk the reason for my visit, she sighed. She wasn't a fan of HR either. Leone told her to put me in the conference room.

"Sorry, Jake," Yolanda said. "Can I get you coffee?"

"No thanks. How about a copy of the *Sun Times*?"

She gave me a look. "You better behave, or I might forget where I put you."

After twenty minutes, when I had started to think that maybe Yolanda had forgotten me, Ms. Leone marched into the room clutching a sheaf of papers. With her half-crescent glasses dangling around her neck, she resembled more than anything a harried librarian.

She didn't bother with the faux-friendly personnel greeting. "You want to borrow money from your retirement plan?" She stood at the end of the table, clearly not planning to sit down for a chat. Her tone made it clear she did not think that was a good idea.

"Yes, I do. Twenty-five thousand."

Her frown deepened as she studied one of the pages. "You only have $48,453, so the maximum you can borrow is fifty percent of that amount. Which we don't advise."

I didn't know who "we" was, and I didn't care. "Okay. Twenty-four thousand, then."

She sighed with practiced condescension. "What is the purpose of the loan?"

I knew the smart thing to do was just answer her questions, but I couldn't resist. "Why do you ask? It's my money."

"The proceeds can't be use for any kind of illegal activity."

"It's for my son's restaurant," I said, this time resisting the impulse to give her another smartass answer.

Her eyebrows peaked. "You know restaurants have a very high failure rate. You have to pay this loan off in five years, and if you lose your job you must pay it off in sixty days. If you don't the loan defaults and your 401(k) will be liquidated, triggering a ten percent penalty and creating a taxable event for you."

"I guess I better not lose my job," I said, offering her some folksy bonhomie.

"You can't make any contributions to the plan while you have a loan outstanding, so you won't have the opportunity to build your retirement nest egg." She glanced down at my file. "And at your age that should be a priority."

"I stopped making contributions when O'Neill stopped matching contributions. I guess he isn't too worried about my nest egg."

She shook her head, dismissing me as a hopeless case. "Complete these forms and give them to Yolanda." She turned to walk out the door.

"When do I get the check?"

Another sigh. "If everything is in order, the funds can be deposited in your bank account tomorrow."

It took me an hour to complete the loan package. I dropped it off with Yolanda, and then I signed back onto Uber and picked up a young woman who needed a ride to Northwestern.

Perfect.

A fifty-dollar fare that brought me within two miles of home. I decided to call it a day.

When I walked into the house, Amanda was on her tri-bike, pedaling furiously. She had set the sleek racing bike up on some sort of stand in front of the television. She was drenched with sweat, and her tri-suit and the exercise mat under the bike were soaked. She stopped pedaling when she spotted me.

"Hi, Jake." Her face was flushed, matching the color of her damp hair. "Hope you don't mind. I need to build my bike endurance. Can't do that outside in this weather."

"Where's Devante?"

"He's building his endurance too. Long run. To the lakefront and back. It's about twelve miles." She glanced at her watch. "He should be back in about an hour."

I walked over to the television. The scene on the screen was a long strip of road on a barren, sun-drenched landscape. "That looks desolate."

"It's Kona, in Hawaii. THE Ironman course. One hundred twelve miles through the desert. It's brutal."

"You're racing there?"

She smiled. "I wish. I have to qualify. I'm doing the Ironman in Madison in August. I need to finish in the top ten percent in my age group to qualify for Kona." She dismounted and started toweling down.

"Don't stop on my account," I said. "I'm not watching TV."

"I'm done. I did thirty miles. I'll go take my shower. Why don't you order us a pizza?" She turned and headed for the stairs.

A pizza? Something was up. "What's going on?" I asked.

"Nothing. No anchovies."

"Amanda!"

She sighed and walked back into the kitchen and sat down. "I wanted to wait until you had your pizza before I told you…"

My mind sorted through the possible announcements that would require pizza to soften the blow: she was leaving; she was pregnant; she was pregnant and leaving; she had some terrible disease. "So tell me, already."

"Charlotte's pregnant."

Oh.

That didn't make sense.

"How do you know?"

"Devante told me this morning. She asked him to go with her when she gets an abortion in two weeks. He wasn't supposed to tell anyone, but he needed someone to talk to and he couldn't talk with you."

"Wait. She's already scheduled it?"

"I sort of think Devante told me so that I would tell you. Or maybe I'm just making excuses for blabbing, but I had to tell you."

"Fuck," I said. It was a tired 'fuck,' not an angry one. I should have been shocked, but I had had this uneasy sense that something wasn't right with Charlotte.

"What are you going to do, Jake?"

I grabbed my coat and car keys. "Go see my daughter."

FOURTEEN

TUESDAY, 7:30 P.M. — FEBRUARY 20, 2018

Charlotte's Apartment

I t took me forty minutes to drive to Old Town. I rehearsed a dozen gems of wisdom I could offer Charlotte. They all sucked. When I rang the buzzer and identified myself, she hesitated a painfully long time before she buzzed me in. Perceptive reporter that I am, I sensed she wasn't happy to see me. I never show up unannounced, so she must have figured out I had been told about her pregnancy.

Charlotte was wearing her standard UChicago sweatshirt and sweatpants. She was paler than normal and had a serious frown when she opened the door. "The house is a mess," she said before I could say hello. "You should have let me know you were coming."

I followed her into her living room/kitchen and sat down on the couch. Her place was messy only by Charlotte's standards. She'd grown up in a house where any surface including the floor was fair game for Tawni's paperwork, clothes, shoes, books, or magazines. The few times I'd been in Charlotte's apartment it reminded me of the photos you see when someone's trying to rent their unit. She was obsessively compulsively tidy—no doubt a reaction to her mother's sloppiness.

Today her apartment resembled a normal single woman's apartment. Her outside shoes had been tossed carelessly by the entrance—not squared away like she normally did, and her winter coat had been hooked on the doorknob to the front closet instead of being hung up. Scattered on her coffee table in the living room were several sections of the Sunday *New York Times*, and piled on the end table next to her reading chair was *We Were Eight Years in Power* by Ta-Nehisi Coates and *What Happened* by Hillary Clinton. Opened and face down in her chair was the book she had obviously been reading when I interrupted her: Michael Connelly's latest Bosch novel, *Two Kinds of Truth.*

She closed the book and dropped into her chair.

"How do you like Coates's new book?" I asked.

She scrunched her face. "I can't get into it. He's too cerebral for me." She puffed out her cheeks and exhaled. "And Hillary's book makes me so damn sad, I can't read it either."

"Connelly's a better writer anyway."

"You remind me of Harry Bosch," she said.

That sounded like a compliment, but I had the feeling it wasn't. "Really?"

"Yeah. He makes a lot of stupid choices, but somehow it all works out for him in the end."

I was tempted to ask her which of my many stupid choices she was referring to, but I decided I didn't really want to know. "How you feeling?" I asked.

Her mouth twisted downward. "Goddamn Devante. I can't believe he told you."

"He didn't. He told Amanda."

"Jesus. He didn't think your girlfriend would tell you?"

"She's not my girlfriend, but I think he probably did think she would tell me. I'm guessing he's conflicted."

Charlotte brought her knees up to her chest and wrapped her arms around her legs. It was her favorite position when she was a kid. "How could anyone want to bring a baby into this fucked up world?" She gazed at the books on her end table. "A place that elects Donald Trump for president?"

"He'll be gone soon. Life has to go on. You can't give up."

"Why not? You did."

"What do you mean?"

She took another sharp exhale. "You should have gone with Monique. You took the easy way out."

My face burned. Charlotte didn't understand. I would have left Tawni (and her) to marry Monique if she had wanted me.

Whatever. No mulligans. I can't undo the past. Like a good politician I had to remember to stay on message. Pregnancy. Abortion. Those were the challenges of the day.

"Where's Greg in all this?" I assumed Greg was the father, so I wasn't asking that question.

Another serious exhalation like she was in labor. "He wants the baby. Mr. No Commitment wants the goddamn baby."

"Does he know your plans?"

"No."

Damn.

That wasn't right. From the years of Tawni and Charlotte battles, I had learned to do whatever I could to avoid conflict. I didn't want a fight with Charlotte, but saying nothing wouldn't work this time.

"I don't think it's fair for you to do this without telling him. He has a right to know."

Charlotte glowered. I'd seen that look a thousand times. "What good is that? He can't stop me. We don't have a future together, and he can't take care of a baby. That would all be on me. And…"

"What?"

"How do I have a chance at Stanford with a goddamn baby to take care of? This is my shot. I know I sound like a selfish bitch, but having a baby fucks everything up."

"There are other options. Nanny. Childcare facilities. Have you considered them?"

"Jesus Christ, Dad. I'm a recovering alcoholic. I'm not a super woman like Mom. I can't handle law school, Greg's needs, your guilt, and a baby. I'm weak. Like you."

Charlotte could be bracingly harsh.

"Okay. Have you scheduled…uh, the procedure?"

"Tuesday after next. Rogers Park Health Center. Devante said he would come with me."

"No," I said. I stood up. "I can't let him do that. It's my job. Come here."

I hugged her and we didn't say anything. I felt my eyes welling. I don't know why. "Maybe I gave up once. But I will never give up on you. Never."

A light snow started to fall as I pulled onto Lake Shore Drive. It should have been a welcome distraction from thinking about Charlotte, but it wasn't. I had spent all those years with Tawni, studiously avoiding any discussion of abortion. She was passionately opposed, and I respected her passion. But I always believed that a woman should have the right to choose.

I guess that was an abstract belief. Now that I was confronted with the issue on a personal level, I was sorely conflicted. I believed the decision had to be Charlotte's, but her not telling Greg was wrong. And my not telling Tawni about her daughter's plan felt like a betrayal. Having a baby and taking on Stanford Law School was, for sure, a huge challenge. But so was beating alcohol. Charlotte was too hard on herself. She was stronger than I.

But it wasn't my call. It was Charlotte's.

Even with the snow and traffic, which should have required my full attention, I couldn't stop replaying the options. But no matter how many times I did so, the choices never got better.

The phone rang. It was Devante. Fuck. He never called me.

"Hey Jake, Mr. Enyart just called you." His voice was strained. Enyart never called anyone either. This had to be really bad news.

"He told me Jamal grabbed Maurice from the home where they were keeping him. They did a drive by—the kid shot up a birthday party for some Latin Kings."

Damn.

I had a sick feeling in my gut. I should have turned Maurice over to the police. "Did the cops grab them?"

"They got Maurice. Jamal got away, But Jake…"
"What?"
"Maurice killed a four-year-old girl."

MONIQUE

That poor little girl. You killed her, Jake.
No. It's not my fault.
You don't need a gun to kill someone.
Go away.
I'm trying, but you won't let me.
I'm waking up now.

Chicago Tribune

Jake's Corner
The Road to Hell
Wednesday, February 21, 2018

I'm writing this at three in the morning. Lately, I have been plagued by a dream. It's something unsettling, something from my past, but it is just out of reach. When I wake up, it's gone. I can't remember it. I don't know what it's about, but it leaves me in a cold sweat.

Some days the world can be a sad, ugly place. Too many days, lately. If you're a police officer, a paramedic, a teacher—every day can be a struggle. But I'm not on the front lines. I'm simply a reporter—an observer—trying to make sense of it all.

Yesterday, Leticia Ribeiro was happily celebrating her fourth birthday when she was killed in a drive-by shooting. Calling her an innocent victim seems woefully inadequate. This was a hate crime. An assault on our humanity. I want to scream, "When will this senseless killing stop?" But I have her blood on my hands.

In my Sunday column I told you about the Devon Boxing Club run by my friend John Enyart. On Friday I was there watching my son train for the Golden Gloves tournament. A 21-year-old gang member entered the club with a 14-year-old boy who he was recruiting for his gang.

The gang member, who had just been released from Danville Correctional after serving two years for armed robbery, ordered the boy to shoot my son. And me. The boy was clearly terrified. He hesitated—and I managed to disarm him. I didn't believe that scared and confused boy was about to shoot us. He had tried to escape the gang life, but he made a wrong turn—got involved with the wrong people. I could have called the police and had him arrested.

Instead, I took him to a home for kids who have no place to go. I thought I was giving him an opportunity for a fresh start.

It was a fatal miscalculation.

Yesterday, the boy was plucked from that safe home by his gang-member handler, and they went on a drive-by shooting spree.

That boy shot and killed Leticia Ribeiro.

My good intentions have cost an innocent young girl her life and sealed the fate of a boy who will now be tried as an adult. If our system of justice works as it usually does, he will be spending the rest of his life behind bars.

I have spent my years as a reporter challenging the system. Questioning the politicians and the police and the bureaucrats who run the city. I would like to think I have done some good things. That I have held the rich and powerful to account and championed those who don't have connections. The underclass. The innocents like Leticia.

Maybe I have. Maybe I haven't.

But this time I was wrong. And there is no way I can ever fix it.

FIFTEEN

WEDNESDAY, 11 A.M. — FEBRUARY 20, 2018

Willis Tower

In the old days, when I submitted my column it would be reviewed by at least two editors. One focused on the content, and the other made sure there weren't any typos or clunky sentences. Those days were gone. Hector was the only one who checked my work, and he was overloaded, so he usually passed it on without comment or change. I uploaded "Road to Hell" at five in the morning, and Hector wasn't available. It went straight to production. It would be in the Thursday print paper and this morning's online paper coming out at nine.

After uploading, I went back to bed. I had to be at Gordon's *Chicago Way* show at eleven, and I didn't want to fall asleep during the broadcast. When I came downstairs at nine, Devante was in the kitchen writing in his planner. Today's *Tribune* was on the counter. The headline read, "Drive-by Mayhem," with a color photo of a smiling little girl above the fold.

"Hey, Jake. You want the paper?" he asked. His voice subdued, sad.

"You read the story?"

"Yeah." He stared down at his planner as though he might find the answer to what was troubling him. "We fucked up, didn't we?"

"I was wrong, D. It wasn't your call." It wasn't, but I knew that me telling him wouldn't make him believe it. I folded up the paper. "I don't want to read it until after this broadcast thing. How come you're not at work?" Devante normally worked Monday to Thursday at Topo Gio and then ran Just Ribs Friday to Sunday.

"I'm taking the day off. I bought a smoker from a rib joint in Niles that closed. They're delivering it this morning; it will double my capacity. I should be jazzed, but today I don't want to do anything."

"I know," I said. "I understand."

Gordon's offices were on the 24th floor of Willis Tower. A windowless conference room had been converted into a broadcast studio for *The Chicago Way*. When the receptionist walked me into the studio, Gordon was at the table studying his laptop. When he saw me, he rose quickly and walked across the room to shake my hand. He was wearing an expensive-looking, well-tailored blue suit with a red tie. I was wearing the same sports jacket I had worn to the banquet—the only one that fit me. I didn't figure he'd notice.

"I just read your column, Jake." He shook his head as though he couldn't believe what he had read. "What an experience." He sounded excited, but his face was grim. "We're going to have a compelling show."

That didn't give me a good feeling. It sounded like what the gladiators might have said when they welcomed the Christians.

I was impressed. Gordon was far more tech-savvy than I was. Okay, a low bar, but he had definitely mastered the technology of putting on a livestream show. Back in the '90s, when I was a hot commodity, I did a few local political talk shows. The studios were large with multiple cameras and a bunch of self-important assistants running around. On the network shows they even had a makeup artist.

Gordon did it all himself. He didn't need a production assistant or an intern or a secretary or even a sidekick to laugh at his jokes. He sat at his desk, like a talk show host, and controlled the production—camera focus, volume, intro music, commercial breaks—all from his laptop.

He wired me up, tested my microphone, did a sound check, and had me sit down in the chair that was angled so that I could look at him or the camera.

"I will introduce you and then I'll start asking questions. You don't have to look at the camera, just talk to me—it'll be easy. Two guys having a conversation. Don't be nervous."

"Got it," I wasn't nervous. Talking was something I'd always been good at.

At ten seconds to noon, he did a countdown and then cued the intro. A stentorian voice came on, "Now from Willis Tower in Chicago, Illinois… Gordon LaPlante and *The Chicago Way*."

Gordon smiled at the camera. "Welcome. I am pleased today to have a timely and very special guest: the veteran columnist for the *Chicago Tribune*, Jake Doyle." He gestured toward me and then delivered an effusive recap of my career, which did not include my fall from grace. I was impressed.

And disarmed.

"I want to get right to it, Mr. Doyle. In this morning's online edition of the *Chicago Tribune*, you have a story about that terrible tragedy—the drive-by murder of four-year-old Leticia Ribeiro."

Hmm. I was now Mr. Doyle, instead of Jake. "Yes. A terrible tragedy." Aargh. I repeated what he said. A totally lame response. I guess I was a little rusty.

"You met the killer the day before. Is that right?"

"Correct. My son was training for the Golden Gloves tournament at a local gym when two young men barged into the gym. The older kid had sparred with my son the day before, and he hadn't liked the outcome. He wanted to settle matters with a street fight."

That was better. A short, punchy response and no 'uh,' 'you know,' or other verbal tics.

"Oh my. What happened?"

"My son picked him up and slammed him to the ground. The gangbanger was shaken up, and I thought that would be the end of the matter. But when he got to his feet, he ordered the younger kid to shoot us."

Gordon masterfully feigned surprise. "That's horrific. You suggested that this was some sort of gang initiation?"

"I believe so. The gangs follow the same handbook as the Mafia. They want their members to have blood on their hands. And the gangs often use juveniles for the dirty stuff because they are usually tried in juvenile court."

Gordon glanced down at his notepad. He had a lot of notes. "So, the gang member says, 'Shoot them!' What happened next?"

"The kid pulled a handgun from his hoodie and was waving it around. He was trying to act tough, but it was clear he was terrified."

"And you disarmed him. Very impressive. How did you manage to do that?"

Gordon panned the camera so it was focused only on me. To the broadcast audience I'm sure he sounded as though he were totally engaged in this dialogue, but he wasn't even looking at me. He was just studying that damn notepad. I like to make eye contact so I can see if the questioner understands, agrees, disagrees, or just thinks I'm rambling. I stared at the top of Gordon's bald head for a moment to see if he would look up, but no luck.

"The owner of the club was an ex-Marine. He approached the boy and asked him if he had chambered a round. It was a distraction. The kid had no idea what he was talking about, and when he turned to look to his handler for some guidance, I was able to step up to him and take the gun away."

"Good on you, Mr. Doyle. That took real guts." His voice was animated, but his stare was angry.

I frowned at him. He was trying to ambush me. "I am not trying to be humble. Any time a gun is pointed at someone there's a real danger—but in this case it was clear that the kid was very frightened. He wasn't about to shoot anyone. When he gave up the gun, it put the onus on the gang member to do something, and he decided flight was the best option."

"He ran off?"

"Yes."

He put down his notepad and leaned toward me. "Okay now. That was gutsy. Even heroic. You protected your son. Very admirable. But you didn't call the police." He had set down his notes and was staring hard at me.

Any vestige of Gordon's faux affability had disappeared. "No. I didn't."

"The lad pointed a loaded gun at you. And your son. Why wouldn't you call the police? I know you're a liberal, Mr. Doyle, but I never thought you were one of those radical anti-police progressives."

He tried to stare me down, but he wasn't in my league. I stared back at him until he folded and picked up his notepad, afraid I would leave him with dead air. "Uh, well—"

I held up my hand to stop him. "He had been a part of the after-school program at the boxing club. He joined that because he wanted to escape the gangs. If we had him arrested he would have been sent to juvenile detention, which is dominated by gang members. It's gladiator school. After six months his chance to escape the gangs would be non-existent."

"Well, it seems to me that if he had been in juvenile detention, he wouldn't have been able to go on a drive-by shooting and kill that poor little girl."

In one sense it was a cheap shot, but it felt cathartic to talk about the tragedy. I guess that's the quirky nature of guilt. "That's correct, Gordon."

He scowled, disappointed with my response, I guess. "I can see from all the flashing lights that we are getting a lot of calls. Why don't we open this up to our listeners. See what they think of Mr. Doyle's good intentions."

He turned away from me to punch some buttons on his console. "Hello, this is *The Chicago Way*. You are on the air. Tell me who's calling and where you're calling from."

"This is Eduard from Berwyn." He had a thick Eastern European accent. "I say bullshit, Mr. Doyle. Those animals need to be locked up. I don't care how old they are. They kill little girls. I say cut off their—"

"Thank you, Eduard. Next caller."

"Tammy, Villa Park. This is outrageous. It's Jake Doyle who should be locked up."

"Vinnie. I drive Yellow Cab. Been robbed three times in the last year. Fucking do-gooder judges keep putting these guys back on the street. I say…"

The callers were angry, vocal, profane. I was glad we didn't have a studio audience; they might have stormed the stage. I wasn't surprised. Despite Gordon's claim of bi-partisanship his audience was hardcore red-state. After ten minutes of non-stop vilification, he finally took a call from someone who had a different perspective.

"My name is Dorthea Gibbs. I'm a retired schoolteacher. Mr. Doyle is correct. The juvenile detention facility is nothing but a school for gangs…"

The calls continued for another thirty minutes. Most of the listeners expressed their outrage and disgust. Many recommended punishments for me ranging from jail time to flogging to castration.

When it was over, Gordon asked me if I had anything to say.

I did.

"In your introduction, you kindly omitted my fall from grace. Twenty years ago, I was a hotshot columnist on the rise. My column was syndicated in two hundred papers, and I was even nominated for a Pulitzer.

"Then the wheels came off.

"I wish I could say I was done in because I got too close to the power brokers and they crushed me. At least that would be a good story. But my fall from grace was all on me. I fell in love with someone I wasn't supposed to fall in love with. She was twenty-one, I was thirty-five and married. She was my intern. She had a baby. We named him Devante.

"I'm supposed to say I was wrong. That I made a mistake and I'm sorry. But I loved Monique and I love my son. My heart wanted something it couldn't have. I don't think that makes it wrong, just impossible.

"Devante's twenty now, and he's a good man. Better than I am. He has big plans, just like his mother did. He's going to be one of those celebrity chefs someday. Even though I didn't raise him, I've been a part of his life and I'm grateful for that.

"Two years after Devante was born, Monique was killed in a drive-by shooting. She was a good person. I grieve for the life that she could have led. The world's a sadder place without her in it."

I was standing, staring at the camera. I don't remember standing up.

"Is it possible to be sorry for a mistake—and my affair was a mistake—and still have no regrets? I think so.

"So why am I telling you all this personal history? I think most people are trying to do the right thing most of the time. We all stumble. We all make mistakes. Some we learn from. We fix the problem. We move on. But some mistakes can't be fixed. We just have to live with those and hope we have enough days left to do better, to balance the scales somehow."

My throat was tight. I needed to finish before I broke down.

"Leticia Ribeiro is dead. I didn't shoot her, but I could have prevented it. I had good intentions, but that means nothing.

"I was wrong. I made a bad decision, and I'm responsible.

"I am profoundly sorry."

Gordon stared at me and tried to speak but couldn't. He cleared his throat and turned toward the camera.

I don't know what he finally said when he regained his voice, and I didn't care. I unclipped my mic and walked out of the studio.

SIXTEEN

WEDNESDAY, 7 P.M. — FEBRUARY 20, 2018

Charcoal Oven

When I got back from the broadcast, I read the *Tribune* story about the slaying of Leticia Ribeiro. It was written by Mary Belton. A poor choice in my opinion. Mary's gift was squeezing emotion out of every scene, no matter how banal. This story just needed to be reported; it didn't require any help from the reporter to break your heart.

I confess there have been so many stories of innocent children being shot in the last few years that I usually avoid them. Not because I'm callous or indifferent—the stories are all heartbreaking—but there is no answer and no justice. The futility overwhelms me. But this time, like Charlotte's abortion decision, it was personal. I read every word from beginning to end, and I knew that Leticia Ribeiro's story would be with me for the rest of my life. The stain might fade, but it would always be a part of me. I'd never be clean.

Amanda had gone to dinner with Bianca, and D was still working on the installation of his new smoker. I grabbed the bottle of Crown

Royal. It was almost full, and I knew if I started I would probably kill the bottle. I had done that before, and nothing good ever came of it. I decided to head over to the Oven, where at least I'd have Enyart to supervise my drinking.

It was a typical Wednesday night there. A half-dozen couples scattered among the tables and booths. They were Skokie regulars, most of them over fifty, sipping Manhattans or Martinis and enjoying the prime rib special or the baked halibut.

Enyart scowled as I sat down at the empty bar. He pulled the Crown off the top shelf and filled an old-fashioned glass to the rim.

"Are we celebrating something?" I asked.

"I figured you might need it after that lynching."

"I don't think you're allowed to say lynching anymore. You listened to the show, I take it."

"Yeah. I know you feel bad about that little girl, but it's not on you."

I swirled the glass and took a sip. The burn felt good. "I think it is."

"Listen. You made a decision with what you knew at the time. One night outside Fallujah, my platoon had traffic control. We had to challenge anyone coming up the road. A kid named Curtis was on forward point. An old LTD came down the road. He shouted for them to stop. They didn't stop. He fired warning shots, but they kept coming. Finally, when they were less than forty yards away, he took them out. It was a husband and wife and three kids. Right decision, tragic result. It happens."

"You were in a war," I said.

"You don't think you're in a war? You made a good call; that kid was scared to death. I don't question what we did."

I had a lump in my throat. It had been my decision, not Enyart's. But he was saying we were in this together. That's true friendship. "Okay. Thanks for the pep talk."

"Fuckers tagged my shop," he said.

"What? The gang?"

"No. Skinheads or some other pathetic white-trash segment. Spray painted, "Nigger-Lover" on the storefront window. "Took me two fucking hours to clean it."

Damn. That was on me. "Because of my column," I said. "Sorry. I shouldn't have identified your club."

Enyart slapped the bar. "If you don't stop being a pussy, I'm taking away your whiskey, giving you a cup of herbal tea."

The door opened. Amanda and Bianca burst into the barroom.

"Jake!" Amanda yelled. Her face was flushed. I don't think it was from the cold. She skipped down the bar and gave me a serious hug. "You were wonderful!"

I glanced over her shoulder at Bianca. "How many drinks has she had?"

Bianca patted Amanda on the back. "Inside voice, Manny. Inside voice." She smiled at me. "More than one. But she's right. You were awesome."

I looked at Enyart to see if he understood what they were saying. He shrugged and started wiping down the bar. "No fucking clue."

Amanda yanked off her parka and sat down on the barstool. "Don't you get it, Jake? You were real. Honest. Nobody every admits mistakes anymore. You left that pompous shithead speechless. It was perfect."

I had left before Gordon did his recap. I guess he didn't have a recap. Sorry I missed that. Sort of.

Amanda pulled out her phone. "Bobby McGee wrote a whole blog post on it."

"Who?"

Amanda gave me one of her "how can you be so clueless" looks. "He's a world-famous blogger. Sort of a Kim Kardashian for left-wing boomers. People hate him, but they follow him. He tweeted a clip of your closing and of that asshole sputtering and stuttering. And..." She started paging through the phone display. "...he included a link to your column!"

Her voice was getting louder. "That tweet has been retweeted by reporters for *USA Today*, the *Washington Post*, and..." She smiled at Bianca, and together they shouted, "...the *New York Times!*"

"What are you talking about?"

"You've gone fucking viral, Jake!"

She handed me her phone. The tweet had one of those hashtags.

"Freedom's just another word?"

"That's the name of McGee's blog. It's a joke 'cause his name's Bobby McGee. You've heard the song, right? McGee's a creepy social-ist, and he hates Gordon LaPlante. So now you're in the *New York Times.*"

"Not exactly. It's just some reporters tweeting."

"Are you kidding? Those guys have millions of followers. Lucy Hall is chump change compared to them. That tweet with your column has been retweeted over ten thousand times."

Enyart handed Bianca a can of Old Style and nodded toward Amanda. "Is your friend drinking, or have you cut her off?"

Bianca settled down on the stool next to Amanda. "Ginger ale," she whispered.

Amanda elbowed her. "I heard that. I'm not drunk. I'm just excit-ed." She tugged on my sleeve. "Check your phone. You must have a ton of messages."

"I turned it off. I'd had enough advice for one day." I turned my phone back on. It beeped for over a minute. I had 185 text messages. Most of them were negative. Not much different from the callers but more profane, and with bad spelling. The voicemail box was full too. Hector had called over a dozen times.

I called him back. He answered immediately. "We need to meet tomorrow morning at ten. O'Neill's going to be there." He didn't sound pissed. He sounded sad. Like his dog had just died. But he didn't own a dog.

As a good reporter, I should have asked him what the meeting was about, but I was pretty sure I knew, and I was positive he wouldn't tell me.

"Okay, Hec. I'll be there."

I swirled the whiskey in my glass. I didn't want to drink anymore. I pushed the glass over to Amanda. "Here. Now you can use that ginger ale and make your favorite drink again. I'm going home. Command performance tomorrow morning."

It was odd to imagine that a million folks might have read my words. Under most circumstances I'd have been buying drinks for the bar all night. But all I could think about was Leticia Ribeiro. And Charlotte. And Devante. My world was swirling out of control.

BobbyMcGee@FreedomsJustAnother Word 6h

Miracles never cease! Pompous prig Gordon LaPlante left speechless by a voice from the past, Jake Doyle! Check out my blog FreedomsJust-AnotherWord.blogspot.com and Jake's column: chicagotribune.com/columns/jake-doyle
#Freedom #NothingLeftToLose

FREEDOM'S JUST ANOTHER WORD...

Volume 9, Issue 5, February 22, 2018

This morning, master of pomposity Gordon LaPlante tried for a hatchet-job takedown of veteran Chicago columnist, Jake Doyle. While Doyle writes for the now-sclerotic *Chicago Tribune*, he himself was in top form.

LaPlante shamelessly tried to crucify Doyle for a tough call. You can read it about it here: <u>Jake's Corner</u>. After a half-hour of abuse from the special needs folks who listen to LaPlante, Gordo made the mistake of asking Jake if he had anything else to say. You can listen to that here: <u>*The Chicago Way*</u>

Gordo undoubtedly expected Doyle to offer some half-baked excuse like most of those overpaid bloviators from the mainstream media, but that wasn't Jake's game.

He owned his decision. To use a phrase we're not allowed to use anymore: He manned up.

And that was more than old Gordo could take. You can listen here to Gordo babbling incoherently for over ten minutes: <u>*The Chicago Way*</u>.

I know, I know. It was only fifteen seconds but that's still a record. I don't think Gordo has shut up that long in the last eighty years.

MONIQUE

A million readers. Jake Doyle is back.
Shut up, Mon. Most of them hate me.
Popularity is overrated. At least they're not ignoring you.
That little girl will haunt me forever.
Don't be so dramatic. You'll get over it. Just like you got over me.
Fuck you, Monique.
See?

SEVENTEEN

THURSDAY, 9 A.M. — FEBRUARY 22, 2018

Tribune Towers

Islept late. When I came downstairs at eight, Devante and Amanda had both left for work. I turned my phone back on. Another hundred text messages and a full voicemail box. I might need to get a new phone number. One of the callers was the op-ed editor for the *New York Times,* Rachel Adams. She asked me to call her back, but she didn't say why. I deleted all the messages except for hers. As much as I resented the attitude of superiority that the *Times* reporters all seemed to possess, I couldn't ignore a call from one of them. I would call Rachel Adams back. But not today.

Amanda had left me a fresh pot of coffee. I settled down with coffee and opened the *Tribune* to check out my column. I know it had already been published online, but it wasn't real to me until I saw it in print.

And it wasn't there.

No Jake's Corner. In its place was a guest column from one of the liberal lady columnists for the *Washington Post.* I checked the online edition for yesterday's paper. The story was gone. No explanation. It was as though it, and I, never existed. Shades of *1984.* I was worried. I didn't love what the *Tribune* had become, but I still loved my job. I didn't want to become a full-time Uber driver.

Hector's office was on the nineteenth floor of the Tribune Tower—an impressive space with a cool view of the river and Lake Michigan. It was the only perk the new owners hadn't taken away from him, but it was only a matter of time. The Tower was a trophy building, too valuable to waste on a bunch of newspapermen. Sooner or later, O'Neill would turn it into condos for rich folks. A place for them to stay when they were in the city.

I got to the Tower at nine forty-five. I wanted a few minutes with Hector before the meeting started. He'd be straight with me. I didn't figure he had the juice to protect me anymore if they were going to fire me, but he would at least let me know the axe was coming so I could prepare myself.

When I got off the elevator and headed down the corridor to his office, Yolanda the receptionist jumped out of her seat, a panicked look on her face. She intercepted me before I turned the corner, and right then I knew I was screwed. Yolanda was a plus-sized sweetheart who welcomed everyone from the governor to the delivery drivers with a warm smile and a kind word.

"Mr. Gonzales wants you to wait in B. He'll be ready for you shortly," she said, her face pinched.

Mr. Gonzales? B? Yolanda had never called Hector "Mr. Gonzales." And conference room B was a windowless closet-size room where they deposited the stringers and freelancers who were too gnarly to hang out in the reception area.

"I'm sorry, Mr. Doyle."

I have no problem being an asshole to most of the folks in the Tower. But not Yolanda. I forced a smile. "Mr. Doyle left town when I was six, Yolanda. I'm still Jake. Don't be sorry. I understand."

They kept me in that closet for almost thirty minutes. Just after ten thirty, Yolanda knocked on the door and stuck her head in. "They're ready for you now, Jake. In A."

"A" was the executive conference room. It had a panoramic view of the city looking south over the river. The conference table could handle twenty easily. But today there were just three folks at the table: Hector, Mary Belton, and Hector's tormentor, James Sullivan. I had never officially met Sullivan, but I could tell he was a prick. My ma would have called him lace-curtain Irish. "Born on third base, thinks he hit a triple." He was skinny and pasty-faced, with wispy brown hair and thin lips.

The group was lined up on the window side of the table like a tribunal or a parole board. Sullivan, who was sitting between a glum Hector and a beaming Mary Belton, beckoned me to sit down on the opposite side of the table.

"Mr. Doyle, my name is James Sullivan. I'm Mr. O'Neill's personal attorney, and he asked me to chair this special meeting because he had an unexpected engagement in Los Angeles."

He slid his business card across the table to me. Timmy's personal attorney was the managing partner of Sullivan and Porter. It's a huge firm; according to his card it was founded in 1903, and there were offices in LA, Chicago, New York, London, and Paris. Sullivan acted so self-important I was tempted to ask him if it was just a coincidence that his name was Sullivan. But I decided this was not the time or place to be a smartass. I pushed the card back to him.

"Keep the card, Mr. Sullivan. I could never afford your services."

So maybe I was a little bit smartass. Hector showed a flicker of a smile—the first sign of life in him since I sat down.

Sullivan's eyebrows pinched. "I wasn't—" he said, and then he caught himself and smiled weakly, as he realized I was joking. I figure he had probably been one of those super serious smart kids in school who could never quite get the joke. He picked up the sheaf of papers in front of him. "This is a press release that will be issued today." He lowered his voice—I guessed that was his lawyer voice—as he started to read. "The *Tribune* recognizes and appreciates the contribution that Hector Gonzales has made in his capacity as interim Managing Editor. Now as we reconfigure our team for the twenty-first century, Mr. Gonzales has been appointed to the position of Community Affairs Liaison."

Any position with community and liaison in its title meant that the job was make-work window-dressing. If a company was too lily-white, as were most of the Chicago companies, they created a Community Affairs job and filled it with a Black man or, preferably, a Black woman. Hector, as a Hispanic, wouldn't get them as many points.

I stared at Hector, whose face was pinched. They must have dumped this on him while I was waiting in the closet.

"Effective immediately, the Managing Editor of the *Chicago Tribune* is Mary Belton."

Damn. Mary Belton had written a column for working women for the last twenty years. She was trim and had a businesslike blonde bob and normally a stern countenance that had been forged by her righteous indignation at the treatment of women. Temporarily, the indignation had been replaced by a smug, fuck-you look.

I would not enjoy having Mary as my editor, but it was better than being fired. Sullivan turned to Belton and said, "Miss Belton, will you explain to Mr. Doyle our plan for column realignment?"

Column realignment did not sound good.

Mary cleared her throat and leaned forward, offering me a shit-eating grin. "Thank you, Mr. Sullivan. Jake, as editor I want to get more involved in the..." She paused, searching for just the right words, "...heartbeat of the community. In these days of belt-tightening, we all must wear multiple hats."

She was pulling out every lame metaphor she could find.

"I'm going to continue to wear my columnist hat, but I want to focus more on the community, the neighborhoods, local politics..."

She wanted my column.

Sullivan jumped back in, impatient with Mary's ramblings. "Mr. O'Neill believes it's time for a new look. You've had the column for..." He studied his notes. "...ten years?"

"Twenty, actually."

"Mr. O'Neill believes it is time for a different perspective. A woman's perspective. We want you to help Miss Belton with her new column."

Mary did another annoying throat clearing. "Jake, you have an impressive coterie of contacts: aldermen, department heads, judges, mob bosses. I need your access so we can have a successful transition."

"Mr. O'Neill sees this as a six-month assignment," Sullivan said.

This was like a mob hit where the hitman makes the victim dig his own grave. They had definitely come up with something worse than being fired.

"And what happens after six months?" I asked.

Sullivan offered me an assholey smile. "What is it they say? 'You will be free to pursue new activities...or spend more time with your family.'"

The thousand-dollar-an-hour man pulled a document from his briefcase and slid it across the table. It had a bunch of those red "sign here" flags stuck to it. "Mr. Doyle, this is your six-month employment agreement. It includes non-disclosure and non-compete provisions, which we need you to initial, in addition to signing the base contract."

"When is all this supposed to start?"

"Today. Mary will be producing the column for tomorrow introducing her. We'll have to come up with a new name," Sullivan said.

"Why did you take down my story?"

Another smug smile from the lawyer. "It didn't reflect the views we want our paper to represent. And we can't have an appearance of disharmony among our people," he said.

"This is a newspaper. We're not all supposed to agree," I said, even though I knew it was pointless.

"Mr. Doyle, the primary reason for that non-compete provision is that we don't want you publishing your opinions elsewhere."

This was a tag-team match, but I didn't have a partner. Hector had remained quiet. Defeated. Now it was Mary's turn. "Jake, not having that boy arrested showed extremely bad judgement. And that will reflect badly on the paper. I recommended taking down your column, and Mr. Sullivan agreed. It's damage control."

Hmm.

"What about O'Neill?"

Sullivan looked discomfited. "Mr. O'Neill has a lot on his plate right now. I'm quite confident he supports Mary's decision."

Mary's decision. Belton flinched. It was the look of someone who just realized she was out on the limb all by herself. She summoned her righteous indignation face. "Your confessional reporting puts our paper at risk," she said.

"At risk of what? Journalism?" I scooped up the agreement and stood up. "Thanks for your time. I'll have my attorney look this over and get back to you."

Sullivan frowned. He was looking much less smug. "Who is your attorney?"

I didn't actually have an attorney. My cousin Tommy had handled my divorce, and I still owed him a grand for that. I blurted out, "Justin Reynolds."

Sullivan sat back in his chair. "From Meyer Waite?" He was clearly impressed and not expecting me to name some high-priced dude like Reynolds.

"That's right. He'll be in touch." I reached across the table and picked up his business card. "I guess I will need your card."

As soon as I got to the parking lot, I called Hector.

He answered like he'd been waiting for my call. "Hey, Jake."

"You got time for lunch, buddy?"

"I'm a community liaison. I got nothing but time. How about The Sign? I could use a good burger."

I laughed. "I wish. I miss those days."

The Sign of the Trader was in the lobby of the Board of Trade. It was the favorite bar of the men and women who spent their days in the pits trading soybeans and cocoa and even newsprint. It was dead at noon, but after two, when the markets closed, it was a raucous scene. The Sign made the best—and by that I mean largest—drinks in the loop. And half-pound cheeseburgers. With tater tots. For years, three vodka gimlets and a Sign Burger had been a once-a-week habit for Hector and me. But the traders had been replaced by computers. They were more extinct than newspapermen. The Sign closed ten years ago.

We decided on Alcocks, a dive bar on South Wells Street under the elevated tracks. We would frequent it after our softball games at Grant Park. I parked in a garage a block away. I felt bad for Hector being kicked into the community affairs position, but that was a better gig than working for Mary Belton. It was a no-win proposition for me. I could give her every contact in the book, but they would either ignore her or feed her their usual bullshit. Mary had a piss-poor bullshit detector. Her column would be a disaster.

I took a seat at the near-empty bar and ordered a Bud from Zelda. I hadn't seen Zelda in five years. She was still rail-skinny with unruly, straw-colored hair and tats that now covered her arms and probably lots of other body parts I couldn't see.

"Good to see ya, Jake. No whiskey? You on the wagon again?" she asked.

"No. I try not to drink the hard stuff before five."

She drew a draught and set it in front of me. "Just four more hours. Pace yourself. I'll be here."

I took a sip of beer and wished I'd ordered a Crown. I had better insights with whiskey. Hector arrived ten minutes later, and he acted ten years younger than when we met at the Italian Village. He practically skipped over to the bar.

"Howdy, Zelda. Crown Royal on the rocks."

"Damn. What happened to your tea with lemon?" I asked with a sing-songy lilt. "You aren't looking all broken up over your new assignment."

He grinned. "I'm not the one who has to carry water for Mary Belton. I'm free, man."

Fuck. "Hey Zelda, I'll have the same."

Zelda grinned. "That's the spirit, Jake."

I lifted the whiskey. "Cheers. And thanks for all your help with Mary and that douchebag Sullivan." It felt good to bust Hector's balls again. I could see that the old Hector was making a comeback.

He held up his hands. "They told me I was getting a new contract, but they hadn't given it to me yet. Didn't want to fuck that up. Nothing I could do, anyway."

"Maybe I should just walk away. I could freelance."

"I don't think so," Hector said.

"Why not?"

"The operative part of that word is 'free,'" he said. "Freelance pay is for shit. You'd make more as an Uber driver."

He was right. I was too fond of that regular paycheck to really do something gutsy.

"You boys celebrating or mourning?" Zelda asked.

"Celebrating. Hector is now the *Chicago Tribune's* community liaison officer. And here he is, already hard at work liaising with the community."

"Very impressive," Zelda said. Her voice flat and sounding very much unimpressed.

"Damn straight," Hector said, downing his drink. "Hit me again, Zelda."

She poured him a shot and moved down the bar to serve another customer.

"Seriously, Hec. How do you feel about the move?"

He shrugged. "I just gotta hang on for five more years. It's a bull-shit job, but no pressure. I report to HR; Sullivan won't bother me there. Belton will be a pain-in-the-ass for you. Sorry, man."

I took a generous taste of the Crown. As promised, it gave me perspective. "After twenty years with Tawni, I figure I can handle anything Mary Belton throws at me."

"You think so?" He didn't believe me.

My phone buzzed. I studied the screen. "Tawni." I turned the phone off. "Hey, I got a call this morning from Rachel Adams."

"The *Times* columnist? What did she want?"

"Don't know. She's the op-ed editor for the *Times* now. I didn't have time to call. I had to meet your tribunal." I waved to Zelda for another drink. "Maybe a couple more Crowns and I'll call her back."

"Yeah, that's a great idea. You're much more articulate when you're half-in-the-bag."

"She's probably writing something about that Bobby McGee blog. That thing got a lot of uh...what do you call it...traction?"

"You become an even greater asshole when you drink."

"Thank you."

Hector's phone started playing "Eye of the Tiger."

"Nice ringtone."

"It's Tawni. She's stalking you."

"Fuck. Give me the phone."

I knew I should answer it. That was the right thing to do, and if I had stuck with beer I probably would have. But after two Crowns, I was much bolder. I turned off the phone.

"Another round, Zelda."

MONIQUE

I thought you weren't getting wasted anymore.
Go away.
Six months. You might need that retirement money you gave away.
It's a loan. Go away. I need to sleep.
I don't think you can last six months with that woman.
I lasted twenty years with Tawni.
Well… not really.
Go away.
You don't enjoy having women tell you what to do.
Fuck you, Monique.
See?
I told you, Jake. A woman knows.
Go away. I didn't give up on you. You didn't want me.
Really?
You were pretty clear.
Are you going to help her like you helped me?
This is different. Goddammit. You're not real.
You always say that when you don't have a good answer.

EIGHTEEN

FRIDAY, 5 A.M. — FEBRUARY 23, 2018

Home

I woke up soaked with sweat even though the room was cold. I looked at my alarm clock.

3:47.

Fuck me. I'd been asleep for only two hours, tops.

I tried to go back to sleep, but I knew it would be hopeless. I couldn't take my mind out of gear.

That little girl was dead and it was my fault.

4:11.

Do I help Charlotte get an abortion? What do I tell Tawni? What do I do with Enyart's gun?

4:42.

Jamal's still out there.

5:02.

What if he comes to the house? Do I use the gun?

5:24.

How do I protect Devante?

. . .

I awoke to the rumble of the garage door. I watched, bleary-eyed, from my window as Amanda backed her Corolla out of the garage and headed toward Golf Road. Where the hell was she headed at five-thirty in the morning? My head was killing me.

I gave up on sleep and took a shower. As I was toweling off, I spotted the digital scale Amanda had "loaned" me. She had a new one and thought I might want this high-tech gadget, which not only gave me my weight, but also let me know how fat I was. Fuck it. I hadn't weighed myself since last summer. I guessed 215.

226.

And body fat of thirty-two percent. Damn. I was almost one-third fat. I turned off the stark overhead lights in the bathroom and went with the kinder light from the shower stall. At least in the dim light my whale-body wasn't quite so frightening.

I vowed to start eating right. I'd have a bowl of that low-fat granola Amanda was so excited about. And exercise! But not today. Too much on my plate. Rome wasn't built in a day.

I finished the bowl of granola, but I was still hungry. I stared with little hope into my nearly empty refrigerator. Amanda had tossed all my comfort foods like cinnamon pop tarts and frozen waffles. Salvation! Devante had brought home a bag of sliders last night. I microwaved a couple. Okay, six. But they were small.

I sat down with a cup of coffee. Amanda had dumped the *Trib* on the table. I didn't really want to look at it, but I couldn't not look at it. I flipped to the op-ed page, where I should have been, and there it was: "My Kind of Town," by Mary Belton.

They had to be fucking kidding. In the corner was a headshot of Mary with that same shit-eating grin she had yesterday. She had used that photo for the last fifteen years. "Readers, I'm thrilled to..." I crumpled the paper and threw it across the room.

"Fuck!!!" I refused to read her sappy drivel. Hector was right about one thing. I could never work for Mary Belton.

Devante came running down the stairs in his boxers. "What's wrong?"

"Nothing. Why?"

He picked up the paper. "Another bad news day? And what's with your eyes? They're all red."

I waved him off. "Where did Amanda go this morning?"

"She joined the Evanston Y so she could use their pool. I think she said she was swimming twenty-five hundred yards. A 'light' workout. That lady is a beast." He picked up the empty White Castle bag. "You ate my sliders?"

"Just a couple."

He sighed and tossed the empty bag in the trash. "Amanda said you talked to Charlotte."

"Yeah. I'll take her to the appointment." I didn't know what I should say to him. He was helping his sister, but somehow "thank you" didn't seem appropriate.

"She's pissed at me, isn't she?"

I shrugged. "Not really. I think she's mostly upset with herself...and me."

Devante nodded. That made sense to him. "Can you drive me to work? Bianca took my truck; she said it needs a valve job. That's why it's smoking so bad."

An hour plus drive on the Edens. I wasn't up for that this morning. "Take my car. I'm not Ubering today."

I was watching CNN broadcast Trump's meeting with the parents of the victims of the Stoneham school shooting when Amanda returned from her swim workout. She frowned at the screen as one of the mothers beseeched the president to put aside politics and support tougher gun control laws.

"Tougher laws wouldn't have saved them," Amanda said. "How's next Tuesday evening sound for our gun lesson?"

She wasn't letting that go. "I don't know. Are you working today?" I asked.

"Leaving in ten."

Her hair was damp and she was wearing a sweatsuit. It would have taken Tawni at least an hour to get ready, and even Charlotte would have needed a half hour. But ten minutes later Amanda emerged in a gray skirt suit and high heels.

"You never cease to amaze me," I said.

My cellphone on the kitchen counter rang. Amanda studied the screen. "It's Tawni," she said as she handed me the phone.

I still didn't want to answer it. Charlotte didn't want her mother to know what she was doing, and I had to respect that. But I felt bad about it, and I didn't want to talk to Tawni right now. I am a master at conflict avoidance. Amanda stared at me, her lips pressed tight. I knew what she was thinking. That girl was pushy even when she didn't say anything.

I picked up after the fourth ring. "Hi, Tawni. What's up?"

"It's about time you answered your phone. Can you meet me at my office? There is something important I need to discuss."

"What?" I asked, even though I knew she wouldn't tell me.

"Not on the phone."

"What time?"

"How quick can you get here?"

"Devante has my car."

"I can give you a ride, Jake," Amanda said.

"Is that your girlfriend?" Tawni asked.

She couldn't help herself. She was a conflict embracer. We were the classic opposites attract, but the attraction had worn out. "I'll be there in an hour," I said.

NINETEEN

FRIDAY, 10 A.M. — FEBRUARY 23, 2018

Willis Tower

For years Tawni had operated out of a cramped office in the West Loop. After our divorce, Justin Reynolds secured for her a courtesy office in his law firm. Meyer Waite had the entire seventy-third floor of the Willis Tower. When I checked in with the receptionist, she escorted me down the corridor to an empty, glass-walled conference room with a panoramic view of Lake Michigan and the loop. A conference room? Something was up.

A moment later Tawni hustled in, clutching a cup of coffee. She flashed her professional smile. That made me even more suspicious.

"Hello, Jake. You want coffee? It's excellent." She extended her arm, directing my attention to the stainless-steel carafe in the center of the table.

"No thanks. I'm coffeed out. Are you trying to sell me something?"

Her face twisted as though I were being foolish. "Isn't that view spectacular? Lake Michigan in winter is so beautiful." Justin Reynolds walked in, followed by Charlotte's boyfriend.

"Hello, Jake." Reynolds strode across the room, hand extended, teeth still movie-star white. He shook my hand and then turned. "I'm sure you know Greg Soler."

"Of course," I said.

I always liked Greg. Maybe because Tawni was so down on him. She claimed it was because he lacked commitment, but what really turned her off was that he was not a particularly exceptional physical specimen. Five eight, probably weighed a buck forty, and he was seriously nearsighted. She said he reminded her of a high school science teacher, which he was.

We exchanged nods of recognition. He licked his lips and stared past me, afraid to make eye contact.

"What's going on, Tawni?" I asked.

Her professional smile got tight. I was interrupting her choreography. "Please. Everyone. Have a seat."

Reynolds and Greg sat on one side of the table, their backs to the window. I was tempted to remain standing just to mess with her plans, but I knew that would be a bad move. I took a seat opposite them, and Tawni sat at the head of the table. She turned to me. Her smile was gone. "Charlotte's pregnant," she said.

"I know," I said.

Her jaw actually dropped. "You know? How...when did you...you didn't think to tell me?"

"That's Charlotte's business."

"It's my business, too!" Greg's voice broke, and his hand went to his mouth to stifle a sob.

Reynolds patted Greg's forearm. "It's okay, Greg. We're here to take care of that," he said.

"When did you find out, Jake?" Tawni asked.

I wasn't playing that game. "Why is Reynolds here? This is a family matter." Reynolds cleared his throat and started to stand up, but then thought better of it. "Greg has hired me to protect his parental rights. And to protect his unborn child."

Tawni had recovered her composure. She leaned toward me, making serious eye contact. "Greg believes that Charlotte intends to abort the baby. Obviously, none of us want that to happen. I know that you, of all people, can appreciate that."

Yes. I could.

I stared out at Lake Michigan. A storm was moving in and the mass of dark clouds was frightening. And beautiful. Greg was breathing hard and staring at me. "Have you told Charlotte how you feel?" I asked.

"We're not together anymore. I thought we would figure out how to raise the baby as separate parents. I'm involved with someone else now. My girlfriend would help me, but now Charlotte won't return my calls."

This was Tawni's world. I wanted to defend Charlotte, but I was out of my league. "I'm not the lawyer here, but Charlotte's an adult. I think what she does or doesn't do is her call, isn't it?"

Tawni exhaled sharply. I had the feeling I was about to understand how Mary Belton felt when Tawni eviscerated her. "That's the sad state of affairs in this country today. Fathers are told they have no legal rights. The unborn child has no legal rights. That will never change if fathers don't fight back."

"Jesus Christ, Tawni. This is not one of your crusades. This is your daughter."

"Your daughter too. And your grandchild."

Reynolds couldn't stay on the sidelines for this free-for-all. "Jake, you are correct that the current case law would suggest that fathers don't have any rights if the mother wants to terminate an unwanted pregnancy. But we have a different line of attack that we believe is promising. We will show that this was not an unwanted pregnancy. Charlotte wanted the baby and now is striking back at Greg because he ended the relationship. With Charlotte's struggles with alcoholism and depression as well as her capacity for violence, that argument will find favor in the right court. It will take us some time to research and develop our brief, so we need to prevent Charlotte from taking any precipitous action before we are ready."

"Violence? What are you talking about?"

"She attacked Greg. More than once. She's a danger to herself and others,"

"Are you fucking serious, Tawni?" I wanted to believe that she wouldn't use her own daughter as a test case, a modern-day Roe in reverse, but I knew better.

"This is bigger than us," she said, her voice rising. "This is a trans-formative opportunity. Some day she will thank us."

Reynolds jumped back in. "We need two weeks. I'm preparing a peti-tion to have Charlotte declared incompetent. Suicidal. A danger to herself and her unborn child. We'll have Tawni declared her legal guardian. That will buy us time to prepare our on-the-merits case, which, if we are success-ful, will change the landscape for fathers' rights. This could go all the way to the Supreme Court." His pretty boy cheeks were flush. This was nearly a sexual experience for him. He probably had a hard-on just thinking about having the chance to argue in front of John Roberts and the gang.

They didn't know that Charlotte had already scheduled the abor-tion. By the time they filed their petition, it would be moot. If I told them about her plans, they would expedite their filing. Tawni was right. I didn't want Charlotte to get an abortion, but I wasn't siding with them against her. There were no good choices here. No winners.

"If you do this, Tawni, you'll destroy any chance for a relationship with your daughter. She'll never forgive you. Ever."

Tawni knew I was right. But that wasn't about to change her mind. Tawni was many annoying things, but she was not a hypocrite. She believed in her cause, and she was prepared for collateral damage, even if she and her daughter were part of the damage. She stared at me, silently for a change. I didn't know what to say. Or do.

My phone rang. Devante. A welcome diversion. I stood up and walked over to the window. "What's up, D?"

"Sir, this is Officer Cahill of the Chicago Police Department. Do you know Devante Baptiste?"

My mouth went dry. I tried to swallow but I couldn't. "He's my son."

"Your son?" she asked.

"Yes, goddammit. Is he alright?"

"He was in an accident on Lake Shore Drive. The tow truck driver discovered his cellphone on the floor of the vehicle."

"Where's Devante?"

"He's in the ambulance. They're probably taking him to Weiss. That's the nearest trauma center."

"What happened? Is he okay?"

"I don't know his condition, sir. When you locate him just send a text to your son's number and I'll drop off his phone."

Jesus. I didn't give a shit about his phone. "They're taking him to Weiss? That's a hospital?" I had never heard of it. I realized I was shouting.

"Yes sir. It's very close. If he's not there, then try Northwestern. That's the closest level-one trauma center."

I hung up the phone.

"Jake?" Tawni said, her eyes wide.

"I have to go. Devante's been in an accident."

I rushed out of the office and Tawni followed me down the corridor. "I'll drive you."

I punched the elevator button hard, as if that would make it come faster. I started to tell her I didn't want her help when I remembered that I didn't have a car. "The cop said that he was probably being taken to someplace called Weiss."

She stepped with me into the elevator and pushed the button for the lower-level parking garage. "Weiss Memorial. It's in Uptown." She wrapped her arms around me. "I'm praying for him."

The warm softness of her body brought back the memories of when we were young and in love. I prayed that prayer would work this time.

TWENTY

FRIDAY, 11:30 A.M. — FEBRUARY 23, 2018

Weiss Memorial Emergency Department

Tawni would have been a five-star Uber driver. She drove fast but under control, anticipating slowdowns and changing lanes seamlessly. We pulled into the Weiss Memorial Emergency Department parking lot in twenty minutes. A burly receptionist with a walrus mustache stood at a podium at the entrance to the unit.

Tawni took the lead. "Devante Baptiste was in a car accident. The police officer said he was probably brought here."

"Are you family?" he asked.

"He's my son," I said. My voice was tight. Desperate.

The man checked his terminal. "He was admitted at eleven fifteen. Stable condition."

"What does that mean? What are his injuries?" Tawni squeezed my hand. I was almost shouting.

"Please have a seat in the waiting room, and a nurse will talk with you shortly."

I started to blurt out something stupid and unhelpful, but Tawni squeezed my hand again and thanked the man for his help.

Clumps of folks were scattered throughout the waiting room. I kept watch on the swinging double doors that led to the emergency room. Behind those doors were a dozen curtained-off cubicles. Most of them appeared to be occupied.

It was warm and stuffy in the waiting room, but I was shivering. I couldn't keep my hands from shaking. No way I could have driven myself to the hospital. Every time someone emerged from the room my stomach clenched.

"Didn't he say a nurse would talk to us right away? Something must be wrong."

"This is a busy place. No news is not bad news."

I knew she was right. It didn't help. But I appreciated the effort.

Twenty minutes later, a petite blonde in blue scrubs walked over to the receptionist. He pointed in our direction.

The moment of truth.

"Mr. Doyle?"

We both stood up. "Yes, ma'am," I said. My voice was a weak croak and my knees were trembling.

Tawni squeezed my hand. "Breathe, Jake."

The woman smiled. I took a breath. "My name is Carol Schmidt. I am a registered nurse in the Emergency Department. Are you Devante's father?"

"Yes. Jake Doyle. This is my wife, Tawni Carter." Not the truth, but close enough for the situation.

"Come with me. Devante is getting some x-rays, but you can wait in his cubicle."

We followed her into a large room lined with curtained-off cubicles. Lots of activity, but it wasn't dramatic like a TV show. No one running around yelling "Code Blue!" or "Clear!"

"Devante had a CT scan," she said as we followed her past several cubicles. "Everything looked fine, so that's good news," she said.

I gasped for air like I had been underwater for too long. Devante was going to be okay. I wanted to cry. I squeezed my eyes shut and tried to compose myself.

"It looks like he's already back from radiology," she said.

She turned into the last cubicle on the left side. Devante was sitting up in the bed, talking to the nurse who had just hooked him up to a heart rate monitor and was now reconnecting his IV. He had two black eyes and both forearms looked sunburned.

"Hi, Jake. Hey, Miz Carter."

Nurse Schmidt checked the monitor. "BP 120 over 76 and a heart rate of 46. "Are you a runner, Devante?" she asked.

"Nah. I'm a boxer. Middleweight. Got the Golden Gloves tournament next month."

"Well, no boxing for a few days."

"Yes, ma'am."

"It looks like you were already in a fight. And lost," I said.

"Dr. Lee will be in to see you, Devante, as soon as she has the results from your x-rays." She turned to us. "It shouldn't be too long."

Sometimes you don't appreciate what you have until you almost lose it. Seeing D alive and kicking, even though his face was all busted up, made me feel like we had finally caught a break. For a moment, anyway, I stopped believing everything was going to hell.

Tawni was studying Devante's face. "What happened?" she asked.

Most women wouldn't have wanted anything to do with their cheating husband's love-child, but Tawni wasn't most women. She was world class at compartmentalizing. She could be disgusted, annoyed, or just plain hate my guts for messing up our marriage; but that was all on me, not Devante. She respected him, and she never resented or complained about the support I provided. She found plenty of other things to complain about, but not Devante.

"I hit that pedestrian bridge at Montrose." He winced. "Sorry, Jake. I think your car is totaled."

Tawni's cellphone vibrated. She pulled it from her purse and glanced at the screen. "I need to take this call. I'll be out in the waiting room." She leaned over the bed and kissed Devante on the forehead. "Thank God you're okay. You gave us a scare."

She hustled out of the cubicle, stage-whispering into her phone. I watched her leave and then turned to Devante. "Okay. Now tell me what really happened. No fucking way you ran into a bridge."

Devante's face was grim. "When I pulled onto the Drive at Devon, I saw a black Lincoln Navigator, tinted windows. The witnesses said that was the car that Jamal was driving when they had that drive-by. Freaked me out.

"I slowed down but it didn't try to pass. I hit the gas and it stayed right behind me. I slowed down again, and this time the Navigator pulled up next to me. The damn driver was wearing a ski mask. Could have been Jamal, but I couldn't see his face. He leaned over toward the passenger window, and I think he pointed a gun at me."

"You think?"

Devante's face tightened. "It just happened so fast. I thought I saw something, and I slammed on the brakes and skidded into the damn bridge."

"Did the police question you?"

"A lady cop. I told her what happened, but she didn't act like she believed me."

An Asian woman walked in quickly, assertively. "Hi, Devante. I'm Dr. Lee. I have your results. Is it okay to discuss them with your visitor?" She looked at me, expressionless. Businesslike.

"This is my dad. You can tell him anything."

She nodded at me and then turned to Devante. "Your head CT is normal. No evidence of bleeding. Chest and rib x-rays look fine. No broken ribs that we can see, and your lungs look good. You lucked out and just have some bruising. Good thing you were wearing your seat belt and that the airbags deployed, or it could have been worse. You will be sore for the next few days. Ice is your friend. Put it on for twenty minutes every few hours for the next couple of days on anyplace that hurts. You can use over-the-counter pain meds like Ibuprofen, Tylenol, or Naproxen for pain. I don't think you need anything stronger for now. We also don't want to make you groggy from strong pain meds because you bumped your head pretty hard. You will probably feel worse tomorrow. Sore and stiff in places you didn't know existed. But usually, any bad injuries hurt immediately, and we looked at your head and chest, which seemed to be the worst."

She paused for a breath. I had the feeling she'd given that speech more than a few times. "What kind of work do you do?"

"I work in a restaurant in the Loop, and on weekends I sell ribs. My restaurant's Just Ribs. Have you heard of it?"

"No." She didn't seem too interested in discussing her culinary interests. "I can write a note for you if you need to take a couple of days off from work. Do you have a primary care physician?"

Devante looked at me. "Dr. Gomez was your pediatrician," I said.

"I haven't seen him in five years."

"Well, you might think about getting a regular doctor. You should have an annual checkup. If you start to feel much worse, have trouble breathing, vomiting, uncontrolled pain, you should come back here. Do you have any questions, Devante?"

"Can I leave now?" he asked.

Dr. Lee almost smiled. "Give me a few minutes to finish up the paperwork. Once that is done, the nurse will come back with written discharge instructions and sign you out. Good luck and take care." She nodded at me. "Nice meeting you, sir."

"Thank you, Doctor," I said. "Do I need to give insurance info to someone?"

"They took care of that when they brought him in. You'll get the bill in a few days," she said as she was halfway out the door. "If you have problems paying, we have financial counselors who can help you set up a payment plan."

"How much?" Devante asked. I could tell he didn't really want to know.

"Don't worry about it. You're still on Antoinette's company plan. It's good coverage," I said. "I'm going to check on Tawni. I'll wait for you out there."

Tawni was pacing nervously in the waiting room. "I've got to get back to the office, Jake. Minor emergency with one of our clients."

"Go. We'll take a cab. I really appreciate your help today," I said.

She waved it off. "Of course. I'm so glad he's okay. We still need to make a plan for Charlotte. I know you don't want her to kill her baby."

Tawni always had to have the final word. She didn't even give me five minutes to appreciate Devante's survival.

They finally released Devante at just after seven. On the cab ride he sat back in the seat with his eyes closed. He didn't say anything. Didn't even make any notes in his planner. But when the cab turned onto Devon, just a few blocks from Enyart's gym, he sat forward and scanned the traffic as if he was looking for something. He didn't sit back in his seat until we headed north on McCormick.

He took a deep breath and exhaled. "I'm sorry about your car. I was scared. I'm still scared."

"Don't worry about the car. I don't blame you for being scared. I'm scared too."

"I thought it was Jamal. Maybe it was all in my head." He took a deep breath. "Damn, I don't know."

Amanda had gone out for the evening, but she left us an impressive chef salad that, despite looking really healthy, tasted great.

"You ought to be paying her to stay here," Devante said. "Maybe I could add salads to my menu. She could be the salad chef."

"So, you'd become, 'Just Ribs and Some Salad'?" I asked.

Devante smiled for the first time today. He got up slowly from the table and walked like an old man over to the sink. "My whole body aches. I'm going to bed."

"Get some rest. I'll take care of the dishes."

"Yeah. All two of them. See you in the morning."

After dinner I made a fire with the few remaining logs that Bianca had brought over and poured myself a short glass of Crown. I sipped the whiskey and tried to make sense of everything that was happening. A week ago I would have believed that Devante had probably just panicked and caused the accident himself.

But he wasn't like that. He was levelheaded, and while he couldn't ID Jamal, he seemed certain that the car that had messed with him was a black Navigator. I think it was Jamal, and I think Devante was damn lucky to escape. Next time he might not be so lucky. Next time we needed to be ready.

Amanda came home just after nine. The fire had gone out, and I was still sitting on the couch, weighing all my options.

"How's Devante?" she asked as she plopped down on the couch next to me. "And what are you doing sitting here in the dark?"

"You said there's a shooting range in Des Plaines?"

"Meron's Gun World. I'm a member."

"Can you take me there and show me how to use that damn gun?"

"How about Sunday? I have a brick in the afternoon, but I'll be finished by four. We could leave here by five."

"A brick?"

"A bike and run workout. I'll do an hour on the bike trainer and then a half-hour run."

I felt more out-of-shape every time I saw her work out. "I have to rent a car, but Sunday at five will work for me."

MONIQUE

So much for your Uber career.
I can replace the car.
Keep helping that boy and you'll go broke.
I don't care.
He panicked. He's the one seeing ghosts now.
Is that what you are?
No. I think I prefer your term.
What term?
Goddess.

TWENTY-ONE

SATURDAY, 7 A.M. — FEBRUARY 24, 2018

Home

Another night of tormented sleep. I was showered and downstairs before seven, but Amanda had already left on her morning run. Twenty degrees outside, dark as midnight, and snow everywhere. The woman was crazy. And she had left me a fresh pot of coffee. Devante was right; I should be paying her to stay here.

I had just poured a cup when the doorbell rang.

Doorbell? Nobody rings a doorbell at 7 a.m. Do gangbangers work this early? I thought about using the peephole but couldn't bring myself to do that. From the living room window, I could see a black limo parked in the driveway. I confess, I was relieved that it wasn't a black Navigator.

I opened the door and was more shocked than if it had been Jamal.

Timmy O'Neill was standing on my porch. The son-of-a-bitch looked like a billionaire—golden wavy hair, just the right amount of tan, and the perfect white teeth you only see on movie stars and TV newscasters. He thrust out his hand, "Hello, Jake, I'm Tim O'Neill."

He had a firm, practiced, politician's handshake. "Come in, Mr.

O'Neill. You look cold." He was wearing a black polo with tan khakis as though he had just wandered in off the eighteenth hole.

"Please. Call me Tim. I'm sorry for this early morning intrusion, but Hector assured me you were an early riser."

O'Neill was taller than I realized—at least six three—and had a look of pampered fitness. I knew from his bio that he was my age, but the years had been kinder to him. "Would you like coffee, Tim?" I asked, demonstrating how well I could follow instructions.

"Love some, thanks. I'm flying back to LA this morning; that's why I'm dressed so foolishly."

"What time is your flight?" I asked.

O'Neill's smile was indulgent, self-satisfied. "Ten minutes after I arrive. Having your own jet makes air travel very convenient."

"I'll bet." I poured him a cup and we sat down at the kitchen table.

He cleared his smile. It was time to get to serious matters. "Hector said your son was in an accident. How is he doing?"

"Bruised and sore, but he'll be okay. My car's totaled, but that's what insurance is for. He was lucky."

He leaned forward and grasped my arm, empathetically. He made serious eye contact, projecting sincere relief. "Wonderful. So glad to hear that." He paused for a respectable moment. "I have a proposition for you." I didn't want to admit it to myself, but he had a commanding presence. "You don't know me, and given the situation with the paper —the cutbacks and everything—it wouldn't surprise me if you hated my guts."

"You don't know me either," I said.

He nodded, acknowledging the point. "I can be an asshole. Myra, my wife, reminds me of that just about every week."

According to *The New Yorker* profile, O'Neill had a beautiful wife, three photogenic kids, and no scandals had touched him. He ticked all the boxes for a viable political candidate.

"My wife used to help me that way too," I said. I think I'm good at reading people, and I can usually anticipate where a conversation is headed, but this time I had no clue why billionaire, aspiring politician Timmy O'Neill was sitting in my kitchen.

O'Neill leaned forward and tapped the table with his finger. "Tawni Carter. That is one impressive woman. Smart and effective."

Again, O'Neill surprised me. I expected a "But..." There was none. "You know Tawni?"

"We're both on the Board of the Gladstone Foundation. She's an extremely effective advocate for her cause. Passionate."

"Yeah, that's Tawni."

O'Neill set his coffee on the table. He rubbed his hands together. "Okay. You're probably wondering what the hell I'm doing here."

Wow. Maybe the guy could read minds. "I am."

"You've seen *The Godfather*, I'm sure. Well, I am here to offer you a deal you can't refuse." He grinned, but not in an evil or assholey way.

I took a sip of coffee and waited.

"Next month I plan to announce that I'm running for president. I'm sure that's not a big surprise to you."

"I've heard rumors."

"This country's in trouble. Trump is a nightmare we have to wake up from. We can't take another four years of that egomaniac, but the Democratic field is a disaster. There is no one out there who can beat Trump."

"You don't think so?"

He held up a finger. "Bernie Sanders. Do you really think the American people are going to elect a goddamn socialist?"

He added another finger.

"Elizabeth Warren. Smart as hell, but she's a policy nerd with no sense of humor. Trump would win in a landslide."

Now he had three fingers out. "Harris. Tough. She was a good prosecutor, but a Black woman without any real experience is a bridge too far. Same goes for that gay guy, Buttigieg. They got no chance."

"What about Biden?"

He snorted and waved his hand dismissively. "Joe ain't running. He's too fucking old."

I had to agree with him there. I shrugged. "Probably right."

"You know why all the pollsters were wrong about the last election?"

"People didn't tell them the truth. Nobody wanted to admit they were voting for Trump."

O'Neill nodded. "That's part of it. But the fact of the matter is that they didn't ask the right people. The media were all following the tweets and the blogs and Facebook discussions. It was a goddamn circle jerk. How many tweets have you shared, Jake?"

"I don't know. Three?"

"Exactly. You still read a newspaper, right?"

"It's sort of a job requirement."

He started counting on his fingers again. "I own newspapers in Baltimore, Dayton, Akron, Nashville, Memphis, St. Louis, Tallahas-see..." He paused, realizing he didn't have enough fingers. "...at least twenty major markets, and over two hundred small-town markets. The average age of the folks reading my newspapers is fifty-three. They don't tweet. And they don't get their news from Facebook. The progressives are killing the Democratic party. My readers don't want to be told they're racists." He was counting on his fingers again. "They don't want the police force defunded. They don't want all their statues toppled. And they goddamn for sure don't want to be told they can't eat meat!"

"I'm with them on that one."

"Trump has a hardcore group of supporters who will vote for him no matter what he does. He starts with a solid base of thirty percent. Any decent Democrat is going to get about the same from those folks who will vote for anyone but Trump. So, the game is won in the middle: that forty percent of independents and moderates, both Republicans and Democrats.

"Harris, Buttigieg, Warren, Booker—they all have a small base of folks who support them. I want to be their second choice. When their guy drops out, I want them to choose me. That's where you come in, Jake."

I had to admit he had my interest. He was an asshole but an artic-ulate one.

"I heard you got a standing ovation at that award ceremony for your wife."

I winced. "Didn't know that made the news. She's my ex-wife."

O'Neill smiled. "When I heard that, it got my attention. And then that show you did with that stuffed shirt LaPlante. My God, that was awesome."

"I don't think your team thought so," I said.

He made a face. "Total fubar by Sullivan. I couldn't believe it when he told me what he did. You got accolades from every major newspaper in the country. I wanted to rip him a new one, but I've been trying to make that transition from asshole real estate developer to newspaperman to uh…"

"Politician?"

He smiled. "I was shooting for statesman, but yeah, politician. I was ready to pick up the phone and apologize to you and reinstate you, and then I had an epiphany."

It's been my experience that epiphanies are usually not good news. I still had no clue what O'Neill was doing in my kitchen.

"Jake, I want you to be my press secretary. Join me on my campaign. We can take this all the way to the White House."

I was speechless. I don't know much about the world of press secretaries, but I'm pretty sure speechlessness is a disqualifying characteristic. I stared at him. Mute. Finally, I mumbled incoherently, "Uh… uh…I don't know what to say. I'm not qualified for that job. As you can see."

"You're not glib, Jake. You're real. And you've got crossover appeal. An old-school liberal who got a standing O from a bunch of right-wing zealots. With that speech to LaPlante you opened my eyes. I've been struggling with how to tell voters what I stand for. These damn political consultants are all telling me what I can't say. Who I have to be careful not to offend. Nobody admits a mistake anymore. All the experts say it's political suicide to do that or to change your mind. You've shown me that's bullshit. The American people respect the truth. People make mistakes. They can accept that. What they can't abide are all the self-righteous hypocrites. If someone offered them a real choice, they'd take it. I know they would. That's what I want to do."

It was a hell of a speech. I was ready to vote for him. "Could I keep my column?" I asked.

He smiled like I was being silly. "No more 'Jake's Corner.' You'll have no time for that. Mary Belton has that progressive shine we need in the Chicago market."

That didn't sound like the guy who was trying to change the political landscape. My confusion must have shown because he waved his hand as if to erase what he had just said.

"Look, I'm not naïve. Mary Belton is a mediocre talent. But she's a survivor. I don't have to tell her to support me or my positions. She'll see the writing on the wall, and her views will magically converge with my positions."

"What if I don't agree with your positions?"

He smiled. I had asked the question he had been waiting for. "Sullivan wanted you to be Mary Belton's gofer for six months. I'll give you a six-month contract. Join me out on the campaign trail. Paid advisor, behind the scenes. As you get to know me and get to see the other candidates up close, I'm convinced you will come to believe I'm the best candidate for the job. At the end of six months, you become my press secretary or you go home."

I couldn't resist. "In six months, you might be going home too."

He smiled, but I didn't think he found the remark humorous. "No. I'm winning this, Jake."

"Your confidence is breathtaking."

"*Forbes* estimated my net worth was ten billion dollars. That's not even close. I could buy and sell Trump ten times over, and I'll beat him like a drum, but I have to get the nomination. And yes, I have a lot of confidence. I have a plan, and you are a part of that plan. I don't apologize for saying this: I love this country and I want to save it. I need your help. Will you help me, Jake?"

I wasn't convinced, but I did believe that he sincerely believed he was the one man who could save the country.

Maybe he was. The idea that I could make a difference in something so important was a siren song not easy to resist.

But I did.

"I'm not the right guy for you. And I've got a full plate right now. I appreciate the offer." With all his stroking, I'd almost forgotten about Charlotte and Devante.

O'Neill stared at his cellphone and then stood up, ready to go. "You're smart, Jake. You know how easy it is to lose everything. You're the man I want, and I make it a point to get what I want. We can do great things together. I'll be in touch."

He turned and walked out the door quickly. Not giving me a chance to tell him no again.

An hour later I was enjoying my fourth cup of coffee as I shared the story of my surprise visit from O'Neill with Devante and Amanda. The doorbell rang again.

The limo was back in the driveway, and a Beemer was parked in front of it. But instead of Tim O'Neill on my porch, this time there were two limo drivers, one who resembled a mob hitman, the other an accountant.

"Sorry to bother you, sir," the hitman said. "Mr. O'Neill thought you might need a car of your own until you replace yours, so he wanted you to borrow this car from our pool." The accountant handed me the keys.

"It's got a full tank of gas," he said.

My first impulse was to say no thanks, but I stifled that response. It was a fine-looking car, and it would take at least a couple weeks to settle with the insurance company and replace the Chrysler. Rental fees, even for a kiddie car, would cost at least a grand—money I didn't have. And I couldn't use a rental for Uber, so I would have no supplemental income.

"Thank you," I said. "And please thank Mr. O'Neill. Much appreciated."

The limo driver tipped his hat and smiled. Sort of. "Have a good day, Mr. Doyle."

Devante had been lurking in the hallway, eavesdropping. "Damn. A BMW. We can drive in style now."

"I don't think O'Neill's generosity includes you driving his car. Your track record's not so good."

Devante grinned. "That's okay. I'll sit in the back and you can drive me around. You need to get one of those little chauffeur beanies."

MONIQUE

Press secretary? Aren't you special. So…you're going to work for Mr. Golden Boy.
I told him no. But he'd make a better president than what we've got now.
You're fooling yourself again.
What are you talking about?
You've already decided. You're just playing hard to get, but you're not very good at it. What are you planning to do about Charlotte?
I'm telling her about you.

TWENTY-TWO

SUNDAY, 1 P.M. — FEBRUARY 25, 2018

Just Ribs

Amanda was riding her bike on the trainer again. A hilly, tree-lined road was displayed on my television. As she pedaled, the bike avatar on the screen moved down the road.

"Are you ready for your shooting lesson?" she asked.

I still didn't want anything to do with that damn gun. I wished I hadn't asked Amanda for her help. "I guess," I said. "What course is that?"

"Madison. The bike segment is two loops of fifty-six miles, but today I'm only riding half of the loop, so twenty-eight miles."

"How long will that take you?"

She shifted to a lower gear as the road started up a steep hill. "With these hills, I'll be lucky to average twenty-four miles per hour. Madison is a tough course. This should take me a little over an hour."

"I'm heading over to help Devante with the phones."

"We need to leave here by five," she said.

"I'll be back before five."

She grinned as she attacked the hill. "You just want to try out your fancy new ride. Say hi for me."

. . .

Devante had two high school girls who took the phone orders and the occasional walk-ins. One of them had called in sick, so I told him I could help him for a few hours. At least six folks were in line just inside the door when I walked in. To my surprise, Charlotte was behind the counter taking phone orders while a tiny Black girl with an impressive braid wrapped on top of her head was handling the walk-in traffic.

Charlotte was trying to handle two phones which were almost literally ringing off the hook. It was the kind of high-stress situation that would normally have sent her into a seriously dark mood, but to my surprise she was smiling.

"Thank God, you're here, Dad. Grab an apron." She punched a button on the circa 1980 office phone. "Just Ribs, please hold." She pushed another button. "Thank you for calling Just Ribs, please hold."

I put on the full-length white apron and slipped behind the counter. "What should I do?" I asked.

She handed me an order pad and pencil and pointed me to the phone at the end of the counter. "Push the flashing buttons. Menu is simple: $25 for a full slab, $15 for a half. Cash only! No delivery today. Make sure you tell them that. No checks, no credit cards. Write down their name, address, cellphone number, and rip off the order ticket and put it in the order tray on the window."

"Why no delivery?"

"No driver."

Devante's rib cooking equipment was in the back, hidden from view by a partition with a small window opening. For the next two hours the phones rang constantly. It was the fastest two hours of work I can remember. And everyone was surprisingly courteous, almost grateful-sounding when I took their order. Like they had won a lottery.

Devante came out from the kitchen, discarded his grease and sweat-stained apron, and grabbed a fresh one. He'd been cooking for at least four hours straight. "Hey, Jake, you gotta take off. It's time for that thing with Amanda."

Charlotte snickered. "When do I get to meet your girlfriend?"

I gave her a look, but I knew it wouldn't shut her up. "She's my tenant. We're going to a shooting range."

Charlotte frowned. She was about to launch into a lecture on the evil of guns, but the phones started ringing again, sparing me.

TWENTY-THREE

SUNDAY, 5 P.M. — FEBRUARY 25, 2018

Meron's Gun World

Amanda was watching for me from the front window when I pulled into the driveway. She walked out to my car carrying a hard-plastic briefcase. She had told me she belonged to a gun club, but for some naïve reason I hadn't thought she really owned a firearm. And that it was in my house. "A gun?" I asked, nodding at the case.

"Glock 19. Very similar to your Sig P20."

"It's not mine," I said.

"It is today. Let's go."

Thirty minutes later we were on the west side of Des Plaines. We drove past a Sam's Club and a furniture warehouse. Amanda directed me to a parking lot next to what looked like a suburban office building. A trio of soccer moms were walking to their cars. Not what I was expecting.

"Part of a neighborhood watch group," Amanda said. "They shoot every Sunday."

"I feel safer already." I grabbed Enyart's gun out from under my seat. For some reason, despite the chill in the air, my hands were clammy. I followed Amanda up the sidewalk to the entrance. The sign on the door read *Open Sunday—11 am to 5 pm.*

"It's closed," I said, trying not to sound relieved.

She gave me a smug smile. "Butch lets me use the range after hours."

"Butch?"

"Butch Meron. He's an ex-cop—a friend of my father's. You're not officially here because you don't have a FOID card."

"A permit?"

"Firearm Ownership ID card. It takes a month to get one, and we don't have a month."

"Yeah, and I don't own a gun either."

"Get over it, Jake."

We walked into the office and stood at the counter. On the wall behind the counter was a poster, "The Four Rules of Firearm Safety."

1. *Always treat a firearm as if it is loaded.*
2. *Keep your finger off the trigger until your sights are on target.*
3. *Always be sure of your target.*

Those rules all made perfect sense. But it was the fourth rule that caught my attention.

4. *Never point a firearm at something you're not willing to destroy.*

Was I willing to destroy Jamal? Was I able?

A lot had changed in a few weeks. A month ago, I would never have believed I would even consider working for Tim O'Neill. And if you'd asked me if I was willing to destroy Jamal, I would have said no. No possible way. But now I wasn't so sure. Damn. Fifty-five years old and I still didn't know who I was.

A wiry man in glasses with a trim beard, wearing camouflage fatigues, emerged from the office behind the counter. He smiled broadly when he spotted Amanda and stepped around the counter to embrace her. "How you doing, Manny?" He released her and extended his hand. "Howdy. Butch Meron."

He had a callused, workingman's grip. "Jake Doyle," I said. I hoped he didn't notice that my hands were still sweaty. "I didn't know she let anyone call her Manny."

Amanda elbowed me. "Butch has special dispensation. Don't get any ideas."

Meron chuckled. "I've known Manny since she was in diapers. Even changed a few. Manny will get you checked out on your handgun. What do you have?"

"Uh…" I didn't know there would be a quiz. "Uh… a Sig?"

"He's got a P20."

"Awesome. Great gun. You've got big hands. Sig's better for you than her Glock."

"Why is that?" I asked.

"Good question. Come on back to the range. I'll show you."

We walked down a corridor to what looked sort of like a bowling alley. Meron had us put both bags on the table at the base of the first lane. At the end of the lane was a paper target with the outline of a half torso.

"Okay, I'll give you my mini-demonstration then turn you over to the expert. This little gal is a certified sharpshooter. She would have made a great sniper."

"Except for that red hair," I said. "And her mouth."

Meron bent over with laughter and actually slapped his knee.

"Fuck you, Jake," Amanda said. "You too, Butch."

Meron held up his hands. "Alright now. Let's see what we got." He zipped open the satchel and turned the bag around. "Want to make sure the gun is always pointed down range." He pulled it out of the bag, ejected the magazine, and checked the chamber. He pointed at the handle. "See, the Sig handle grip is smooth, whereas the Glock has recesses for each finger. That's not so good if you got big hands. Makes it harder to get the firm grip that you need."

He ran through the safety rules for the range and demonstrated how to load and unload the magazine, and then he placed the empty gun back on the table. "Okay. I have to finish closing, so you're up, Manny. How are you fixed for ammo?"

"Two hundred rounds. We're good."

Two hundred rounds? I didn't say anything, but that sounded like a lot of bullets.

"It's not that much, Jake. We'll fire a hundred rounds today."

Amanda picked up the Sig, checked to make sure it was empty, and then set it back down. "I'll show you how to use a two-handed grip. You want to get as much leverage on the gun as possible. There are two points of leverage with your gun hand. First is the web between your thumb and forefinger. You want the web to be high on the backstrap of the pistol." She picked up the gun and demonstrated the proper position. "The second point of contact will be just in front of the middle knuckle area, underneath the trigger guard. Again, you're trying to get maximum leverage so the gun doesn't kick when you shoot.

"The third point of contact I'm looking for is the index finger of my non-firing hand directly under the trigger guard. Keep the thumb on the gun hand pointing up so you have room for your support hand, which does most of the work. You should have thirty or forty percent pressure with your firing hand and sixty to seventy percent pressure with your non-firing hand."

"Hold on," I said. This was a lot more complicated than I expected. "What does thirty percent pressure mean?"

She paused to consider the question. "You ever use a hammer?" she asked.

"Not if I can avoid it."

She sighed. "Okay. Like you were holding a glass of milk."

"Got it." That was the same rule of thumb I had heard from Jack Nicklaus on the Golf Channel when asked how tight to grip the club.

"You want less pressure with your shooting hand so you can pull the trigger nice and smooth. That way you'll be more accurate, and you can shoot more rapidly."

Shoot more rapidly?

"Okay. Now your stance. You shoot left-handed?" she asked. She stared at my left hand as though it were deformed.

I shrugged. "I guess."

She tilted her head from side to side. "It would be easier to teach you to shoot right-handed. The safety is on the left side so you can flick it off easily with your gun hand."

"I don't think that's a good idea. When I broke my left hand in college, I had a cast for a month. I had trouble just brushing my teeth with my right hand."

She fluttered her lips. "Okay." She faced me, her hands on her hips. "You want a wide stance with your knees flexed. Keep your weight in the balls of your feet, with your left foot slightly to the rear. Raise the gun to eye level and extend your arms. You should have a slight bend in your arms so they can act as shock absorbers when you fire. Keep your torso relaxed, hips pushed back, chest forward, head upright. Ready?"

Learning the tango would have been easier. And safer. "I guess," I said.

The lane had a computer screen next to the firing table where she set the gun. "Okay, let's start at fifteen feet." She tapped on the screen, and the paper target moved up the track toward us. Fifteen feet was damn close. The torso target had oblong concentric circles drawn on the chest. A two-inch circle in the center was red. The close-in circles were gray, and the border circle was black. "Put these on." She handed me earmuffs. "Load your weapon and assume the shooting position. I'll tell you when to fire."

She stepped back and I entered the booth. I picked up the gun and slipped the magazine into the handle. It clicked. So far so good. I gripped the gun with my left hand, trying to remember all those leverage points she talked about. I took the wide stance and brought my right hand up, being careful to keep the gun pointed down range.

"That looks good, Jake. Now raise the gun and sight the target. Aim for the red. Exhale and fire."

Even with those sound muffs on, the gunshot was deafening. The gun had jumped in my hand, and the bullet tore a hole six inches above the silhouette. Damn. A total miss from fifteen lousy feet.

"That's good, Jake. You were on line. More bend in your arms. Shock absorbers. And not so tight with your grip. A glass of milk, remember? Take three shots."

I exhaled and did my best to relax. Three quick shots. I was surprised at how easy it was to fire the gun. Two shots were in the gray, and one was just outside the red."

"Awesome. You're a natural."

I went through two of the four magazines in no time. Thirty rounds. It was a kick. My last five shots were all around the red.

"Want to try from thirty feet?" Amanda asked.

"No thank you." The mental energy of trying to learn something new and the adrenalin rush of firing that damn gun were exhausting. "Your turn," I said. I stepped out of the booth and swept my arm, inviting her to step up.

Amanda picked up her gun case and set it on the table. She quickly assembled and loaded the Glock and slipped on the sound muffs. She brought the target forward and snapped a new silhouette into place. She tapped on the touchscreen, and the target retreated down the range. The red bullseye was now just a barely visible dot.

"How far away is that?" I asked.

"Seventy-five feet."

She picked up the Glock, took her stance, and fired five shots in less than two seconds. She brought the target back. All the bullet holes were in the red.

"Damn, Amanda. Did your father teach you to shoot?" It was a stupid question. She had just been a kid when her father was killed.

"No. He wouldn't have approved. He didn't like guns either." Her expression was grim. I was sorry I had stirred up a bad memory for her. She studied the target. "I think we're done here."

Meron had returned with a rifle. He set his weapon down in the next booth. The affable look with which he had greeted us had vanished. "That kid who was involved in that drive-by shooting?" It wasn't really a question.

"Jamal? Did they catch him?" I asked, but I could tell by Meron's expression that they hadn't.

"Carjacked a lady in Kokomo. Killed her. They're not certain it was him, but he fits the description."

"That's in Indiana?" Amanda asked.

"A hundred miles east," I said. Damn. Another innocent slaughtered because of my decision.

"They issued a statewide BOLO. He won't get far," Meron said. He picked up his rifle and loaded a large magazine.

"I hope you're right," I said. But I didn't have his confidence in law enforcement. "What kind of gun is that?"

He assumed a shooting position, his cheek pressed into the stock of the rifle as he aimed at the target. "This is an AR-15."

"An assault rifle?" I was pretty sure those guns were illegal, but I didn't say anything.

Meron set the rifle down on the table. He shook his head emphatically. "No, sir. Not an assault rifle. AR stands for Armalite Rifle. It's a semi-automatic."

"That's the gun used in that Florida school shooting," Amanda said.

That was just a week ago. It seemed longer.

"It's the weapon of choice for those mass shootings," Meron said. "Sandy Hook. The Pulse. That Las Vegas massacre. And at least a half-dozen other places." He moved his target to the end of the range and started shooting. It took him less than ten seconds to shred the target.

"My god. That's a lot of bullets," I said.

"Thirty rounds," Amanda said.

Meron ejected the magazine and clicked in another one. I couldn't imagine trying to defend against that much firepower with a puny handgun.

My ears were still ringing as we drove home. I had my handgun training, but I felt less confident now than I had before. Jamal was still out there, and he wasn't taking prisoners.

"What's wrong, Jake?" Amanda asked as we turned off Golf Road on to Kedvale.

"I'm worried about D. That guy is a killer."

Amanda nodded. "I know. Let's hope the cops find him."

She wasn't someone who offered bullshit reassurances. I liked that about her. As I was pulling into the driveway, my cellphone buzzed. It was Charlotte.

"I fucking hate her!" Charlotte said before I could speak.

There was only one person on earth who could inspire that kind of rage in Charlotte. "What happened?"

"Some asshole so-called deputy just knocked on my door and handed me a summons. Mom's trying to have me declared incompetent. They're holding an emergency hearing. I hate her! I hate her! I fucking, fucking hate her!"

Damn. All through high school Charlotte and Tawni would have almost weekly rage battles. I could usually placate Charlotte, but now the stakes were a lot higher.

"Okay, Charlotte. Calm down. When is the hearing?"

"Thursday. I need a lawyer."

"Come over tomorrow after school. We'll figure this out."

"I am not incompetent! She can't do this."

"I know, honey. Don't worry. Tomorrow. Get some rest."

I clicked off the phone. "You heard all that?" I asked Amanda.

"Oh yeah. You didn't need the speakerphone."

"I have to find her a lawyer." I laughed bitterly.

"What's so funny?"

"I told that asshole Sullivan that my attorney was Justin Reynolds. Tawni's guy. I guess I can't use him. And after that loan to D, I'm tapped out. Fuck."

"Bianca," Amanda said.

"What? She's a legal aid lawyer."

"She's perfect. She helps people who can't afford a lawyer. She's tough and smart. You should see her in court. She's a barracuda."

She would, for sure, be better than my cousin Tommy. And I didn't owe her $1,000.

"Do you think she could come over tomorrow after work?"

"Sure. I'll tell her you're ordering a deep-dish from LaRosa."

MONIQUE

You liked shooting that gun, didn't you? Turned you on.
No.
You know you can't lie to me, Jake.
Okay. It was exciting.
That gun will get you killed.
Guns don't kill. People kill.
That gun will get you killed.
I know.

TWENTY-FOUR

MONDAY, 6 P.M. — FEBRUARY 26, 2018

Home

Five minutes after Charlotte arrived, Bianca and Amanda showed up with two large pan pizzas from LaRosa's. Both meat-lover specials, at Bianca's insistence. I was liking her more all the time. Thirty minutes later, one pizza was gone, and the women were chattering like they had been friends for years. I could tell Charlotte liked them—she was not what you would call inscrutable—and for the last ten minutes she had been relating for them her version of growing up with Tawni and Jake. It was exaggerated and inaccurate…but amusing.

"…and whenever Mom and I started fighting, Dad would sneak off to work on his novel."

Amanda looked over at me. "You wrote a novel?"

I have written several novels. Well, actually five versions of the same novel. I trashed them all. They were too real. "Never finished it, but I was present for many, many of those mother-daughter battles."

Bianca set her '80s vintage Samsonite briefcase on the coffee table and opened it. "Let's talk about this petition and our strategy."

Amanda stood up. "I'll go upstairs, give you some privacy. Anyone need another Coke?"

"Please stay, Amanda," Charlotte said. She reached out and touched Amanda's sleeve. An uncharacteristic move for Charlotte. "I need all the help I can get."

Amanda flushed. "Sure thing." She gathered up the paper plates and cans and returned with another six-pack of Coke.

Bianca frowned as she flipped through the petition. "Forrest Boswell has been assigned as the judge for the case."

"Do you know him?" Charlotte asked.

"*Sí*. He's not my favorite. Patronizing. Hardcore right-to-lifer. Belongs to that group where your mom got an award."

"You mean the Thomas More Society?" I asked.

"*Sí*. That's the one."

"Can we get him removed?"

"I don't think so. No basis." She flipped another page. "Who is this Dr. Russo? He examined you, Charlotte?"

She pronounced Charlotte as "Charlit." With this judge, her accent was probably another strike against us.

"He's Mom's shrink. After my DUI I was having trouble sleeping, and Mom got me an appointment with him so he could prescribe Doxeprin. Mom seemed so understanding. I should have known better."

"Tawni has a shrink?" I asked. How could I not know that?

"Everyone has a shrink, Dad." She glanced at Amanda and Bianca. "Well, everyone with money. This is the twenty-first century."

"Why would this doctor say you were suicidal?" Bianca asked.

Charlotte shrugged. "I don't know. I told him I couldn't sleep. He asked me about my dreams. I don't remember what I said. I just wanted to get the script and get out of there."

Bianca made some notes. "They will need more than that to make their case. What about your mother or Greg? What kind of testimony can they offer?"

"Tawni said you attacked Greg," I said.

Charlotte scowled at me as if I were making the accusation. "Bullshit. I shoved the wimp when he got in my face."

"Any blood or bruises?" Amanda asked.

Charlotte's face twisted. "No. He fell back on the bed."

"Good for you, girlfriend," Bianca said. "Never leave a mark." She grinned and the women all laughed. Bianca had a knack for working with temperamental clients.

"Do you want me to testify?" I asked. "I can attest to your competence. For Christ's sake, you've been accepted at Stanford Law School."

Bianca's jaw dropped. "You're going to Stanford?"

Charlotte beamed. "I got the notice two weeks ago."

Bianca tossed the petition back on the table. She laughed. "Why didn't you tell me this? It changes everything."

"It does?" she asked.

"First year law students might want to kill themselves after six months of law school, but not when they get their acceptance. You're not competent—you're super competent."

Amanda raised her hand like she was in school. "But that judge is a zealot. Won't he think you want to have an abortion because you got into law school?"

Bianca shrugged. "It's a legitimate reason for an abortion. Here's something to think about. When you testify, I might suggest that it will be hard for you to take care of a baby while going to law school."

"Why say that?" I asked. "You're just playing into his hands."

Bianca gave me a withering look, not unlike Tawni. She turned her attention to Charlotte. "Maybe when I ask that question, you have decided you can handle a baby and law school. You've considered options, such as daycare or a babysitter, and decided those will work. So…" she paused and stared at Charlotte, "…at that moment, you are planning to have the baby and go to law school."

"But—" Charlotte's face revealed her confusion.

"That's what you think on Thursday. Friday is another day. Maybe you change your mind again. It's just a hypothetical. Not a recommendation…of course."

We all sat silently at the table, digesting her suggestion.

"Fucking-A, Bianca," Amanda said, breaking the silence.

Bianca raised her Coke can. "To super, super competent Charlotte. Goddamn. Stanford. You go girl."

MONIQUE

Monique?

...

What's wrong?

...

Don't look at me like that.

...

Are you angry because I'm helping her?

...

Hey! Don't turn your back on me. Monique come on.

...

This is not the same. And the world has changed.

...

Monique! Goddammit!

....

Fuck you too.

TWENTY-FIVE

TUESDAY, 10 A.M. — FEBRUARY 27, 2018

Appleton, Wisconsin

 text from Mary Belton was waiting for me when I woke up this morning.

> Can we meet this morning? 9 a.m.
> IMPORTANT!

She had sent it at 5 a.m. The caps suggested an air of desperation. Mary was not an early riser. I figured it had something to do with my contract, so I made sure not to bring it with me.

I must have had an upgrade in status because when I showed up at the front desk Yolanda ushered me into panoramic conference room A instead of the closet. Mary was twenty minutes late for our meeting, but I think that was more incompetence than showmanship. She looked like she had been up all night. Her usually tightly wrapped hair bun was struggling to stay together, and her face was etched with stress.

She trudged into the room with a stack of files and a cup of coffee.

"I'm so sorry, Jake. I'm running way behind. I never realized how many people need to talk to the editor."

I actually felt a little sorry for her. "Not a problem. Just enjoying the view and the fresh coffee."

She sat down at the table and started sorting through her files. "Mr. Sullivan asked me to do a Sunday feature on Mr. O'Neill. A background story on how he got where he is today. Something that wasn't already covered in this *New Yorker* piece." She pushed the magazine across the table to me.

Sullivan, as expected, had no idea what he was asking for. *The New Yorker* spends months on their stories, and the one on O'Neill was 5,000 words.

"How can I help?"

"I'm buried. So much to do. Could you do a draft and I'll polish it on Friday?"

I was being promoted from gofer to ghostwriter. Not sure that was a promotion.

"Sure, I can do that," I said.

Mary was more than a little surprised at my affability, but this was a good assignment. I needed to find out more about the golden boy who wanted me to be his press secretary; and while the thought of Mary "polishing" my work was hard to swallow, the story wouldn't have my name on it.

Mary pulled out a paper from one of the folders. "Mr. Sullivan gave me a list of men and women who are available to be interviewed."

It was mostly business associates and guys who knew him in college. The kind of people you might interview for a *People* magazine puff piece. I paged through *The New Yorker* article. It focused on O'Neill's life after college. It wasn't an origin story, but it mentioned that he grew up in Appleton, Wisconsin.

"To get something fresh," I said, "we need to discover the boy who became the man. I'll drive up to Appleton and talk to some of the folks who knew him back then. I'll be back here on Friday with a draft story for you."

I figured to have a draft by Wednesday and give it to Mary after Charlotte's hearing on Thursday. A classic slacker move—promise to finish a one-day assignment in four days and then get credit for beating the deadline.

Belton took a deep breath and poured herself a fresh cup of coffee. "Yes. Yes. The boyhood angle. That's perfect, Jake. Thank you so much."

"Sure thing, Mary. Appleton's a three-hour drive, so if I take off now I can get there by one." I grabbed up Sullivan's list and *The New Yorker* and headed for the exit. Mary started to get up. I held up my hand. "Take a five-minute break. Enjoy the coffee and the view. Don't burn yourself out."

I guess I was getting soft in my old age.

I made it to Appleton before one o'clock. It was a blast driving that Beemer on the highway.

I have a system for this kind of where-they-came-from investigation. I start with a local retirement community or assisted-living facility. River Heights, forty acres on the Fox River on the outskirts, looked promising. I introduced myself as a newspaper reporter for the *Chicago Tribune* and told them I was working on a story about Tim O'Neill.

These places are always looking for diversions for their seniors. Lunch was over, but there was a large group playing bingo, and when they announced between games that I wanted to interview folks who knew Tim O'Neill I found four prospects. I talked for over an hour with his former next-door neighbor (he used to shovel her walk for free), his barber (good kid, kept his hair short), his fourth-grade teacher (a sweet boy, very polite), and his Boy Scout troop leader (he knew that kid was going places).

Not exactly Woodward and Bernstein revelations, but not unexpected. Those folks represented the adult perspective. I needed to talk to some of the kids he grew up with. After retirement homes, I look for a promising coffee shop or diner. So, I stopped at Schreiner's Diner and ordered a cup of coffee and a slice of cherry pie. (Appleton was apparently known for its cherries, not its apples).

It was good pie. When Doris refilled my cup, I told her about my mission and asked if she had known Tim O'Neill.

She scowled good-naturedly. "I'm much younger. My cousin

Bonnie dated him. She's got a picture in her office of them sitting on some damn float for a homecoming parade, waving to the crowd."

"Her office?"

"She works for Century 21. It's a couple blocks from here."

Old girlfriends are often a good source; however, Bonnie was a bit of a disappointment. I had to wait an hour for her to come back from an appointment, and then she had the same bland assessment that all the old folks had. Nice boy. Courteous. Serious. They weren't really dating. They had been voted sophomore king and queen for homecoming. She put up the photo in her office after O'Neill made the cover of the *Forbes* issue where they profiled all the billionaires. "One of my lost opportunities," she said with a smile.

The man, the boy I mean, was nearly flawless. I wasn't looking for dirt, but I was hoping for some rough edges, some youthful callowness, something readers could relate to. Perfection is boring.

By five, I had had enough. Tim's barber, Bobby Martino, had recommended McGuinness's Irish Pub. "Try the Reuben!" An Italian recommending a Reuben in an Irish pub, it had to be good.

I took a seat at the near-empty bar and ordered a Harp's draft. The bartender, who resembled a gray-haired Frankie Avalon, had a smooth, unlined face and a cocky grin as he carefully positioned the beer on a coaster. "You're that reporter who's asking questions about Timmy O'Neill?"

I extended my hand. "Jake Doyle. Did you know him?"

His hand shook slightly, and the back of his hand was age-spotted. He was older than I had thought. "Dan Coots. Pleased to meet you, Mr. Doyle. I used to read your column in the *Post*. Haven't seen it for a while."

The *Appleton Post* had been part of the *Tribune's* syndication that I lost twenty years ago. "Yeah. I'm no longer syndicated. Column's just in the *Tribune* now."

"Things change. I get it. Young folks aren't reading newspapers. I taught phys-ed at the high school for forty years. Coached girls' soccer. Nowadays all the kids are trying to get out of gym class." He grabbed a menu from under the bar and set it next to me. "I recommend the Reuben."

He was still grinning, but I had the sense that the grin was permanent. He hadn't answered my question, but something in his non-answer made me suspect I had finally found someone who didn't belong to the Tim O'Neill fan club.

"I'll try the Reuben," I said.

"Want fries?"

"No thanks. Do you remember him?"

"Who? O'Neill? Everyone knows him. I hear he's running for president."

This is usually the place where the others would share some heartwarming recollection of young Tim, but Coots didn't offer anything. "Would you vote for him?"

Coots stopped grinning. He ran his hand through his hair, considering the question. "Depends. Who's running against him?"

"Well, I guess that would be our current president."

He snorted and started rubbing the bar down like Enyart always did when I pissed him off. "Fucking great choices you're giving me." He turned and walked over to the order window. "One Reuben! No fries."

"I'm going out on limb here," I said. "It doesn't appear that Tim O'Neill is one of your favorites."

Coots shrugged. "I don't know the man. But I knew the boy. He wasn't what everybody thought he was. Maybe he's changed. I don't know." He walked down to the end of the bar to serve another customer. His walk was unsteady, as though the floor were slippery and he was afraid of falling.

A bell rang. "Reuben up!" someone yelled from the kitchen and set the sandwich on the food counter. Coots' hands trembled as he carried the plate over and set it in front of me. He grabbed a napkin that was pre-wrapped with silverware and set it next to the plate.

"Anything else? Want another Harp?"

"Thanks. Could you share some memories of the younger Tim? I'm not trying to do a hatchet job on him, I just want a true picture. Everyone I talk to raves about the boy. That happens a lot when the boy grows up to be a billionaire. Or president. Memories change."

Coots put down his bar towel and started twisting his hands, as if he could twist away the shakes. "Not my place. If you want to learn about Tim O'Neill, you need to talk to his high school girlfriend."

I glanced at my notes. "I did talk to Bonnie...uh...Merritt. They were sophomore class homecoming king and queen."

Coots waved his hand dismissively. "No. Not Bonnie. Anny. Anny Rush. She was his girlfriend the summer after he graduated."

"Do you know where I could find her?"

I was wrong about Dan Coots having a permanent grin. His smile had vanished, and he seemed lost in some long-ago memory.

"Anny Rush could have been an all-state soccer player. Fast. Agile. She made everything look effortless. I used to love watching her play." He bit down on his lip and the tremor in his hands got worse.

"Are you okay, Dan?" I asked. "What happened to her?"

He picked up the towel and started wiping the bar down again. It didn't need wiping.

"That Reuben's good, isn't it?"

"Excellent. What happened to Anny?"

He scowled. "You'll have to talk to her. She's a bartender at the Elk Room in Elkhart Lake. It's part of the Oshtoff Resort. Mighty fine place. I used to take the wife there in the summer."

"Where's that?"

"Damn. You're from Chicago, and you don't know where Elkhart Lake is?"

He was back in ball-busting mode. "I don't get out much."

"An hour south of here. You can probably get a room there tonight. Not a lot of tourists in February."

"Thanks. I'll check it out."

TWENTY-SIX

TUESDAY, 7 P.M. — FEBRUARY 27, 2018

Elkhart Lake

E lkhart Lake was only forty-five miles from Appleton, but to get there I had to navigate several county roads. I was used to driving in Chicago where every highway is lit up like Las Vegas. The wind was picking up, and the swirling snow on the dark roads made the drive challenging. Wouldn't want to be an Uber driver here.

Ninety minutes later, I was sitting on a barstool in the Elk Room, a large country club space with a gleaming mahogany bar, a wall of windows that looked out on the golf course, and a forest-worth of walnut paneling.

The bartender was strikingly attractive. Slender, with long blonde hair that was streaked with gray, she had light blue eyes and moved up and down the bar like an athlete. I was about to order a Spotted Cow draft and ask her if her name was Anny, but she beat me to it.

"Are you that nosy reporter Coots warned me about?" She acted serious, but I had the feeling she was putting me on.

"I wouldn't say nosy. Maybe inquisitive? Name's Jake Doyle." She smiled as we shook hands.

LEN JOY

"Anny Rush. Danny called and told me you were coming."

"I was hoping to talk to you about Tim O'Neill."

She frowned. "Danny just won't let that go. What would you like? From the bar."

"I'll try the Spotted Cow." Always good to go with the local option when you're trying to make a good impression.

Anny returned with a draft and set it in front of me.

"Thanks. Mr. Coots wanted me to hear your story. I just want background." I gave her my most sincere I'm-just-a-guy-trying-to-do-his-job look.

She studied me, trying to decide if I was worth the time.. "I have a break in five minutes. Why don't you grab that table in the back, and we can talk there. It's not a long story."

I took the Spotted Cow, which was a more than passable local lager, and sat at a table in the back corner of the bar looking out at the patio that bordered the eighteenth green. Only three of the other dozen tables were occupied. Anny joined me ten minutes later. She nodded at my nearly empty glass. "Do you want another beer?"

I shook my head. "I might drive back to Chicago tonight. It's only about two hours from here, right?" Just as I said that a blast of wind rattled the huge window.

Anny winced. "Winds are picking up. Highway 57 will be a challenge. You might want to stay here tonight. Plenty of rooms available."

She was right, I didn't want to drive two hours in the dark with a winter storm coming on. If I were working for Hector, it wouldn't have been a problem. But I could just imagine Mary Belton's reaction if I tried to expense a room from this place. Even off-season it was probably $300 a night.

"Let's see how things go," I said. I had spotted a Motel 6 just off the highway. That fit my budget better.

"How was Coach Coots?" she asked. "Was he shaking bad?"

"Not too bad. Parkinson's?"

She nodded. "He's been fighting it for five years. You should have seen that man in his prime."

"He said you were a world-class soccer player."

Anny huffed and gave me serious eye contact. "Danny Coots was my greatest fan. I was never as exceptional as he remembers me. He thinks I was cheated out of some great opportunity—like if I had been able to play for him my senior year, I'd have made the Olympic team." She gave a slight shake of her head as if to clear it of that notion. "I wasn't that good."

"What happened? This has something to do with O'Neill?"

She sipped her coffee and surveyed the near-empty barroom. "Tim was a year ahead of me. He had graduated and was leaving for Harvard in the fall. He was a typical high school big deal. Lettered in three sports, National Honor Society, president of the class. Total heart-throb, bigshot. He didn't know I existed."

"And..."

"There used to be an amusement park called Cherryland on Lake Winnebago. They hired dozens of kids from Appleton High for summer jobs. I ran the whirling teacups, and Tim had the highly coveted job managing the bumper cars, right next to the teacups."

"I'm guessing he learned of your existence."

She smiled. She had a great smile, and with those light blue eyes the effect was hypnotic. "We would go for late-night swims after work. I had never had a real boyfriend before, and I'm not sure he counted. Nobody knew we were going out. All we did was swim and have sex on the beach. It was crazy." She closed her eyes like she was imagining the scene.

I tried not to imagine the scene.

"First week on the job, Tim discovered weed. I don't think he ever drank or smoked anything before that summer, but one of the ride operators was a dealer, and he was selling all the kids dime bags. Tim was always looking for an angle or a better deal. After a few weeks of paying retail as he put it, he went to the dealer's supplier and bought a kilo. He said it was for his own use; he was taking it to Harvard if he didn't use it all."

I was dubious. "He wasn't planning to resell it?" The guy I had read about loved making a profit.

Anny shrugged. "I guess we'll never know. That same night he made the buy, we got caught on the beach fooling around, and the cops found the grass. Back then holding that much pot was a felony. It was seen as intent to distribute."

"Damn."

"Tim had turned eighteen in July, so he was legally an adult. The cops put us in the back of the squad car, but they left us alone for a few minutes as they searched the area for other teenagers making out. While they were gone, Tim begged me to tell them it was my pot."

"A real standup guy."

Anny waved her hand. "It made sense. I was a juvenile. I wouldn't be facing prison time. I wasn't on my way to the Ivy League. I wasn't planning to be president. And I was crazy in-love with him."

"So, you took the fall for him?"

"Told me he'd be back next summer and we'd be together. Get married when I turned eighteen. It was all teenage nonsense. I got slapped with a juvie rap, got suspended from school, and missed my chance for soccer fame and fortune."

She tried to make light of it, but I wasn't buying it.

"That's what really upset Coach Coots," I said.

"He hates Tim. I don't hate him. I understand him."

"What do you mean?"

"Tim O'Neill has a gift for getting people to do what he wants. He'll probably make a great president."

"That's sort of cynical."

"Hey, Jake. Look at who we have now. O'Neill's not a saint, but he's better than the alternative. I'd vote for him."

"You're better than he is, Anny. He didn't deserve you."

Her face flushed. "Thank you. You're a nice man…for a reporter."

I laughed. "Nicest thing anyone has said to me today."

A gust of wind rattled the windows and whipped up the snow on the patio, creating little tornado-like swirls.

"No way you're driving home tonight," she said.

"You're right. There's a Motel 6 just down the road. Newspaper business isn't that flush anymore. We can't afford to stay in these luxury hotels."

She leaned forward and grasped my hands. Her spooky eyes were mesmerizing. "No way. Stay here. I'll comp your room. Have another

Spotted Cow. When my shift ends at nine, I'll join you, and you can tell me the Jake Doyle story."

That was an offer I couldn't refuse. Women used to make proposals like that when I was almost famous and almost handsome, and they often meant something. But now I'm neither of those things. I knew it simply meant she wanted to hear my story because I am a mesmerizing storyteller.

I remembered that I was trying to lose weight, so I ignored the entrée offerings and focused on the appetizer menu. I went with the sliders: three delicious mini-burgers. Okay, they weren't that mini, and I added cheese. I hadn't eaten all day, unless you count that cherry pie at the diner and the Reuben at the bar. I was finishing my second Spotted Cow when Anny headed back to the table. She wasn't smiling.

"Here's the room key, Jake." She huffed. "The other bartender hasn't shown yet—probably blaming the weather, which is bullshit as he has four-wheel drive. So I have to work his shift. The room's on the second floor. Enjoy." She forced a smile and acted genuinely disappointed, which only made my disappointment worse. I was really looking forward to spending more time with her.

It was a very posh room. Hardwood bed frame, gleaming granite countertops in the bathroom, and an actual kitchen. I had just pulled my travel kit from my bag when someone knocked on the door. My first thought was that I was getting busted for my free room. I opened the door, and there was Anny with a bottle of Crown Royal.

"Surprise! They closed the bar because of the weather."

Idiot-like, I stared in disbelief.

"Aren't you going to ask me in?" she asked, her smile starting to fade.

"Wow! Anny! Yes, please come in." I was babbling, and to make matters worse, as she stepped into the room I kissed her. On the lips. The kiss brought me back to full consciousness. "Oh my god, I'm sorry. Uh...I didn't...uh...I was just uh…"

She kissed me back, probably just to shut me up. "I brought your favorite." She waved the bottle of Crown Royal. It was half-empty.

"Did you steal that bottle from the bar? And how'd you know that's my whiskey?"

"Borrowed it. And I know because I'm a huge fan of "Jake's Corner." Crown Royal and Enyart were frequently mentioned in your column. Enyart's my favorite." She walked over to the dresser and grabbed two glasses. Real glass, not plastic. She poured a shot in each and handed me one. She dropped down on the bed and scooched up to the headboard. "Cheers!" she said, raising her glass.

"Thanks," I said. I sat down next to her. "I'll be sure to let Enyart know. They run my column in the local paper?" I asked. That seemed unlikely.

"No. I used to live in Chicago. Moved there after high school. Escaping the 'scandal' I suppose. Took a job at Blue Cross/Blue Shield. I didn't figure to stay, but I never got around to leaving. Before I knew it, I'd been there twenty years."

"I know. That happens."

"So, one day I'm in Grant Park having lunch. Someone had left a section of the *Tribune* on the bench where I was sitting. I checked out 'Jake's Corner.'" She took a breath. "It was the story you wrote about the day your lover died."

I swallowed hard. "'Waiting for the Bus,'" I said, my voice barely a whisper. "That was the title. Hardest thing I ever wrote."

Anny squeezed my hand. "Your story was heartbreaking and beautiful, and it changed my life."

I took a shallow breath. I was feeling unreasonably emotional. "Really?"

"You made her seem so alive. All those plans she had. It made me cry to think she would never have a chance to live the life she wanted. And deserved."

"Thank you," I said. I hoped she would tell me how it changed her life, but I didn't want to ask.

"Your column made me realize I wasn't living the life I wanted. My older brother had a tourist business in northeast Australia. Kimberly— it's a paradise of waterfalls and rapids. I used to spend a week there every year and kept telling myself that I was going to move there someday. After I read your column, I finally listened.

"I quit my job and two weeks later I was giving rich tourists the river ride of their lives. Came back here when my mom got sick. Now I'm a massage therapist and a bartender. I have great hours, usually, and I can ski in the winter and swim in the summer. I love being outdoors. I love my life."

"It sounds wonderful. You're a lucky woman."

"Right. I'm not a victim. Tim O'Neill didn't ruin my life."

"Massage therapist, huh?" I looked at her with what was probably an Enyart-like leer.

She arched her eyebrows. "You know what would be better than a massage right now?"

I had some thoughts, but I was smart enough to keep them to myself.

"Have you seen the shower?" she asked. "Come on." She walked me into the bathroom, turned on the twin-jet, state-of-the-art shower, and peeled off her clothes like we were in the YMCA locker room.

"Come on in, Jake. Soap my back."

Later as we lay in bed savoring the last of the Crown, Anny told me she had read my column on the shooting of Leticia Ribeiro. "It wasn't your fault, you know that, right?"

"On some level, I suppose. It's been a rough two weeks." I told her about Jamal stalking Devante, Charlotte's pregnancy, the whole ugly situation with Tawni, and my *Tribune* demotion. I don't normally share, but I was surprised at how good it felt. Anny was a good listener. When I finally shut up, Anny wrapped her arms around me and buried her face in my neck.

"You need a break."

I smiled. "I think I just had one."

She rolled over and straddled me. "Are you going to tell your new boss lady that you fucked Tim O'Neill's high school girlfriend?"

I rolled her onto her back and kissed her. "Not if you're good."

We made love again, and afterward, when Anny snuggled close, she was more serious. "Do you need my story?"

"No. It belongs to you."

"We were kids. I know I've changed," Anny said. "Maybe Tim's changed too. You should think some more about working for him. He could use you on his campaign. You could keep him honest."

She was serious. "I've already turned him down. It's over," I said.

But neither of us believed that.

Anny leaned over and kissed me softly on the lips. "Remember what I said, Jake. He's very good at getting what he wants."

MONIQUE

You're welcome.
What do you mean?
You got lucky because of my story.
She's a good person.
You've always had a thing for blondes.
Uh…not always…
Don't fall in love with her.
I don't fall in love anymore.
She won't be there when you wake up.
You don't know.
Don't be so hard on your golden boy.
He sacrificed her. He was a selfish prick.
It happens all the time. At least he was just a boy.
What do you mean?
You know what I mean.
I didn't sacrifice you. I loved you.
That's always your answer.

TWENTY-SEVEN

WEDNESDAY, 9 A.M. — FEBRUARY 28, 2018

Home

Anny was gone when I woke up. I'm a light sleeper. I don't know how she could have left without waking me. She left a note in the bathroom: *You're a good man, Jake Doyle. Take care of yourself. Anny.*

No number, which told me she wasn't looking for me to call her. A wave of sadness washed over me. But not in a bad way. It was invigorating. A parting-is-such-sweet-sorrow kind of sadness that made me feel like I was still alive. Maybe I've been wrong. Maybe I could still fall in love.

The winter storm had moved on. It was a beautiful day with the sun sparkling on the fresh snow that had fallen in the night. I was definitely falling in love...with the Beemer. I pulled into my driveway before nine. There was a FedEx envelope on the front steps.

Devante was at the kitchen table, an array of glossy equipment brochures spread out in front of him.

"How come you're not at work? You buying equipment?"

"Just doing some planning for when I get my financing. I'm leaving in five. I finished the questionnaire Mr. Reynolds gave me for that grant thing. He wants to make the proposal next week." Devante frowned. "Should I be doing this with him, Jake?"

"You mean because of Charlotte?"

"Yeah."

It was a good question. "Did you ask her?"

"You know Charlotte. She would never tell me not to do it."

It was true. Charlotte would always be in D's corner. She'd never want to hold him back. "This grant's a good thing. If the lawyer can help you get it, then use him."

Devante bit down on his lip, considering that. "Cool. What's in the FedEx?"

"I don't know." I opened the letter. It was a $45,000 settlement check from the Land of Lincoln Insurance company for my Chrysler. To describe that as generous would have been a gross understatement. That's what I paid for the car four years ago. A note attached to the check read, "Expedited settlement as requested by Mr. O'Neill."

I handed it to D.

"Damn. That was fast. Mr. O'Neill is trying to get your attention." He stared longingly at the check. "What kind of car you gonna buy? Not another Chrysler."

I gave him a look. "There's nothing wrong with the Chrysler."

Devante screwed up his face. "It's a boring White-man car. Get something with some style. How about a Miata?"

"I need a four-door for Uber. I can buy a new Chrysler for $5,000 down and then repay most of my 401(k) loan. That gives me some cushion in case somebody's rib business needs a little more capital."

Devante grinned. "I always liked that Chrysler." He scooped up his papers and headed for the door. "See you tonight."

I sat down at the kitchen table with a cup of coffee and the *Tribune*. I wanted to check out the dealership ads, but I had to check out the columns and the front page. It was a habit I couldn't break. Mary, in her column, had profiled a Black alderwoman who was raising funds for the Bud Billiken parade. I couldn't finish it. A cheerleader piece for a parade that wasn't taking place until August. We all have to fill space sometimes, but that alderwoman was about to be indicted. Mary should have asked me.

On the front page, the lead story (from the wire service, of course) was the students returning to school at Marjory Stoneham Douglas High School, "to find police officers with heavy artillery and teachers with open arms." One of the students who had been lobbying for tougher gun control tweeted, "I try not to think about all the people I miss. That's the hardest part."

Below the fold was a story by a local *Trib* reporter about Dick's Sporting Goods. The chain had announced they were no longer selling assault-style guns or high-capacity magazines, and they would prohibit gun sales to anyone under twenty-one.

A small gesture, but something. I liked the image of the teachers with open arms. That was courage, and it didn't require a gun.

Enyart pulled into the driveway just as I was starting to look through the car ads. He walked in through the back door, not bothering to knock. He rubbed his hands together and stomped the snow off his shoes. "You need to shovel your walk," he said.

"I save that for Amanda. She enjoys the workout. You might want to upgrade to your winter wardrobe now. It's ten degrees out." Enyart had no hat or gloves and wore a ridiculously thin leather jacket over his signature white polo shirt.

He waved me off. "Cold's a state of mind. How'd your trip to cheese-land go?"

"I met a woman who said you were one of her favorite things in my column."

He nodded as if that was no surprise. "Was she promising? Did you get her number?"

"Nope. She's not your type anyway."

He scowled. "They're all my type. I contain multitudes."

"You want coffee, Mr. Whitman?" I reached for the pot.

He waved it off. "Carlos called me. They found the guy who killed that lady in Kokomo. It wasn't Jamal."

That was sort of a good-news-bad-news development. That poor lady was still dead, but it wasn't on me anymore. On the other hand, that meant Jamal was still out there. Someplace.

"I don't know what to say to that. No idea where Jamal is then?"

"Carlos thinks he's probably in Mexico."

Until they catch him, it doesn't matter what they think. Every time I see a black Navigator I'm going to want to reach for that gun under my seat.

"Hang on a second," I said.

I walked upstairs to my bedroom, and from the nightstand I grabbed the Sig and the bag with the four magazines Amanda had insisted I keep with it. I carried it down to Enyart and put it on the counter, carefully—the way I had been taught. "Take this. I don't want it."

Enyart stared hard at me, but he didn't say anything. He just nodded, checked the gun to make sure it was unloaded, and put it in the sack with the ammo. "Okay, Jake."

Three hours later I was the somewhat proud owner of a 2016 Chrysler 300 with 30,000 miles. It cost me $26,000, and I put $5,000 down. With a pang of regret, I left the BMW at the dealership and called the limo service to pick it up.

It took me only an hour to draft the O'Neill story. I put in every awestruck compliment I had collected, and I kept Dan Coots and Anny out of it. I would upload it after the hearing tomorrow.

All things considered, it had been a good day.

I had rid myself of the gun that was tormenting me, and, thanks to O'Neill's generosity, I had a newer car with fewer miles and $40,000 with which I could almost repay my 401(k) loan. Now we just had to win that hearing.

MONIQUE

You did the right thing, Jake.
You mean about the gun. Yeah, I think so.
No. I meant the car. Good idea going for the heated seats.
Fuck you, Monique.
I'm serious. You'll want that comfort when you're a full-time driver.
I still have a job. And don't forget that offer from O'Neill.
Golden Boy is not hiring you once he learns you fucked his girlfriend.
She's not his girlfriend.
Okay.
She's not.
Tell him that.

TWENTY-EIGHT

THURSDAY, 9 A.M. — MARCH 1, 2018

Circuit Court of Cook County, Skokie

Charlotte's hearing was scheduled to begin at ten in the morning in the Cook County Circuit Court in Skokie. I had been to the Skokie courthouse a few times in the last twenty years for traffic court, which is always a flurry of activity. Our courtroom on the second floor was much smaller than traffic court, and it felt like a church without the stained-glass windows. It had the kind of quiet that makes you whisper. When Amanda and I arrived at nine forty-five, Charlotte and Bianca were sitting at the defense table. No sign of Tawni or attorney Reynolds.

A heavyset woman in a blue blazer and dark slacks was the only other person in the courtroom. She had a lantern jaw, bleached blonde hair, and a scowl. "That's the court clerk," Amanda whispered.

We filed into the first row of the gallery, behind Charlotte and Bianca. Charlotte smiled nervously. I leaned over the railing and gave her a hug. "You got this, Charlotte. No sweat." I hope I sounded more confident than I felt. From everything Charlotte had told us, this should be a slam dunk dismissal, but Tawni doesn't pick fights she can't win. Especially with Charlotte.

Bianca didn't look any more confident than Charlotte. She glanced over at the empty petitioner's table. "Maybe they're not coming."

Charlotte and I knew better. "No, that's Mom," Charlotte said. "Five minutes late is on time for her. Being early is inefficient."

Bianca patted Charlotte's hand. "Remember, Char. You don't say nothing to your mother. No reactions. *¿Bien portado. Comprende?*"

"What?" Charlotte asked.

"Sorry," Bianca said. "Be a perfect lady. Okay?"

Charlotte nodded and swallowed hard. I could tell she was in turmoil. It had to be a hard thing to have your own mother trying to have you declared incompetent. I suppose it would be a hard thing for a mother, too, but in Tawni's case I wasn't so sure.

A deputy sheriff entered the room from the door just to the left of the judge's bench. He whispered something to the clerk. Her scowl deepened, and she glanced up at the clock, which indicated a minute after ten. On cue, the door to the courtroom opened, and Tawni and Justin Reynolds hustled down the aisle. Charlotte turned away from them and stared straight ahead. Bianca stepped into the aisle and introduced herself to Reynolds as Tawni took a seat at the petitioner's table.

"I wonder where Greg is," I said to Amanda.

"He's probably being called as a witness, so he has to stay outside," she said.

The clerk stood up. "All rise. The Circuit Court of Cook County is in session, Judge Forrest Boswell presiding. Be seated. No talking. Silence all cell phones."

Forrest Boswell looked like someone named Forrest Boswell. Gray and imperious, with wire-rims and thin lips. He was tall and commanding, and while it was hard to tell with his black robe on, I was certain he had an annoyingly flat belly. A country club guy for sure. I bet he had a killer forehand.

He nodded to the clerk and she announced our case. "In re: Charlotte Doyle."

The judge surveyed the courtroom. "Will the lawyers please identify yourselves for the record?"

Reynolds rose quickly. "Your Honor, Justin Reynolds for the petitioner, Tawni Carter, who is the mother of the respondent, Charlotte Doyle."

The judge smiled. "Nice to see you again, Mr. Reynolds. It's been a while."

Reynolds returned the smile. "Yes, Your Honor. Always my privilege."

Bianca stood. "Bianca Pujols, Judge. I represent Charlotte Doyle."

The judge scowled and appeared mildly perplexed. No preppy greeting for Bianca. "Mr. Reynolds, please proceed with your opening statement."

Reynolds stood up. He could have been a model for a Brooks Brothers ad. Conservative-cut, light-gray suit; crisp white shirt with just the right amount of cuff showing; and a muted purple tie for a splash of color. His wheat-colored hair was insouciantly long but groomed. He came from generations of privilege and had inherited not just wealth but style. Also, very white, perfectly straight teeth.

"Your Honor, Ms. Carter is seeking an emergency temporary plenary guardianship for her daughter, who is suffering from paranoid schizophrenia as diagnosed by Dr. Carl Russo. She is episodically delusional and a danger to herself and others. She is not capable of handling her affairs, business or personal. Today you will hear testimony from Charlotte's own mother as well as from Ms. Doyle's former boyfriend, Greg Soler. We will enter in evidence an expert medical report from Dr. Russo. This evidence will confirm these sad circumstances, and we will ask the court to appoint Ms. Carter as her daughter's temporary guardian. Thank you."

Paranoid schizophrenia? What a crock. I stared at Tawni, but she kept her eyes on the judge.

Bianca did not look like a model for Brooks Brothers. She wore loose-fitting, dark slacks and a tent-like white button-down. Judge Boswell frowned as she began her opening statement.

"Your Honor, there is no evidence—"

The judge held up his hand. "Wait! We have rules in this courtroom, young lady. The court has not yet called for the Respondent's opening."

Bianca's eyes flashed, and I held my breath fearing an outburst, but she kept it together. "Sorry, Your Honor."

"Don't you work for the Legal Aid Society?" the judge asked.

"Yes, Your Honor, but I am representing Ms. Doyle as an independent attorney."

The judge waved his hand dismissively. "Proceed, Ms. Pugh."

"It's Pujols, Your Honor."

"Excuse me."

"My name is Bianca Pujols, not Pugh."

The judge's nostrils flared, and he cast a withering stare at Bianca, angry at her for not being named Pugh, I guess. "Proceed, Ms. Pujols."

"Thank you, Your Honor. There is utterly no evidence—"

Another stop sign from the judge. "Ms. Pujols, an opening statement is not the place for argument. Tell us what evidence you intend to present to disprove the petitioner's case."

"Ms. Doyle will testify to her competence," Bianca said. There was an edge to her voice. She stared hard at the judge and then sat down. It had to be the shortest opening statement on record.

We were at the mercy of Judge Boswell. We were already losing, and they hadn't even presented their evidence.

"Call your first witness, Mr. Reynolds."

Reynolds ran his hand through his mop of hair. "Petitioner calls Dr. Carl Russo."

Russo was a rotund fop who dressed like a mobster trying to make an impression. His blue suit was a fancy Italian job, and his monogrammed shirt was light blue with a white collar. He had pointed shoes and, to complete his ensemble, a diamond pinky ring.

He announced with inexplicable pride that he had a D.O. from the University of Curacao and was accredited by The International Academy of Psychiatric Dream Diagnostics. He needed a heavy dose of that cologne he was wearing to cover up the stench of his bullshit resume.

"Dr. Russo, you filed an affidavit with the court stating that, 'Charlotte Russo is episodically delusional and a danger to herself and others. She is not capable of handling her affairs, personal or business.' What led you to that conclusion?"

"Thirty years of experience dealing with patients like Ms. Doyle. She manifests acute syndromes of suicidal ideation. I used my unique technique of dream analysis which made it clear that Ms. Doyle was seriously troubled and a danger to herself and others."

"Your exam led you to believe that she was a paranoid schizophrenic?"

"Exactly. Without a doubt. One of the clearest examples I've encountered in all my years of practice."

"Judge, I move to enter Doctor Russo's report as Exhibit 1."

Bianca started to object, but then thought better of it.

"Proceed," the judge said nodding to the clerk. She marked the report and set it on her table.

"Thank you, Doctor. No further questions."

"Any questions for Dr. Russo, Ms. Pujols?"

"Yes, Your Honor." Bianca stood but remained behind the table like she wasn't planning a lengthy cross-examination. "Dr. Russo, you say you graduated from the University of uh…Curacao? Did I pronounce that right?"

Russo smiled smugly. "Sounds right to me. But you'd know better than I would."

"Is that a correspondence school?"

"Objection, Your Honor. Relevance."

"Sustained. I'm aware of Dr. Russo's background. He's testified in my court several times."

I had a sense that Dr. Russo wasn't part of the judge's country club crowd.

"Dr. Russo, you based your diagnosis on the dreams that Ms. Doyle shared with you?"

"I interpreted her dreams on the Hardin-Morgan matrix of psychological disorders."

Bianca pulled out a journal from her briefcase. "Is that the matrix they introduce in this article from the *Journal of Dream Psychology*?"

"Yes. It was."

"Are you aware that this journal does not require peer review for the articles they publish?"

"Objection. Again, relevance."

This doctor was a quack pushing junk science in bogus journals. But that didn't matter to the esteemed judge. "Move on, Ms. Pujols."

"Dr. Russo, you prescribed Doxepin for Charlotte, correct?"

"It's part of my regimen to help foster a rich dream environment."

"Are you aware of this article in *Lancet*..." she grabbed another journal from her case, "...that reports on a study from research doctors at NYU that suggests Doxepin can induce hallucinogenic dream-like episodes?"

Russo folded his arms. "The operative word is 'suggests.' Sloppy research, not persuasive," he said.

The guy was shame-proof and had probably been accused so many times that he had a bullshit answer for every allegation suggesting he was an incompetent quack.

"I see," Bianca said, oozing Tawni-like fake sincerity. "Is it your testimony that the article from the leading medical journal in the world was sloppy? Not up to the standards of uh, what was it... *The Journal of Wild Dreams?*"

"Objection—"

"Withdrawn. Are you being paid for your opinion, Dr. Russo?"

Russo offered up his most patronizing smile for Bianca. "Young lady, I am *not* paid for my opinions. I am paid for my time, same as any other physician."

"No further questions, Your Honor."

The judge dismissed the doctor and asked Reynolds to call his next witness.

"Petitioner calls Tawni Carter."

Tawni had dressed down for this occasion. Her charcoal gray sheath dress and a single string of pearls were the essence of simplicity and style. She wanted to project humble, but that's a challenge for a beauty queen. She walked slowly to the witness stand. "Good morning, Judge Boswell," she said as she took her seat. I couldn't see her face, but I swear she winked at him.

The judge nodded. "Miss Carter," he said with an avuncular twinkle in his eye.

It was so obvious that they knew each other that I wanted to stand up and object.

The clerk recited the oath in a rapid monotone and asked Tawni if her testimony would be the complete truth.

Tawni stared intently at the clerk. "I will tell the truth. Absolutely." The clerk told her to be seated, indifferent to Tawni's charm.

Reynolds stood up. "Ms. Carter, please tell the court who you are and how you are related to Miss Doyle."

"My name is Tawni Carter. I am the executive director of the Carter Institute, which has been protecting the life of the unborn for twenty-five years. I have a bachelor's degree from Wheaton College and an honorary doctorate from Claremont University. Most importantly, I am Charlotte's mother."

"Tell the court about your relationship with your daughter."

Tawni smiled wistfully, as if she were imagining fond childhood memories. "I gave her life. We were very close as she was growing up. We had to be, because of her father's rather notorious uh…difficulties."

"I know this is not something you want to discuss, but could you be more specific about Mr. Doyle's difficulties?"

Tawni did her best to pretend she didn't want to share my past. "He had an affair with a young intern. They had a baby. It cost him his career. Nearly lost his job. I had to devote more time to building my organization, as we couldn't count on him to support us. I did it for Charlotte."

"Are you still close to Charlotte?"

Tawni blinked trying to make herself cry, but she was never any good at that. A bridge too far, I guess. "Not as close as I would like. In her rebellious college years, she took up more with her father. Young people are sometimes attracted to the outlaw types. Jake…uh, Mr. Doyle, had a reputation as a hard-drinking partygoer. It pains me to say this, but I think it was her father's influence that had a great deal to do with Charlotte's drinking and depression."

Bianca rose from her seat. "Your Honor, I object to the narrative. Let's get back to a question-and-answer format, please."

The judge, who had been staring raptly as Tawni delivered her fantasy recollection, didn't even look at Bianca. "Witness may proceed."

Reynolds must have figured he had had enough of Tawni's make-believe backstory. He moved on. "Did you receive a call from your daughter on the night of January 15 of this year?"

"Yes. She called me from the Evanston police department. She had been in an accident."

"Why was she at the police department?"

"They had arrested her for drunk driving."

"Objection. This witness doesn't have first-hand—"

"Overruled. Ms. Pujols, there is no jury here. Let the petitioners present their case without so many unnecessary interruptions. I can sort out the wheat from the chaff. Continue, Mr. Reynolds."

"Did your daughter tell you that the police charged her with driving under the influence?"

"Yes."

"Did that concern you?"

"Of course. She's an alcoholic. She's not supposed to drink."

Bianca sighed. "Objection, lacks foundation, calls for an opinion she's unqualified to give, assumes facts not in evidence." She said it rotely, knowing the answer. She didn't bother to stand.

"Overruled."

"Has your daughter ever participated in an alcoholic rehabilitation program?"

"Yes. She attended the Carpenter Program run by the Evanston Hospital from February to April 2016."

"While your daughter was in rehab, did you have occasion to meet with her and her counselor?"

"Yes. I met twice with the counselor, Mrs. Marjorie Guthrie. She told us that Charlotte had episodes of suicidal ideation when she drank."

Bianca tried again. "Object to the hearsay."

"Overruled."

Reynolds hardly paused for the objection or the ruling. He kept his focus on Tawni. "So, it was important that she not drink, is that correct?"

"Yes. Critically important." Tawni did her best to project sincere empathy and concern.

Reynolds stepped out from behind the table where he had been standing and took a few steps toward Tawni. "Ms. Carter, did you receive a subsequent call from Charlotte on Sunday, February 11?"

"Yes. Charlotte was angry that Dr. Russo would not refill her prescription for Doxepin."

"Doxepin is a sleeping pill?"

"Yes. It's an opioid," Tawni said, her eyes wide with faux alarm.

Bianca stood up. "Objection. It's not an opioid. It's an anti-depressant."

"I'm sorry, Judge. I misspoke. I meant anti-depressant," Tawni said.

The judge waved his hand, as if the medical debate was of no import.

"How would you describe your daughter's temperament during the call?"

"She was angry. She called me a bitch and a few other things I won't mention."

"Why was she angry at you?"

"She wanted me to persuade the doctor to write the prescription. She was quite hysterical. When I refused, she screamed and said she was going to kill herself, and then she hung up."

"What did you do then?"

"I called her ex-boyfriend—they had just broken up after her DUI —and I asked him to go over and check on her."

"Thank you, Ms. Carter. No further questions at this time."

"Do you have any questions for this witness, Ms. Pujols?"

"Yes, Your Honor." Bianca walked over and stood two feet from the witness stand. Much closer than Reynolds had stood. Tawni was good at reading people. She didn't smile at Bianca. The two women stared at each other like gunfighters at high noon.

"Do you know if Mr. Soler went over and checked on your daughter?"

"He said he would."

"But you don't know if he did, is that correct? You didn't call him up and say, 'How's my daughter doing,' did you?"

"No. He said he would do it."

"Would it surprise you to learn that he did not check on her?"

Tawni's face wrinkled with confusion, and she looked to Reynolds for help. Reynolds was flipping through his notes trying to catch up.

He rose tentatively. "Uh, objection, Your Honor. Uh…relevance?"

"Overruled."

Wow. We won one.

"He said he would. I assumed he did."

"Did you call the police and ask them to check on your daughter?"

Tawni made one of her don't-be-ridiculous faces. "No."

"Ms. Carter, you initiated this petition on February 25, correct?"

"Yes."

"Because you were concerned about your daughter's welfare. Worried that she might harm herself."

"Yes."

"But back on February 11, when you say your daughter claimed she was going to kill herself, you didn't bother to take any extra measures to prevent her threatened suicide, did you? You depended on the ex-boyfriend who had just dumped your daughter because he was disgusted about her DUI."

Reynolds stood up. "Is there a question here?"

Bianca stared at Reynolds. She didn't look angry, she looked like a cold-blooded assassin. "Ms. Carter, what happened between February 11 and February 25 that made you decide that your daughter now needed a guardian?"

"I don't understand."

"Come on, Ms. Carter. Isn't it true that your concerns for your daughter's well-being changed when you learned that she was pregnant? Isn't it true you're seeking to become your daughter's guardian not because you care for her well-being, but because you wish to protect her fetus?"

Tawni's face was florid. "It's a child!" she said.

"Thank you. No further questions."

Bianca had done a nice job of portraying Tawni as a hypocrite. But I wasn't sure that would win us any points with this right-to-life judge. It was, however, schadenfreude to see Tawni on the receiving end of an interrogation for a change.

Reynolds patted Tawni's hand as she took her seat. She yanked it away from him. Her jaw was set, and there was still a lot of color in her cheeks. She stared straight ahead. On the pissed off scale she was at eight, maybe even nine. Reynolds stood up and called Greg Soler to the stand.

Soler had been out of the courtroom, so he had not heard Tawni's testimony or Bianca's withering cross-examination. That was probably a good thing for him, as he acted like a man who wanted to be someplace else. He was pasty-faced, and he licked his lips and slowly rocked back and forth as the clerk swore him in.

He stated his name and connection to Charlotte, and then Reynolds asked him, "Mr. Soler, how long did you have a relationship with Charlotte Doyle?"

His eyes rolled back in his head, like that was a question he wasn't expecting. "Uh, I guess, uh…a year?"

Reynolds looked slightly discomfited. "Isn't it correct you were together from the time she left rehab in June 2016 until early this year?"

"Uh…that sounds right."

"Over the course of the nearly two years you were together, did you notice a change in her behavior?"

"She had a lot of anger issues."

"Could you be more specific regarding Ms. Doyle's behavior?"

Soler leaned forward and started rocking faster. I couldn't see, but I suspected his feet were tapping too. "One time I left some clothes on the floor. I planned to pick them up, but I forgot, and she came home from work and swooped all the clothes up and tried to throw them in the trash."

"What happened?"

"I tried to stop her, and she shoved me. Hard. Caught me off guard. Knocked my glasses off."

Reynolds paused. "Any other incidents that were exceptional?"

"After we had the fight over her getting a DUI, we broke up. A few nights later she called and left an angry voicemail. It worried me because she sounded…uh, crazy."

"With the court's permission, we wish to play that voicemail message from the third of February."

Bianca stood up. "Objection, Your Honor. We have not had the opportunity to hear this message."

"Your Honor, this just came to our attention. We didn't have time to share it in advance," Reynolds said.

Bianca gave him her most disgusted look. "If you hadn't so conveniently showed up five minutes late, you could have shared it with us before the hearing commenced."

"Enough!" Judge Boswell said.

I think he knew Reynolds was full of shit, but he obviously wanted to hear the voicemail. Charlotte hadn't told us about this message, but she had given her mother dozens of voicemail blasts over the years, so the existence of this voicemail was not a surprise to me. I suspect it was to Bianca, though. I had my fingers crossed that the content wouldn't be too damning.

But of course, it was.

Greg. Greg. Greg!!! Pick up, you fucking pussy. You are such a fucking coward! I hate you. I fucking, fucking hate you...

Mercifully, iPhone voicemail messages cut off after three minutes. In addition to calling him a bitch and a pussy, toward the end she got more creative, calling him a "miserable cunt." But the most damning part was that she threatened to kill him and herself. I could see by the look on the judge's face that he was shaken.

Charlotte drilled her ex-boyfriend with her eye lasers. If looks could kill... But Bianca seemed unfazed. I am certain this voicemail was a surprise, but she was proving to be a good poker player.

Reynolds stood in the docket, his head down, as if praying for this poor lost soul. "Thank you, Greg. No further questions," he said softly.

Bianca jumped up immediately and walked aggressively toward Greg. He leaned back in his chair and stopped rocking. His eyes went wide. Bianca stopped at the rail and put her hands on her hips. "*Santa mierda!*" she said, shaking her head in disbelief. "That message was awful. If somebody said all those nasty things to me, I'd be *muy enojada*. And hurt. What was her phrase? 'A miserable little cunt.' *Oy, Dios mío.* Where I come from, those are fighting words."

Reynolds stood up, wearily. "Your Honor, is there a question…"

Bianca plowed ahead before the judge could rule. "Mr. Soler, are you a voluntary member of the petitioner's team?"

Greg wrinkled up his face. "I'm sorry, I don't—"

"Did they have to subpoena you to testify, or did you volunteer?"

He swallowed hard, hoping for a lifeline from Reynolds. "Uh…I guess I volunteered."

"Did you know that Ms. Doyle is pregnant?"

"Yes."

"Did you impregnate her?"

"It's my baby," he said.

Bianca nodded. "Your baby, huh? Interesting. So, Mr. Soler, are you testifying against your ex-girlfriend because of your concern for her welfare, or because you are angry that she called you a miserable little cunt and you fear she will have an abortion and deprive you of your baby?"

Reynolds jumped up. "Objection, Your Honor. Counsel is taunting the—"

"—I withdraw the question," Bianca said. "No further questions for this…witness." She paused long enough for all of us to fill in the blanks.

Reynolds looked at Bianca, clearly exasperated. He had underestimated her. "Petitioner rests."

Judge Boswell took off his wire rims and rubbed his face. "Respondent, are you ready?"

"Yes, Your Honor. We call Charlotte Doyle."

My stomach was clenched. I don't think I would've been this nervous if I had been the one up on the stand. Charlotte was sworn in and at Bianca's request gave a brief summary of her background.

"Charlotte, are you a patient of Dr. Russo's?"

She wrinkled up her face. "No. He's my mother's doctor. She gets sleeping pills from him. She sent me to him because I was having trouble sleeping. He prescribed Doxepin. It gave me weird dreams."

"You mentioned that you are a teacher at Evanston High School. What do you teach?"

"Journalism."

"Your father is a journalist, is he not?"

"He's a columnist for the *Tribune*. 'Jake's Corner.'"

The judge looked over at me, surprised. Not the look of an adoring fan, but not an enemy either. Mildly respectful…maybe.

"As a journalist, has he been helpful to you in your career?"

Charlotte smiled sort of sadly. I wished I hadn't turned her down every time she asked me to speak to her class.

"Not terribly," she said. "He's not optimistic about the future of the newspaper business. But he's a great dad. He's always been there for me. Not judgmental. He listens." She choked up on "listens," and I felt my eyes starting to well.

"Your mother has suggested that your father contributed to your drinking problem. Would you agree with that?"

Charlotte clenched her jaw and took a calming breath. "No. He helped me. He didn't have mother's self-righteous sanctimony. His father and uncle were alcoholics. He always told me that alcoholism is something you have, not something you are."

"Are you drinking now?"

"No. I've had one drinking episode in the last two years. It was stupid. I was celebrating some good news."

"What was that news?"

Her frown transformed into a thousand-watt smile. "I've been admitted to Stanford Law School and I'm starting in September."

Tawni gasped. "Stanford?" She swiveled around and gave me the classic Tawni stare. As if I had some obligation to share her daughter's plans with her. I gave her my most beatific, shit-eating grin. She bit her lip, because she couldn't bite me, and turned back in her seat.

It got better.

Judge Boswell leaned over. "That's my alma mater. Congratulations."

"Yes, congratulations, Charlotte," Bianca said. "So, you're not suicidal or incompetent, are you?"

Charlotte broke with her lawyer's advice and drilled Tawni with a stare that was every bit as lethal as Tawni's. "No," she said.

"Are you pregnant?" Bianca asked.

"Yes."

Bianca stepped back. "I went to Kent for law school. It was really tough. Time-consuming. I'll bet Stanford's even tougher. Hard to navigate with a baby. How do you plan to handle it?"

Charlotte lost her evil stare and smiled at Bianca like a young mother-to-be. "They have excellent childcare services and there are many nannies in the area. It will be a challenge with an infant, but manageable."

"Thank you, Charlotte. No further questions."

Reynolds stood up and looked over at Tawni, who appeared genuinely confused. "No cross-examination, Your Honor. We're ready for our closing argument."

The judge smiled at Charlotte, who he now saw as a future alum. "You're dismissed, Ms. Doyle." He cleared his throat. "I've heard enough. No need for closing statements. Petition denied."

Amanda leaped from her seat and clapped her hands. "Yes!" She leaned over the rail to embrace Bianca, who was hugging Charlotte. I was still planted in my seat, trying to process everything. Charlotte had won. She had beaten her mother. Thanks to Bianca.

Tawni was standing in the aisle, a peculiar expression on her face. Not one I had seen before. A mix of shock and respect and maybe even love. She walked over to Charlotte. "Honey, that is very impressive. Stanford. I will help you any way I can."

Charlotte stared at her mother, not saying anything. The courtroom had returned to its church-like quiet. No one breathed.

Finally, after what seemed an eternity, Charlotte pushed past her mother and started for the door.

"Go. To. Hell," she said.

Her voice was barely a whisper, but I'm sure Tawni heard her.

As we filed out, a woman who had been seated in the last row of the gallery approached me. "Jake, can we talk?"

An attractive forty-something brunette, dressed for comfort not style, wearing a navy pullover and nondescript slacks and walking shoes. She had to be a reporter, but I couldn't place her.

"Uh…"

"Rachel Adams, *New York Times*. We met a few years back at the Media Fest convention in San Diego."

I had a foggy recollection of that conference. "Yes, of course. Good to see you, Rachel." Then I remembered: the voicemail. "Ah, you called me last week."

She smiled benignly. "I'm doing a feature on Tim O'Neill. I want talk to you about your experience. Background. Not on the record."

So much for my fantasy that the *New York Times* wanted me. But something didn't add up. "I don't have time," I said. I sounded annoyed, and I guess I was. "Why are you at this hearing. It's not news."

She gave me a look that suggested I was being naïve. "I was looking for you. But this is news. A right-to-life advocate tries to get her daughter committed to prevent an abortion. Definitely newsworthy, Jake. But it's not the story I'm working on. Have dinner with me Saturday and give me some useful background on O'Neill. I'm dying for some Chicago-style pizza. We could go to Giordano's or Pizzeria Uno?"

"Tourist traps," I said. "We don't need to go into Chicago. How about The Village Inn right here in Skokie? Might be a little loud on Saturday night, but the pizza's great."

"Wonderful. I'll meet you there at eight." Her cellphone buzzed.

I mouthed the words, "See you, Saturday," and left her in the courtroom.

Amanda and Bianca were waiting for me in the corridor. "Where's Charlotte?" I asked.

"She went home. She didn't feel good. I don't think she slept much the last few days," Amanda said.

"You did a wonderful job, Bianca. Thank you so much. I should have hired you for my divorce."

"I'm staying with Bianca tonight," Amanda said. "Are you going to the Oven to celebrate?"

I shook my head. "I have to write up my story for my new boss."

Not exactly true.

I was feeling unsettled. Winning the right to have an abortion didn't seem like a great victory. At least not one I wanted to celebrate.

It was a short drive to the house. I uploaded the O'Neill story to Belton and dropped onto my bed. Despite having done nothing all day, I was exhausted.

MONIQUE

Someone finally stood up to Tawni.
Yeah.
You don't seem happy with your victory.
I don't want her to have the procedure.
God, you can't even say the word.
Abortion! Satisfied?
You should be happy. The New York Times. *You ARE going to be famous.*
They don't want me. They just want dirt on O'Neill.
You still can't read between the lines.
What are you talking about?
Give them what they want.

TWENTY-NINE

FRIDAY, 9 A.M. — MARCH 2, 2018

Home

I could hear voices in the kitchen when I got out of the shower. Devante was talking with a woman, but it wasn't Amanda. The voice was familiar, but in my fog-brain I couldn't place it. I checked my phone. I had a text from Mary Belton:

> The O'Neill story — great work, Jake.
> Sullivan loves it. Wants to meet with us at
> Univ Club. Noon?

Damn. Lunch with Mary would be bad enough. But to eat at that stuffed shirt club with that prick Sullivan after he had yanked Hector's membership really sucked. If I kept getting invited to those fancy clubs, I'd have to buy another sports jacket. I found a clean white shirt and decided my black jeans would probably not be challenged by the wardrobe police at the club so long as I wore a tie.

I walked downstairs. Seated at the table, enjoying a cup of coffee and chatting with Devante like they were old friends, was Anny Rush. In an instant, my foul, negative mood vanished.

"Hey, Jake! You slept late," Devante said, grinning like the proverbial Cheshire cat.

"Hello, Jake." Anny stood up.

Seeing Anny, in my kitchen, talking with my son, it just felt so right. I walked over and kissed her. I wanted her to be a part of my life, but of course she had her own life, and I was letting my heart take me to that fantasy land where the intrepid reporter wins the fair maiden.

"Damn, Jake. Bold move," Devante said.

"Hey! What did I tell you about talking to strangers?"

"I told her she must have the wrong Jake Doyle. No way she could be looking for you. I guess I was wrong."

Anny laughed. "Devante was telling me about Just Ribs. Very impressive."

Devante carried his empty cup to the sink. "I'm installing a new smoker this morning. Stop by tonight and I'll give you a slab on the house."

She smiled in that way that I knew she wouldn't be around for any rib dinner. "I wish I could do that. I'm leaving today." She looked at me. "Australia. I wanted to talk with you before I left."

Devante grabbed his hoodie from the coat rack. "Australia? Cool." He headed for the door. "Talk to you later, Jake."

I poured myself a cup of coffee and sat down across the table from Anny.

"You must be proud," Anny said.

"You're going back to your brother's place?"

"His business is booming. He needs help. I think it's the right thing for me to do. I'm not leaving for a couple weeks, but I have to go to St. Louis to see my other brother. I'm giving him the keys to my cabin."

She sipped her coffee and then reached across the table and grasped my hand. "I missed you, Jake. I wish we had met some other time or place. Or world." She smiled sadly.

"Yeah. I know…" I reached for her other hand and I closed my eyes. That sweet pang of regret for what might have been enveloped me.

"Reporters have been coming around asking about O'Neill. It will only get worse. I don't want to spend my life talking about him. I don't want to be the woman who brought down Tim O'Neill…or who got him elected president."

"I understand. *The New York Times* contacted me. They're doing a story on him, too."

"Did you write your story?" she asked.

"It's not my story. I gave her the background. She'll do a puff piece."

Anny nodded. "I'll be off the grid. Far from annoying reporters. If you want to write my story, you have my permission."

"I've been thinking about what you said—that O'Neill would probably make a good president."

She sighed. "Well, better than what we have now, anyway."

"The question I keep asking myself is whether that's good enough. By that standard almost everyone's qualified."

She let go of my hand and stared up at the ceiling. "It was a lifetime ago, Jake. He was just a kid. People change. They grow up."

I took hold of her hand again. I wanted her to look at me. "I know, Anny. But that was his first real test—his chance to be standup —and he failed. Thirty years later, is he a better man?" I shrugged. "Is he?"

Her mouth twisted into a frown. "I don't know. If the story comes out, he'll have a chance to own it. I believe in second chances. Even for the rich and famous."

I remembered what O'Neill had told me about how nobody apologized anymore. He wanted to be different. If I told Anny's story, he would have his chance to show voters he was a different kind of politician.

"You're dressed up. Are you going into the office today?" Anny asked.

"I have to meet my new boss for lunch. Not looking forward to it."

"Oh…" She had a sly look on her face. "It will only take me five hours to get to St. Louis. I don't have to leave for a couple hours."

I know I was grinning like an idiot. "Want a tour of the house?"

She took hold of my hand. "Let's start with the bedroom."

. . .

After we made love, Anny showed me photos of Kimberley. I had always thought the outback part of Australia was a wasteland. But the place was incredible. Beautiful wild rivers, deep canyons, majestic waterfalls. It was a pristine wilderness.

As I drove down Lake Shore Drive to the dreaded luncheon, I fantasized about living there with Anny. We would be like Humphrey Bogart and Katherine Hepburn on *The African Queen*. Of course, she'd have to be the boat captain.

THIRTY

SATURDAY, 7 P.M. — MARCH 3, 2018

The Village Inn, Skokie

R achel Adams was sitting at the bar, wearing a Mets warmup jacket, arguing with a burly guy in a Cubs hat.

"You can't still be upset about '69," she said, smacking the dude in the shoulder. "That was fifty years ago. You weren't even born yet."

He grinned good-naturedly. "It's a legacy hatred," he said as he paid his tab. "Nice talking with you, ma'am. Mets suck."

"True enough," she said. She turned in her seat and smiled at me. "Hey, Jake. Want to sit at the bar?"

I slipped onto the vacated barstool. "Nice jacket. Good way to make new friends."

The barmaid, Molly, flashed her sparkling Irish eyes as she set a Harp draft in front of me. "Haven't seen you for a while, Jake. You on the wagon, again?"

"I'm on a diet."

Molly loved to flirt with the old men like me. "You don't need to diet, babe." She turned to Rachel. "Another Bud?"

"Sure." She finished her beer and pushed it to the edge. "This is a friendly bar, Jake. Pizza smells great too."

"Not a Yankee fan, huh?"

"I grew up on Long Island, can't you tell?" she said, parodying her accent. "Mets are our home team."

We ordered a medium deep dish with sausage and mushrooms and killed a half hour talking baseball. When Molly brought our pizza, I decided it was time to get down to business. "You wanted to talk about Tim O'Neill?" I asked.

She nodded. "His campaign is getting a lot of attention. He's saying all the right things. With his resources, he could be a formidable candidate. Is he as good as he looks?"

I studied the condensation on the beer stein. "No," I said. "He's not."

Rachel put down her beer. Engaged. "Good lede, Jake. What's the story? This is just background."

I pulled out of my jacket the story I had just written. "I was thinking you could use something like this as a sidebar to your feature on O'Neill. You know, put it in your own words. It will all check out, I promise."

She read it fast. Then reread it. Then she set it down and drained her beer. "Molly, could we have another round? With a shot chaser?"

"You like the pizza?" I asked.

"Holy shit, Jake. This is dynamite. This story could change the whole dynamic of the presidential race. Wow. Just wow. The *Trib* won't print this?"

"No. They're conflicted. You can have the story. Rewrite it. I guarantee it will hold up."

"No, no, no, no." She shook her head violently. "This is your story, Jake. I'll print it, but you deserve the byline." She glanced at her watch. "We can make the Sunday edition. Tomorrow. Okay?"

There would be no turning back if *The New York Times* printed my story. Molly brought us two beers and two shots. "Crown Royal, right, Jake?" she said.

I downed the shot.

"Are we a go, Jake?" Rachel asked.

I took a deep breath and slowly exhaled. "Okay," I said.

Rachel pushed her glass next to mine. "Here. You need another shot."

MONIQUE

You've really done it this time.
You were wrong.
Courage in a bottle. You'll be sorry when you sober up.
I don't think so.
Good thing you got that car.
Why?
Cause you're about to become a fulltime Uber driver.
Fuck you.

THIRTY-ONE

SUNDAY, 8 A.M. — MARCH 4, 2018

Walker Pancake House

I woke up with a serious Crown Royal hangover and a nagging feeling I had fucked up big-time. Did I really agree to have that story published in *The New York Times*? Maybe it was all just part of those crazy dreams I've been having.

No chance.

Rachel had texted me at five this morning.

> Here's a link to the story.
>
> "Tim O'Neill — Feet of Clay?"
>
> This is going to be huge.

I couldn't bring myself to open the story. I wasn't ready yet. If I didn't see it, I could pretend for a little longer that I hadn't totally shit-canned my career.

Devante and Amanda were already up, but something was off. Amanda wasn't in her workout gear, and no coffee had been made.

"What's going on?" I asked.

"Walker Pancakes. With Enyart," Amanda said. "Get your coat."

"Enyart doesn't do breakfast," I said.

"He said he wanted to hear about Charlotte's victory," Devante said, "but I think he really wants to get the down-low on your new girlfriend."

"Yeah. Me too," Amanda said. "D said she was hot."

"Fuck you both, very much."

Enyart had secured a booth in the back. He was sipping his cup of coffee and admiring the stained glass that decorated the windows and gave the place a special warmth. The diner didn't normally seat parties until everyone arrived.

"Did you annoy the receptionist so much that she gave you a table just to get rid of you?" I asked. Amanda slipped in next to him, and D and I sat down on the other side.

The waitress who served us the last time we stopped here stepped over with a pot of coffee. "Good morning, Mr. Doyle. Coffee?"

"Kinga looks out for me," Enyart said. "I told her the famous Jake Doyle was joining me. Got seated immediately."

"He's not good at waiting," Kinga whispered to me.

"Who's your new lady friend?" Enyart asked after Kinga left with our orders.

They were busting my balls, but I could tell they all cared. They wanted me to have a girlfriend. I'm not sure I wanted one, but I wanted Anny. A life lesson I learned long ago: we usually don't get what we want.

"Her name's Anny. She's a nice lady, but she's gone. Off to Australia, so there's no story. Didn't even leave a phone number."

Amanda's face turned pouty. "Ah, Jake, I'm sorry." Then she brightened. "Hey. What about WhatsApp?"

Devante laughed. "Jake doesn't even tweet."

"No. I taught him how. He even knows how to use hashtags," Amanda said.

I happened to know what WhatsApp was. "Guys, just let it go, okay?"

It must have been my tone because this time they did. Kinga brought our pancakes, waffles, and for Enyart his three-egg omelet. We ate in silence until Enyart put down his fork and said, "I have some news. Good news, I think."

I was offline again, thinking about the shitstorm that was about to hit and imagining the headlines.

Jake Doyle, sexual predator, strikes again.

Jake Doyle, ingrate, sells his boss down the river.

Jake Doyle—

"Hey! Did you hear what I just said?" Enyart asked. "Carlos called me. Chicago PD caught Jamal."

Now that was good news.

"Wow, that's a relief," Devante said. "I've been trying not to think about him, but I think I see him everywhere."

Me too.

"He didn't go to Mexico?" Amanda asked.

"That was a bullshit rumor. He was at his uncle's place in Wicker Park. Been hiding out there since the shooting."

"Will that help Maurice?" Devante asked.

Enyart held his cup while Kinga refilled it. "Don't know. They charged Jamal with murder." He set his coffee cup down. "I heard Bianca did a good job at the hearing."

"She was awesome," Amanda said. "That girl is an assassin."

"I want to hire her to defend Maurice. Maybe she can help him."

That was the thing folks didn't get about Enyart. He believed in second chances. And redemption.

"Do you want me to ask her?" Amanda asked.

"No, just give me her number. I'll call her."

My phone vibrated. A call from Sullivan. I had twenty-five text messages. I let Sullivan's call go to voicemail. Another call came in and five more text messages.

"What's happening, Jake?" Devante asked.

I turned off the phone. "Just work stuff. It can wait until Monday."

MONIQUE

You wouldn't have liked being press secretary.
I know.
You wouldn't have been any good at it either.
You're right.
You don't suck up. You're too honest.
That's the nicest thing you've said to me in a while.
I'm not real, Jake. Remember?

THIRTY-TWO

MONDAY, 10 A.M. — MARCH 5, 2018

Tribune Towers

Devante and Amanda were still out on their long run to the Bahai Temple and back, so I kept my phone turned off and enjoyed a peaceful breakfast. Well, tried to enjoy it. Amanda had been insisting I eat heathier, so I had a bowl of her low-fat granola with her beloved strawberries. I hunted through the refrigerator hoping Devante had brought home some takeout sliders or leftover ribs but no luck. I poured a second cup of coffee and turned on my phone—carefully—like it might explode.

That was close to accurate. Ten voicemail messages and forty-seven text messages. The one from Sullivan was a demand that I come to his office at ten o'clock. The rest of the text messages were from other reporters who wanted to talk to me about my story. I was about to screen the voicemail messages when Charlotte called.

"Hi, honey."

"Holy shit, Dad! You've gone viral again! I wonder what Lucy Hall has to say now!"

"Who?"

"The bitch who trashed you last week for shitting on the resistance."

"I didn't...never mind. I just turned my phone on, so I'm not up-to-speed on the Twitterverse."

"You didn't see the *Times* follow up article?"

"No. I don't read the *Times.*"

"Another woman has come forward. Someone O'Neill dated when he was at Harvard. She got busted for smuggling pot from Canada for him. He left her holding the bag too."

"Damn." I had the sick feeling it would now be open season on Tim O'Neill. I didn't want that, but I'm not sure what I wanted.

"You sound upset. It was a good story. You did the right thing."

"I guess. What time do you want me to pick you up tomorrow?"

"My appointment is at ten. Can you pick me up at nine?"

"I'll be there." Not likely that I would be getting any conflicting work assignments.

I hung up the phone, and the sadness that had been hanging around felt like it had moved in and set up a permanent residence.

I didn't want Anny to leave.

I didn't want to destroy Tim O'Neill.

I didn't want to lose my job at the *Tribune.*

And I didn't want Charlotte to get an abortion.

But there was nothing I could do about any of those events.

Some days life really sucked.

Yolanda welcomed me with a sad smile, as though someone in my family had died. "Hello, Jake. Mr. Sullivan and Hector are in the conference room."

Sullivan was standing, staring out the window at the Chicago River. Hector was sitting at the table, wishing he was someplace else. I didn't figure Sullivan would have the guts to meet me without backup, and he probably didn't figure Mary Belton was up to the task.

Sullivan didn't hear me enter. "Hello, Jake," Hector said. He shrugged and had an I-don't-know-what-I'm-doing-here look.

Sullivan wheeled around. "Mr. Doyle, you are being terminated, effective immediately. For cause. You have violated your contract, and we will be pursuing litigation."

No surprises, other than the very upset demeanor of James Sullivan. I thought a high-priced lawyer would be more dispassionate.

"For what?" I asked.

"That libelous piece of crap you had published in the *Times.*"

"The truth is a defense in any libel case," I said, exhausting my legal knowledge.

Sullivan sneered. "You just picked a fight with a man who has more fucking money than God. We will bury you in litigation. You will be ruined financially and professionally." He spat out the last word. "Not that that means anything to you."

I figured my best tactic was to adopt the rope-a-dope strategy Ali used against George Foreman. Let the guy punch himself out. "Anything else?" I asked.

"You're nothing, Doyle. You think you can bring down Tim O'Neill?"

I smiled, which really annoyed him. "I don't think that at all. I like Tim."

"You disgust me." He pressed a button on his phone. "Get security in here."

Hector stared at Sullivan. "Security?"

"To escort Mr. Doyle off the premises."

"Are you thinking I might steal the artwork off the walls?" I asked.

I had known Bob Wilkins, the *Trib* security guard, for thirty years. "Sorry, Mr. Doyle," he said as we waited for the elevator.

"No sweat, Bob." Dwayne Smith saw me waiting and quick-stepped over. Sotto voce he said, "Sorry about the Best Ribs thing. Damn shame."

"What do you mean?"

"You didn't hear?" he asked, looking like a man who wished he had kept his mouth shut. "Uh...Mary Belton cancelled the whole thing. No Best of Chicago awards this year."

Mary Belton didn't have the juice to even validate parking. But Smitty was right about one thing—it was a damn shame.

MONIQUE

Tomorrow's the big day.
Just let me sleep, will you?
You are asleep. It's not my fault your conscience is bothering you.
It's not.
Admit it. You don't want her to have an abortion.
It's not my decision.
I see.
It was different with you.
That's what you always say, Jake.

THIRTY-THREE

TUESDAY, 10 A.M. — MARCH 6, 2018

Rogers Park Health Center

When I buzzed Charlotte's apartment she told me she'd be right down. She stepped off the elevator clutching a backpack. With her knit cap and a ski jacket she looked like a scared high school girl. I could imagine how she felt; I was scared too. We rode in silence.

It was a damp gray morning, which seemed appropriate. I found parking on Howard Street, a block from the clinic. We walked carefully; frozen snow and salt crystals dotted the sidewalk. A grandmotherly gray-haired lady stood in front of the clinic. As we turned toward the entrance, she offered Charlotte a pamphlet. On the cover was a photo of a baby and a banner that read, *It's a child, not a choice.* Charlotte kept walking. The woman nodded at me as we passed. Her face was sad, not angry.

The clinic was a storefront on Howard Street. In the waiting room were a middle-aged Asian couple, a young Black woman with earbuds who was staring at her iPhone, and a skinny dude in a blue blazer and khakis who was tapping his foot, looking as though he were ready to bolt out the door.

. . .

Charlotte told the receptionist her name and she ushered us into another room. "We're running a little behind," she said. "The nurse will be in to talk to you in about twenty minutes. Just try to relax."

It wasn't an exam room. There were three comfortable chairs and a coffee table with well-thumbed copies of *People*, *Entertainment Tonight*, and *Essence*. We sat down.

"Thank you for coming with me, Dad." She picked up the copy of *People* and plopped down in one of the armchairs. She tossed the magazine back on the table and covered her face with her hands. "Oh, God."

"Are you okay, Char?" A dumb question, but I'm a master at that.

She moaned and uncovered her face. "Am I making a mistake, Daddy?"

She hadn't called me Daddy in twenty years. But she was asking for my help.

"I've been thinking a lot about what you said last week about me giving up. Or taking the easy path."

Charlotte's face was creased with pain. "I didn't—"

I raised my hand. "It's okay. Let me tell you my story before I lose my nerve. When Monique discovered she was pregnant, she was devastated. She had a ten-year plan, and it didn't include having a baby at twenty-two. Devante is just like her. Ambitious. Always in a hurry. It wasn't in my plans either, but I told her we could make it work. She didn't want to hear that. She said she wanted an abortion. She asked me to take her to the clinic."

Charlotte stared at me, trying to catch up on the importance of my revelation.

I took a deep breath and stared down at the floor. Charlotte was studying me, her forehead wrinkled with confusion. "I betrayed her," I said. I had never thought of it that way before. But that was the truth.

Her surprised look morphed into confusion. "Betrayed her?"

"I told Antoinette. I knew Monique's mother would never countenance an abortion. Under any circumstances. And I knew Monique would never go against her mother's wishes. I was right."

"Monique was angry?"

"I would have married her. I would have left Tawni, and I would have abandoned you. I know that's an awful thing to say and for you to hear, but I think you need to know that. I would never have stopped loving you. And I never will. But I wanted to be with Monique. I loved her, but she didn't forgive me, even after Devante was born. She loved the boy and she changed her plan. She was a good mother. I thought over time she would give me another chance; I was willing to be patient. Turned out we didn't have more time."

"I'm sorry, Dad. I didn't know."

"I don't regret my decision. I mean, I can't. Devante..." I stopped. I didn't really know what to say. "I gave up the world for him. It was worth it." My voice had gone husky. A tear leaked from my eye. I swiped at it with the back of my hand.

Charlotte was silent. She stared at me, her eyes glistening.

"I'm not telling you this to change your mind. Monique should have had a chance to pursue the life she had planned. I took that away from her. She wasn't being selfish, and neither are you. I want you to pursue your dream, but you've asked me if I think you are making a mistake, so this time I'm going to be honest.

"Yes. I think you are making a mistake. You are strong and capable. You can have this baby and go to law school. Life is precious. You will love this child more every day, and he or she will be such a wonderful part of your life that you will be eternally grateful that you brought this child into the world. This I believe with all my heart."

I took a breath. Charlotte was staring at me. I couldn't read her.

"If you have this baby, I will move to California and help you raise the child. I wasn't the greatest father in the world, but I will make it my mission to be the world's greatest grandfather."

Charlotte took a tissue from the box on the table. She blew her nose and dabbed her eyes. "I love you, Dad."

I got up from my chair and wrapped my arms around her. "I love you, too, honey."

There was a knock on the door. I sat back down, and Charlotte said, "Come in."

A nurse entered the room. "Charlotte?"

Charlotte nodded.

"Hello, Charlotte. My name is Angela Ramos. I have a few questions." She smiled warmly and turned toward me. "And you are…?"

"That's my father," Charlotte said. "Jake Doyle."

Nurse Ramos made a note on her clipboard. "Well, he can stay here if it is okay with you."

Charlotte breathed deeply and she seemed to sit up straighter in her chair. "I am sorry, but I've decided not to have the abortion."

I think I stopped breathing. I wasn't sure I heard her correctly. But Nurse Ramos had. She set down her clipboard and took hold of Charlotte's hands. "Don't be sorry, Charlotte. The whole purpose of my questions was to make sure that this is what you want to do. Now I have some different questions, if you don't mind."

I started breathing again. My vision had become blurry. Nurse Ramos pushed the box of tissues over to my side of the table. "Here, Mr. Doyle."

I didn't say anything. I was afraid I'd start blubbering. I took a long cleansing breath and tried to rein in my emotions. The nurse was questioning Charlotte. Did she have an OB-GYN? Was she planning to keep the baby? I couldn't focus.

All the other issues that had been troubling me—the impossibility of a life with Anny, the loss of my job, the Tim O'Neill debacle, Devante's lost opportunity, the Jamal situation—were still out there, but now I felt like it would be okay. I would survive. We all would.

THIRTY-FOUR
TUESDAY, 6 P.M. — MARCH 6, 2018

Home

I brought Charlotte home with me, and we spent the afternoon binging on the last five episodes of the last season of *The Sopranos*—when everything falls apart. We'd seen it before, but it was more fun the second time.

"Damn, I thought I had problems," I said as Tony scrambled to keep his empire intact.

"You could have used a good therapist," Charlotte said.

"Can you imagine your mother in couples' therapy?"

Charlotte laughed. "The therapist would kill her."

"Are you telling your mom about your decision?"

She wrinkled up her face. She looked almost as pained as when she was in the clinic struggling with her decision. "Would you tell her? I don't want to deal with her. Ever."

"Sure. Tomorrow. Let's enjoy the finale."

The Soprano family had gathered for dinner at a diner. Meadow was struggling to parallel park her car. It was excruciating to watch, knowing what was about to happen. In the diner the family chatted amiably while the camera panned to the other customers. A Black man gets up and goes to the rest room. Meadow finally parks the car. The man returns from the restroom and approaches the table. Tony looks up and smiles and the screen goes black. For two minutes.

"I love that ending," I said. "I guess there won't be any sequels."

"The producer wanted the blackout scene to last five minutes," Charlotte said. "But the studio wouldn't let him. There were huge debates on Twitter as to what really happened."

"Seriously? More evidence for why Twitter is a waste of time."

"I'm hungry. Can we order a celebratory pizza from La Rosa's?" Charlotte asked.

Pizza wasn't on the diet plan Amanda had prepared for me, but this was a special occasion. "Let's order two—D and Amanda will be home soon."

They arrived at the same time as the pizzas. Both were ecstatic at Charlotte's news. We were having such a good time, I hated to dampen the celebration, but I had to deliver the rest of the news of the week.

"As you might have guessed, the *Tribune* owners didn't take kindly to my story in *The Times.*"

"That was an awesome column. Everyone's talking about it," Amanda said.

"Yeah, Jake. Nice work," D said.

Charlotte was silent. She knew what was coming.

"D, I'm sorry to tell you that the *Tribune* has decided not to have any 'Chicago's Best' awards this year."

Devante looked at me, confused momentarily, and then the recognition hit him. "Damn. That sucks." He bit down on his lip.

"What petty assholes..." Amanda said.

"You're right. It's retaliation, plain and simple. I'm sorry, D."

Devante sat back in his chair. "No biggie." He grabbed another slice of pizza. He took a large bite and then set it down. "I have an idea. Let's invite the other rib places and have a Ribfest. Not a competition. A celebration of ribs! Open it to all the rib joints in the area."

Amanda clapped her hands. "I love that idea. When?"

D grabbed his planner. "How about March 31? That gives us almost three weeks."

"You could have it at the high school. On the infield of the track. I'm sure I could get permission," Charlotte said.

It was like a scene from an Andy Hardy movie, where the gang decides to put on a show. An hour later Devante had an action plan written out. Over my objections, I was made the honorary chairman of the event and would be expected to give the opening remarks.

"You've got a bad-ass rep now, Jake. You're a headliner," Devante said. "And tomorrow I start training with Enyart again. Golden Gloves the week after the Ribfest."

MONIQUE

I'll let you sleep tonight, Jake.
Thank you.

THIRTY-FIVE

WEDNESDAY, 4 P.M. — MARCH 7, 2018

Devon Boxing Club

E nyart was wearing the Everlast boxing mitts, calling out combinations for Devante. "Jab, jab, cross-lead, uppercut. Jab, cross, lead hook. Stay balanced. That's it."

It was exhausting to watch. Each punch made a whomping sound as Devante smacked Enyart's mitts. His movements were smooth and powerful. The week off from training didn't appear to have affected him.

"Okay. That's good," Enyart said, putting down the mitts. "Time for road work. Three miles."

Devante grinned. "Want to run with me, Jake?"

I had worn my workout gear, which D found particularly amusing. Told me I looked like Rocky. He said nobody wore cotton sweatpants. He's a clothes snob.

"Not today. My coach says I'm not ready to run yet." In addition to a diet, Amanda had come up with a training plan for me. I was to start with brisk walking and not try running for at least a month.

D pulled off his gloves and slipped into his warmup jacket, which was gaudy and synthetic. "Stay on the sidewalk," Enyart said. "This ain't Evanston. Runners don't have any rights."

"He looks pretty good," I said to Enyart after D had left.

Enyart nodded. "He's got skills. And great stamina. If he gets a lucky draw, he could make it through a few rounds in the tournament."

"Did you talk to Bianca about Maurice?"

"Oh yeah. Amanda's right. That lady could be a Marine. We met yesterday. She's trying to get a deal for him. If Maurice testifies against Jamal, she thinks he has a chance to regain juvenile status."

"Will he testify?"

"She's trying to get him released on bail. He can stay with me. She wants to work out a deal with the prosecutor so that he gets sentenced to some juvie facility out-of-state, away from Jamal and the gang."

"Do you think you could train me?" I asked.

"For the tournament?" To his credit, he didn't laugh.

I laughed. "No. I just want to get in better shape. Lose some pounds. I have time now."

"When you're not driving for that damn Uber, you could hang out here. Help me with the school program. And Jake..."

"What?"

"Next year, you can sign up for the tournament. You were a brawler, but you can take a punch. That's half the battle. I'll have you ready."

I hadn't told anyone about my plans to help Charlotte. We had decided we would move out together after her teaching contract was over and rent a three-bedroom apartment near campus in California. I was excited about the whole idea—and scared too.

"I won't be here next spring. I'm moving to Palo Alto with Charlotte to help her raise her kid." I had the feeling Enyart would understand.

He did.

"Goddamn, Jake. You finally did it."

"Did what?"

"Got your head out of your ass and made a decision that makes sense. Oorah!"

That's high-level compassion on the Enyart scale.

MONIQUE

Jake? Are you there? Come on, Jake, answer me.

THIRTY-SIX

THURSDAY, 3 P.M. — MARCH 8, 2018

Home

This was the first day of the rest of my life. Okay, maybe it was the second day, but today was the official start. I got up at six o'clock when Devante and Amanda got up—it's still totally dark at that crazy hour—and I put on my Rocky sweats and met them in the kitchen. Amanda gave me my workout for the day: a brisk walk down Kedvale to Dempster and back. Two miles. I told her I could jog that, but she insisted I start with just walking. When I returned, I feasted on a bowl of low-fat granola and yogurt.

The *Tribune* didn't have any more Tim O'Neill reports, but the online version of the *Sun-Times* had two articles—a reprint of my *New York Times* piece, which the *Sun-Times* helpfully introduced with a sidebar on my "notorious, scandalous past," and an AP flash poll in which only thirty percent of those polled thought O'Neill was qualified to be president, down from sixty percent two weeks ago. His ship was sinking fast.

I was about to check the listings for apartments in Palo Alto—just to get an idea of what I could expect—when my phone rang.

Tawni.

I wasn't ready to talk to her. Before, I would have let the phone ring, but this was the new, hopefully improved, version of me—the one that didn't duck uncomfortable calls.

"Hi, Tawni."

"Did you forget what day this is?"

"I guess I must have."

"It's our anniversary, Jake."

Tawni never cared about our anniversary, even when we were married. "We don't have anniversaries anymore. Remember?"

"I know Charlotte didn't have the abortion. I'm sure you were planning to tell me sooner or later, but I couldn't wait. Let's have dinner at The Alcove for old time's sake. I made reservations for seven."

We had gone to the Alcove for our twentieth anniversary. Rack of lamb to die for. Maybe if I hadn't been so hungry—that granola just doesn't do the trick—I would have resisted her invitation (it was more of a command).

"Are you buying? I'm no longer employed. You probably know that too."

"I do. And I want to talk about that. Tonight. Yes. I'll buy."

Now I was really suspicious. And hungry.

The Alcove has an intimate dining room tucked under the elevated tracks in Evanston. I got there at six fifty-five and Tawni was already seated. In the thirty years I have known Tawni, that had never happened. My suspicion level was off the chart.

She stood up as the host brought me to her table in the back corner—the most private and intimate location. She gave me a smile that was very hard to resist. It seemed so genuine, but I knew better.

She had ordered us both martinis. "For old time's sake. It used to be our drink." She raised her glass. "Happy Anniversary."

The Alcove makes a great martini. "You seem to be in an exceptionally good mood," I said.

"I am happy. But sad, too. I am sorry about the whole competency hearing. I was desperate. That was a mistake."

"Yes, it was." I picked up the menu. They still had the rack of lamb. My stomach was growling. "Are you ready to order? I'm starving."

That kind of change of subject normally would have pissed her off, but she just smiled and picked up the menu. "I think I'll have the Caesar salad. I've gained a few pounds; it's all those damn banquets."

"You look great." She did. She always looked great.

I ordered us a bottle of wine. Tawni insisted on the eighty-dollar Cab from some Napa winery she had visited. We had a great dinner talking about the old days. We had a lot of good times in the years before Charlotte was born.

I told her how Sullivan had killed the Best of Chicago awards. She was genuinely disappointed for Devante. "He's a very talented young man. You should be proud of him. He is going to do be a huge success, I just know it."

Her generosity toward D was one of those things about Tawni that made it so hard for me to dislike her, despite all the shitty things she had done.

"James Sullivan is a cretin," she said. "I can't believe he killed those awards just to hurt you. You should file a lawsuit against the *Tribune* for wrongful termination. Justin's firm could represent you."

"They threatened to sue me, but they haven't, yet. Best not to poke a bear. Especially one with billions."

She tilted her head and smiled. "Point taken," she said. "But keep it in mind if they do sue you."

We ordered coffee and decided to split a flourless chocolate cake. I was starting to think I had been wrong. Maybe Tawni didn't have any special agenda. Maybe she just missed me.

"We're going to be grandparents. Can you believe it?"

Uh oh.

"I'm moving to Palo Alto with Charlotte," I said. "I'll help her take care of the baby."

When Charlotte was a baby, Tawni took care of almost all the parenting tasks. I was often absent, or angry, or drunk. I was not a good father to Charlotte, and I expected Tawni to remind me of that now. She was never one to pull her punches.

"Oh my. That's wonderful, Jake. What a relief."

"A relief?"

"It's so hard to find quality childcare. Charlotte isn't really the nurturing type." She paused. "But she'll learn. You can help her. She has a good heart. So do you, Jake."

"Thank you." I didn't know what else to say.

"Charlotte hates me right now. She won't take my calls." She took a deep breath, and I swear her eyes were misting. "I want to be a part of our grandchild's life. Can you help me, Jake?"

I had loved Tawni once. I didn't love her anymore, but I still cared for her, and I know that being cut off from a grandchild was heartbreaking for her. I'm not a strong man. I know that. The easy thing would be to just say I would help and then get out of town. Kick the can down the road like a good politician. But if I wanted to be a better grandfather than I was a father, I needed to start now.

"You made a serious mistake, Tawni. Some mistakes you can fix. Some you just to have to live with. Charlotte is your daughter. She has your stubborn will. I'm not saying she won't ever forgive you because I know people can change. And maybe after the baby arrives, she'll feel different. Maybe not.

"I can't help you. That will be up to you and Charlotte. My advice is don't push it. You need to be patient. It might take years."

Now she was crying. Real tears. If it was an act, it was Oscar-worthy. "Okay, Jake. Thank you."

She paid the bill and I walked her to the car. "Send me pictures?" she asked.

I nodded and swallowed hard. "Of course."

THIRTY-SEVEN

SATURDAY, 1 P.M. — MARCH 31, 2018

Ribfest

Things were happening fast.

I learned that all those stories I had read about how expensive it was to live in California were false. Expensive was a wholly inadequate term. Palo Alto was out of reach. I kept searching farther east and found a two-bedroom apartment that had seen better days, in Emerald Hills, about thirty minutes from the law school. A "steal," the realtor assured me for only $3,400 per month. I signed the lease and prayed that I could make enough money with Uber to keep us afloat.

I might actually start believing in the power of prayer. An hour after I signed the lease, I got a call from Rachel Adams. In typical New York fashion she got right to the point. She wanted me to write a weekly column for the *Times*. She knew about my plan to move to Palo Alto, and she liked the "optics" of an old school Chicago columnist moving to California to help his daughter raise a child.

"Grandpa in the land of fruit and nuts." She laughed at the notion, as though I didn't know what I was getting into—which was true. On hearing her offer I hesitated. I had been making fun of the pretentious

Times for decades, but I quickly came to my senses and said yes. I didn't even try to negotiate the salary. I knew it would be enough that I wouldn't have to be an Uber driver in California.

Devante, Amanda, and Charlotte worked nonstop on the Ribfest. All the finalists signed up as well as ten other rib joints. The school made the field available, and over five hundred tickets had already sold. Even the weather cooperated: it was supposed to be in the fifties and sunny.

They still insisted that I had to give a speech. I promised them it would be the shortest welcoming address on record.

Bianca got the court to allow bail for Maurice, and he was released into Enyart's custody. For the last two weeks he and I were co-trainers for Enyart's afterschool program. Maurice was a natural athlete like Devante, and he enjoyed helping the kids. But yesterday I could tell something was bothering him.

"What's up, Mo?" I asked as we were packing up after the kids had left for the day.

His face creased with worry. "Miss Pujols made a deal. You hear about it?"

Bianca had made a deal with the prosecutors that in exchange for Maurice's testimony against Jamal, they would sentence him as a juvenile and he'd be sent to a facility in southern Indiana. Two years and then he would have a second chance.

"I did. It's a good deal."

"I have to be a rat. Put my man J-dog down."

"Jamal is not your man. He abandoned you."

"He ain't going to like it. He could hurt me."

"He won't know where you are, and besides, he'll be in Stateville for the rest of his life."

I understood his fear. I had been looking over my shoulder every day until they caught Jamal. But he was not a powerful gang leader with associates to do his bidding. We had succeeded in getting Maurice out of jail, where he would have been in danger.

Maurice's frown deepened.

"How is it living with Mr. Enyart?" I asked.

He shrugged. "It's cool."

"Remember what Jamal did when Mr. Enyart threatened him?"

"Yeah. He split."

"Well, even if he could get out of jail—which he can't—you think he would mess with you when you have Mr. Enyart as a bodyguard?"

He bit down on his lip. "Jamal don't want no part of Mr. Enyart."

It was a beautiful day for Ribfest, and folks were lined up from the entrance to the track all the way to Church Street. A five-dollar ticket would get you three sample ribs. You could buy as many tickets as you wanted. It wasn't meant to be a money-making proposition. It was to be, in Devante's words, "A celebration of ribs."

A reviewing stand had been erected in the center of the track. At one thirty Devante got up on the stand and blasted an airhorn for a good ten seconds. "Okay, now that I have your attention, I want to introduce the chairman of Ribfest 2018, the celebrated columnist, and my father, Jake Doyle! Come on up, Jake!"

I climbed up. He had done a surprisingly good job at silencing the crowd. I am guessing they had figured out that there would be no ribs until I finished talking.

"Thank you all for coming. I've been on a diet for the last two weeks. Trust me, I am as hungry as anyone here, so I promise to be brief." That brought a bleat of airhorns and cheers.

"I heard a country song the other day: an old man giving career advice to his son. We do that a lot. He tells his boy to find something he loves and call it work. I know from my own personal experience that when you are working at something you love, even if the hours are long and the pay is low, it's rewarding. That's what we have here today. Hardworking folks doing something they love. Let's all celebrate that."

I stared out at the crowd; there had to be over a thousand people. Standing next to the *Just Ribs* booth was a tall blonde wearing a cowboy hat.

Anny.

Even from a distance I recognized her piercing blue eyes.

I closed my eyes and when I opened them, she was still there. The crowd had gone silent, not sure whether I had finished my speech.

"So again, thank you all for coming. I declare Ribfest 2018 to be officially opened."

Devante jumped back up on the stand and gave another blast of his airhorn as the crowd cheered—thankful I had stopped talking.

"Good job, Jake."

"Anny's here," I said.

"I know. I comped her a ticket." He had a shit-eating grin. Way too proud of himself.

"But...how...never mind." I didn't care how he pulled this off. I jumped down from the stand and wove my way through the crowd. Anny had just finished her rib sample and was licking her fingers.

"These are awesome!" she said.

"You're back?"

"Devante tells me you're going to be a grandfather. Congratulations."

The crowd was pressing in, anxious to get their ribs. "Walk with me," I said.

We walked out of the track area over to the girls' softball field, which had been taken over by an army of geese. They ignored us. I told Anny about losing my job and my plan to move to California. She already knew.

"It looks as though O'Neill's presidential campaign is over. Or it will be soon. What's happening with Australia?" I hated to ruin the good time vibe, but I had to know.

She stopped walking and kissed me. "This isn't the end of the fairy-tale, Jake. This is not where we live happily-ever-after. But maybe it's the start of our story. I'm still leaving. I have a flight in two hours, but I wanted to see you before I left. I love you, Jake Doyle. You're a good man. You deserve me."

My throat was tight. "I don't know if I deserve you. I just know I love you. But I can't go to Australia."

She smiled. "I know, Jake. I understand. This isn't goodbye. This is see you later, Grandpa. Law school is three years. Your daughter won't need your help forever. Come and visit next year. We have time."

I walked her to her car and stood in the parking lot as she drove out of sight. She was playing the long game. I had played that game before and it hadn't worked out.

But this time it would be different.

I walked around the fest wondering how it was possible to feel sad and happy at the same time. I sampled ribs from the other rib joints that had been nominated for Best Ribs. They were good, but, of course, not as good as Devante's ribs. I made my way back to his stand. Charlotte, Amanda, and Bianca were helping serve while D worked the grill.

"Great speech, Dad!" Charlotte said.

"We love your girlfriend," Amanda said.

Bianca nodded her agreement. "A very nice woman, Mr. Doyle." Seeing Bianca reminded me that Enyart was supposed to be here.

"Have you seen Enyart?"

Devante looked up. "I forgot. Enyart called me. He said he had to pick up Mo from his brother's place. He didn't sound too happy."

"Happy's not his strong suit," I said. I didn't know Maurice had a brother, but I know Enyart didn't want him visiting any of his so-called friends or anyone in his dysfunctional family.

I killed another hour wandering from booth to booth, just enjoying the day and feeling good about my future for the first time in weeks. Maybe months. Maybe years. I walked back to the *Just Ribs* booth. The crowd had thinned.

"I thought I would take off if you don't need me. Did you hear anything more from Enyart?"

Devante shook his head. "Take off, Jake. We got it covered here."

My good-time feeling dissipated the moment I pulled into my driveway. Enyart's pickup truck was parked in front of the house.

The house was dark, but a fire was burning in the fireplace. Enyart was sitting on my couch staring at the fire. The bottle of Crown Royal was on the coffee table, and he had a full tumbler of whiskey in his hand.

"Hey," I said. "Everything okay?"

His face was red, but it wasn't his angry red. Unbelievably, it appeared he had been crying. He stared at the glass of whiskey. "This stuff doesn't work for shit."

Enyart didn't drink. Ever.

"What happened, John?" I held my breath.

He put down the tumbler and covered his face with his hands.

"Goddammit!" He pounded the table with his fist. "Maurice is dead. OD'd." He sobbed. It sounded almost inhuman. "I thought I could keep him safe from Jamal, and his own miserable family killed him." He picked up the glass and hurled it into the fire.

I stepped next to him and put my hand on his back. "I'm sorry, John." I wanted to tell him he did his best, but I knew he would have none of that, even though we both knew it was true.

THIRTY-EIGHT

SATURDAY, 7 P.M. — APRIL 7, 2022

Golden Gloves Tournament, Cicero Stadium

The day after Maurice died the prosecutor dropped the charges against Jamal, and he was released from jail. No witnesses were willing to testify to the murder of Leticia Ribeiro. It was as if it never happened.

Enyart worked Devante hard all week, getting him ready for his bout. He didn't say a word about Maurice or Jamal. I guess that was a skill he learned as a soldier. You lose someone and you just keep going. A day at a time. It was a tough code.

Devante was fighting in the novice 168-pound category, which included anyone from eighteen to forty with fewer than nine fights. Devante was eighteen and had zero fights. His opponent, Jim Collins, was twenty-four and had won all nine of his matches. He was five-eight and had a muscular compact frame. A classic middleweight.

I waited in the locker room with Devante as Enyart wrapped his fists and helped him put on his boxing gloves.

"That dude's undefeated," Devante said. "Damn. I heard his uncle was middleweight champ."

Enyart gave him his look. "Wrong. John Collins lost the title fight. TKO in the first round. And you ain't fighting his uncle."

The intercom squawked. "Baptiste and Collins, you're up."

The Golden Gloves was nonstop bouts. There had already been four matches, and another six were scheduled. We walked down the gangway to the red corner of the ring. Devante climbed through the ropes. Collins was waiting in the blue corner. He acted bored but menacing.

The referee gave both boxers their instructions, and then Devante returned to our corner. "Fight your fight," Enyart said. "Keep moving and don't let him tie you up. Use your jab."

The bell rang and, unlike Jamal, Collins approached cautiously. He fired a couple of jabs; Devante parried them and slid to the side. Collins had good footwork, and he stayed on D, backing him into a corner.

D tried to slide to the left, but Collins cut him off and then fired a right hook to the jaw followed by a straight left hand that snapped D's head back. His knees buckled and he fell back into the ropes, then slid down to the canvas. He tried to get up, but the world was spinning too fast for him. D got to one knee and was trying to use the ropes to pull himself up when Enyart threw a towel into the ring.

The ref waved his hands over his head and pushed Collins to his corner. Devante staggered to his feet, his eyes still glassy. He walked slowly to his corner. "Damn. What hit me?"

Enyart squeezed his neck. "Just breathe, son."

The referee brought the two fighters back to the center of the ring. "Winner by a TKO in one minute twenty-two seconds of the first round, Jim Collins!" He raised Collins' hand, and then Devante walked back to the corner, slightly less dazed than a moment ago. "Sorry, guys."

"Nothing to be sorry for," Enyart said. "You ran into a buzzsaw. It can happen to anyone."

"Come on, D," I said. "Get cleaned up and we'll go to Gibson's. My treat."

"Those are words you don't hear too often," Enyart said. "I'll meet you there. You don't need a long shower, son. You didn't work that hard." He grinned and gave Devante's shoulder a squeeze.

Devante and I walked across the stadium parking lot. "I'm giving up on my boxing career," Devante said. "Getting knocked senseless is no fun."

I was thrilled to hear that. "Good idea. You're going to be a world-class chef, so you don't need to get your brains scrambled."

A shadowy figure emerged from a row of cars, twenty yards ahead of us.

Jamal.

Devante saw him too. "Damn," he said.

He pointed his gun at Devante. "Time's up, motherfucker."

I saw the flash from the gun as I shoved Devante. "Run, D!" I screamed.

I turned toward Jamal waving my arms like a mad man, hoping that—

Don't open your eyes, Jake.
Monique?
It's me, babe.
I can't see you.
I wasn't expecting you so soon.
I have to get back. I need to find Devante. Make sure he's okay.
That's out of your hands. You can't save him.
No. You're wrong. I couldn't save you, but I can save him. I have to.
You fought the good fight, Jake. I'm proud of you. Come with me.
Not until I know he's okay.
Oh, Jake. You never learn. Your story has no heroes.
I know.
Take my hand. It's time.
You're hurting me.
Take my hand. We can be together now. No more pain, Jake.
Where is Devante? Tell me the truth.
The truth is elusive.

Tell me!
Come with me and I will tell you everything.
Okay. I will, Monique. But...
Don't open your eyes, Jake!

I open my eyes.

A gauzy angel is staring at me.

I want to ask if Devante is okay, but there's a tube stuck down my throat and I can't talk. Someone squeezes my hand.

"I'm here, Dad."

END

A NOTE FROM THE AUTHOR

I would love to hear what you thought of *Freedom's Just Another Word...* Please consider leaving a review on Amazon.

Please join my newsletter for news about new writing projects, my reviews of other indie authors, and my ongoing multi-sport adventures: <u>Do Not Go Gentle...</u>

PART 1

DRY HEAT EXCERPT

ONE

JOEY

3 p.m. – Saturday – November 20, 1999
Roadrunner Park – Phoenix, AZ

The gangs were always stealing the nylon basketball nets, so the park director had replaced them with galvanized steel chain, which rattled obnoxiously on every bad shot. Joey frowned as his jump shot clanked off the front rim.

"Your shot sucks today, Joey Blade," Mallory said as she bounced the ball back to him.

"Your boobs are distracting me. Maybe it's time you started wearing a bra." Blonde, with a pixie cut that framed her cute little-girl face, Mallory could have passed for a twelve-year-old if it hadn't been for her huge breasts. She was fifteen, two years younger than Joey, and they had been playground buddies for ten years. She lived with her creepy father in a rundown brick house a block away and escaped to the park most afternoons.

"Come on, concentrate, Mr. All American." She lifted up her sweatshirt, flashing him as he took his next shot. An airball.

"Aargh." Joey chased after the errant shot, hip-checking Mallory as he grabbed the ball. He dribbled out to the corner and swished a turn-around jumper. "Yes! No distractions that time." He pumped his fist.

Mallory smirked. "Better get used to it. You'll have plenty of distractions when you're in Lala Land next week."

Lala Land.

Joey was out of time. He had to make a decision about his trip to USC and he had to make it now. He clanked another free throw off the rim.

"What's wrong, Joey?"

"Dutch."

Mallory scowled as she bounced the ball to him. She knew what Joey's dad was like. Dutch Blade was an unfiltered, heart-on-his-sleeve guy. He could chew someone out one moment and be hugging them the next.

"He doesn't want you following in the immortal footsteps of O.J.?"

Joey gave her a look. Mallory was always a smartass. Three weeks ago, in his last high school football game, the Shadow Mountain Matadors had defeated Apache Junction, last year's state champion, 28 to 24. Joey rushed for 264 yards and scored all four touchdowns for Shadow Mountain. After the game, he was contacted by every school in the PAC 10, all promising that he would have a bright future playing football for their university.

He thought it would be cool to have all that attention, but it was really like trying to date five girls at once. Everyone insisted their school was the best choice for Joey. He didn't like disappointing people and he didn't want to string anyone along, so he quickly narrowed the search to USC in Los Angeles and the University of Arizona in Tucson.

He dribbled out to the foul line and took another turnaround jumper. The shot was a foot short and wide left.

Mallory scampered over and picked it up. "You can't blame that one on me."

Joey tried spinning the ball on his index finger, but he couldn't keep his focus. "Dutch grew up in Tucson. He loves the Wildcats. He's always said that if his folks had had the money, he would have gone to

U of A instead of Vietnam." He glided out to the corner again. "Ball!" he shouted. Mallory fired a chest high pass to him and he swished a fifteen-footer.

"Maybe he just wants to keep you close so you can help with the family business," Mallory said with a faux expression of innocence.

Dutch had started Blade Engine and Crankshaft when he returned from Vietnam. With the help of Joey's mom, Callie, it had become the largest engine rebuilder in the southwest.

"My dad thinks anyone who goes to California just wants to be a movie star."

Mallory tilted her head and squinted at him. "You're pretty cute with that curly hair and those girly eyelashes. I could definitely see you in the movies."

"Shut up, Mallory. This is serious."

"What do you want to be when you grow up? A football player? Or are you planning to take over the business?"

Joey gave her the finger. They'd had that discussion before. "I want to be a writer. USC would be better for that, but to my dad, a writer is even worse than a movie star. He doesn't think it's a real job unless you're sweating."

"So, your big problem is deciding between a free education in California or Arizona?" Mallory arched her eyebrows, suggesting that was the kind of problem most people would love to have. Then she grinned and said, "You want to come over to my place for a glass of ice tea?"

"Uh . . ." Joey stared down at his feet. Mallory was cool, but he couldn't stand her father. Donny Stewart worked at Blade Engine as a mechanic doing engine installs. He thought he was some kind of comedian. He was always telling stupid, dirty jokes and his delivery sucked. He acted like Joey was disrespecting him for not laughing his ass off. Joey knew Stewart resented him because he was the boss's kid. Donny Stewart was an all-around creepy guy.

"My dad's running the install center today." Mallory said. "He won't be home for two hours."

"Ice tea sounds great," Joey said.

Joey sat down on the yoga mat on Mallory's screened porch. She brought out two glasses of ice tea and handed one to him. "This is my workout studio," she said. "You okay with the floor? I can get you a chair."

"No, this is good." He took a gulp. "Thanks. I really sucked today."

"You were definitely not Joey Blade, All-American."

Joey shook his head. "It's Solita's fault. She came home today from ASU with her latest boyfriend. I'm pretty sure he's gay. We all sit down for a special family lunch and she tells me how cool it is that I'm visiting USC next weekend. She wasn't supposed to blab that because I haven't told Dutch yet. She did it just to get a rise out of him. She's been fighting with him all her life."

"Solita's cool. I wish I had a sister who could tell my old man to go fuck himself."

Joey shifted his position, trying to get comfortable. "I love Solita, but she makes it so difficult. When Dutch heard about USC he blew a gasket. Told Solita that no kid of his is attending some granola-munching fag school. I thought her boyfriend was going to faint. So then Mom got angry and told Dutch to watch his language. Callie Blade's the only person on earth who can stop Dutch in his tracks. He got all contrite and told the boyfriend that there was nothing wrong with granola."

Mallory laughed so hard she snorted tea through her nose. "Your family meals sound like so much fun."

"After dinner, Dutch drags me into his office and starts giving me the hard sell. Telling me all the reasons I should go to U of A. "Closer to home he says." Joey shuddered. "That's not a good reason. He tries to tell me it has a better football program, but he knows that's not even close to true. So then he tries the career angle. Tells me I'll make better connections. But that's only true if my career is working for Blade Engine, and that's never going to happen. So then – get this – he says the weather is better. The weather! Can you believe that?" Joey took another gulp of ice tea. "I say, 'The weather, Dad, come on.' And he says 'It's a dry heat. Very comfortable.'"

Mallory laughed again. "Dry heat. Your dad's a trip."

"He even tries reason. Says the Wildcats need me. Says I'll get lost in the shuffle cause USC drafts ten tailbacks a year. But the USC recruiter compared me to Marcus Allen. Probably because we're both six two and neither of us are speedsters. Not like O.J. Hah! They never talk about O.J. That's what happens when you fuck up as badly as he did. Anyway, Dutch wants me to go down to Tucson for a meet and greet next Saturday and I want to go to that USC game." Joey paused to catch his breath.

Mallory giggled.

"What's so funny?" Joey asked.

She set her ice tea on the floor and cupped his face in her hands. "You talk too much." Then she tongue-kissed him. Joey's heart raced. He had ignored most of the stories, but he knew Mallory had a reputation.

He slipped his hands under her T-shirt as she tugged down his cargo shorts. He unsnapped her shorts and she wiggled out of them. They lay together on the mat, their naked bodies pressed together. It was really going to happen.

Joey tried not to show how nervous he was. He rolled on top. He wasn't sure how to proceed, but Mallory helped him. Joey came in ten seconds.

"Sorry," he said, embarrassed.

Mallory was cool. "That's okay. Have another ice tea and I'll bet you'll be ready for another round."

He was, and it was much better the second time. Afterward, they spooned on the yoga mat. Joey cupped her breasts and tried to think of something to say, but he'd already talked too much and he couldn't think of anything that wasn't lame so he kept his mouth shut.

Mallory scrunched around and rolled on top of him, pinning him to the mat. "You don't have to say anything, Joey. That was nice."

"Nice?" Joey said. He was hoping for more than nice.

"Nice is good."

As he was heading out the door, Mallory wrapped her arms around him again. "I think your father is right."

"About what?"

"Arizona. That's where you should go."

"Why?"

"Because then we could do this again. Have more nice times." She giggled and Joey had to admit it sounded appealing.

TWO

SIX WEEKS LATER

8 p.m. – Friday – December 31, 1999
Shadow Mountain High School – Phoenix, Arizona

Joey parked Dutch's pickup in the teacher's parking lot at the far corner of the school property. The millennium celebration bonfire wasn't an official school event so there would be no teachers using the lot tonight. All the other high school kids were parking in the visitor's lot next to the football field, but Joey didn't want to park there with this ugly truck and its stupid BLADE ENGINE & CRANKSHAFT logo plastered on the doors.

The little S-10 was a '93 with over six hundred thousand miles on it. The engine was tired—a Corolla passed him on the way over—and the cabin stunk. Even after Joey hung three New Car Scent tree deodorizers on the rearview and under the visors it still carried the smell of dried sweat, cigarette smoke, and fast food from the three dozen drivers who had used it to deliver parts over the last seven years. Blade Engine was only using it now for emergency deliveries, so his dad let him drive it on the weekends. It was most definitely not a cool ride, but better than walking.

Wendy Chang, Joey's new girlfriend, refused to ride in it. "It's disgusting, Joey. We'll take my car to the party." Wendy's father was some big-time lawyer. For her seventeenth birthday, he had given her a '99 Infiniti J—a lady car for sure—but a nice ride. He had met Wendy at a party at Lookout Mountain the weekend after Thanksgiving – the week after he had been with Mallory. He hadn't seen Mallory since that day, and he never saw her in school. He felt like he should say something to her about Wendy, but he wasn't sure what.

Joey walked past the tennis courts and entered the football field at the north end. He hadn't been on the field since the big game with Apache Junction. This morning he had called Coach Meyer at the University of Arizona and told him he was signing the letter of intent and would be heading to Tucson in the fall. He couldn't go against his father's wishes. Tomorrow he would let USC know of his decision.

Today was his eighteenth birthday. He was officially an adult. A man with a full-ride scholarship. Even Wendy would be impressed. A sex breakthrough was definitely a possibility tonight. Thanks to Mallory, he wasn't totally inexperienced. He felt a little guilty that he was grateful for that.

The bonfire was being built just beyond the south end zone near the pole vault pit. Lua Tupola pulled up towing a hay wagon loaded with wood and scrub brush. Lua was a giant. Six foot four, two hundred forty pounds. As nose tackle, he anchored the Shadow Mountain Matadors' defensive line. Lua had corralled a bunch of younger kids to unload the wagon. A swarm of them were streaming from the wagon carrying armloads of wood and brush for the fire.

Wendy, with her legs tucked, was perched on a hay bale. She was wearing white jeans and a powder-blue cashmere sweater. Her long black hair was gathered into a silky ponytail and designer sunglasses wrapped the top of her head like a tiara. She reminded Joey of one of those Disney princesses, except for the joint she was smoking. She spotted Joey and gave a little finger wave with a coy smile he hadn't figured out how to read yet. TJ Grimes, her pot supplier, sat next to her on the bale holding a pint of Southern Comfort.

TJ was a scrawny, freckle-faced redhead with greasy long hair. He moved to Phoenix a year ago and lived with his older brother, who everyone said was a serious drug dealer. He was a year behind them in school and had the hots for Wendy.

"Joey!" TJ jumped up from the bale. "Just keeping it warm for you, buddy. Have a seat."

Joey ignored TJ and sat down next to Wendy. "Sorry I'm late. You know how my mom is."

Wendy draped her arms around Joey's neck and ran her fingers through his hair. "I would die for those caramel curls." She feathered a kiss on his neck and whispered in his ear,

"I was worried that you'd stood me up on your birthday."

"Dude, it's your birthday?" A trickle of a Southern Comfort slipped down TJ's chin. "You're eighteen? Congratulations." He held out his pint. "Take a hit. Get your birthday buzz started."

"No thanks," Joey said. He glared at TJ, hoping he would get the message to disappear, but the kid was too drunk to notice.

Lua was walking toward them. The giant Samoan moved with the grace of a big cat. "Happy Birthday, Joey Blade. Come here, brother." Lua's voice, like his walk, was smooth and light and soft. He held his arms opened wide. Joey couldn't help but smile when Lua was around.

Joey stood up and braced himself. "Don't hurt me, man."

Lua wrapped his meaty arms around Joey and lifted him off the ground. "Don't be a pussy, Blade." He gently set Joey back on his feet and turned to TJ. "Hey, Grimes, I hear you got good weed."

"Absolutely. Primo Mexican Red."

Lua scowled. "Don't shine me, shitbird."

TJ rubbed his hands together. "It's true. I got a connection in Rocky Point. I'll give you a dime bag for five bucks. New customer special."

Wendy handed her joint to Lua. "Try it, Lulu. It's good stuff."

Lua took a deep hit. The joint disappeared between Lua's huge thumb and forefinger. "That's tight," he said, his eyes watering. "You got a bag in your little purse there?"

TJ clutched his fanny pack protectively. "No, I don't carry. It's in my car."

"Okay. I'll take two of those discount dime bags."

TJ screwed up his face to complain, but then thought better of it. "Okay, ten bucks. Special favor. Don't tell no one. Come with me. It's in my car."

Lua had turned to look at the crew building the fire. He shouted at the group, "Hey, dipshits, start with the small stuff." The fire was more smoke than flame.

"Come on. I got lighter fluid," TJ said.

Lua scowled. "Bring it to me. I gotta go help those numbnuts before they smoke us all out."

TJ shrugged and started to settle down next to Wendy on the hay bale. "You better get Lua his grass before he throws you on the fire," Joey said.

"You don't want to disappoint a new customer," Wendy said.

TJ was all attention when Wendy acknowledged his existence. "Yeah. You're right, Wendy. I'll be right back."

He did a quick about-face and stumbled into a face plant. The pint of Southern Comfort bounced out of his hand. "Goddammit." He jumped up and grabbed the bottle. It was unbroken, but most of the whiskey was gone. He took one last pull from the bottle and tossed it aside. "Fucking Lua. Screw's me on the price and now he wants free delivery." When he saw Joey staring at him, he blanched. "Just kidding, man. Me and Lua—we're cool."

Joey stared at him walking away. "Grimes is too stupid to be a drug dealer."

"I know," Wendy said. "But he does have good weed." She kissed him with feeling. "Happy birthday, babe."

Her lips tasted faintly of strawberries and Joey's heart raced as her tongue probed teasingly. He tried to prolong the kiss, but she pulled back. "Hold that thought. I have to talk to Lawrence about something. It won't take long." Lawrence Darville was Wendy's old boyfriend. She pushed herself up from the bale and kissed him again. "Keep an eye on the fire." She grinned as if running off to talk to her ex-boyfriend was a big joke.

Darville had pulled into the student lot in his new midnight-blue Toyota Tacoma. A super cool ride. A model year 2000. Fresh from the factory. He stood in the bed of his pickup wearing a leather bomber jacket looking disinterestedly at the kids building the bonfire. With his mop of white-blond hair and his pretty face, he looked like a young David Bowie. When Wendy approached, he jumped down and climbed into the cab. Wendy got in the truck.

Damn thing probably still had a real new car smell. Joey thought about his piece-of-shit S-10 with its sweat and taco smells and its duct-taped upholstery. He didn't blame Wendy for not wanting to ride in it.

Wendy and Darville had been on and off all throughout high school. Even after she dumped Darville and started dating Joey, there were more than a few times when she had run off to talk to him about something. Joey didn't really care. He never expected to date someone like Wendy. He wasn't in her league. She was a snob, but she was beautiful. Exotic. She had a right to be stuck up. She was a preppy, like Darville, but smart like all the Asians. She applied to Harvard and didn't even bother with a backup school. Her bigshot old man told her there was no need to. Harvard was his school. End of story.

Joey Blade wasn't part of her long-term plan, but that was okay with Joey. Wendy would be a perfect end-of-the-school-year girlfriend. In the fall she'd go east and Joey would head down to Tucson. He didn't need to hassle her if she wanted to gossip with Mr. Too Cool. After the bonfire, some of Wendy's preppy friends were having a party at Darville's home. His parents were in Cabo for the New Year. Joey would have preferred making out over at Squaw Peak.

It was a typical Phoenix winter night. Once the sun went down the temperature dropped quickly. Lua had managed to organize the fire-builders and the dark clear sky was now dotted with sparks. Joey shivered. He should have worn something more than his flannel shirt, but all he had was his varsity letter jacket. He was so proud of that jacket when he earned it as a freshman, but now he felt silly wearing it. Maybe that was Wendy's influence. She wasn't into sports. The wind was whipping up and he was getting cold. He was about to get up and move closer to the fire when he spotted Mallory walking toward him.

Damn.

When he started dating Wendy, Joey forgot about everything else.

He should have at least called Mallory. Now as she headed toward him, he felt like a shit.

Mallory looked different. Serious. She sat down on the bale next to him. Close. The heat of her body took the edge off the chill Joey was feeling.

"I saw your girlfriend leave you to go talk to her old boyfriend." She was staring at the fire, not looking at him.

"Yeah. They're still friends."

Like you and me. We're still friends, right?

She was still staring at the fire. Not looking at him. "I'm pregnant."

A simple declaration, delivered as information, not an accusation.

Joey's throat tightened, like some invisible specter was choking him. Even if he had known what he wanted to say, he wouldn't have been able to get the words out. He hesitantly lifted his hand and covered Mallory's hand that was resting on her thigh. "Uh . . . what . . ."

Mallory flipped her hand over and squeezed his hand. "I'm keeping the baby. I don't want anything from you. I'm not telling anyone that you're the father. I just wanted to let you know. You have a right."

A father. A baby. . "You . . . you have to tell someone," he said. "I can help."

Mallory jumped up from the bale. "If you tell your parents, my father will find out and he will make trouble."

"Are you sure?"

Mallory looked fierce, not angry. "He's an evil man," she said. Her voice level, but determined. "I will never tell him. Now go enjoy your bonfire. And your beautiful girlfriend. Everything will be fine." She turned and walked quickly away toward the parking lot without giving Joey a chance to say anything more.

THREE

8:30 p.m. – Friday – December 31, 1999
Shadow Mountain High School – Phoenix, Arizona

Joey watched Mallory walk away. He tried to gather his thoughts. Everything wasn't going to be fine, that much he could figure out. It was hard to breathe, like the wind had been knocked out of him by a blindside tackle.

His father would go ballistic.

Dutch had been giving Joey sex lectures since he was twelve years old. "Don't be thinking with your little head, Joey. Get a girl pregnant and you can kiss your fancy dreams good-bye."

No one knew he had been with Mallory, but there was no way that this would stay a secret.

A baby? He shouldn't be thinking about himself or worrying about what his father would say. He knew he was being selfish. Mallory was having a baby, *his* baby. How could that be possible? Who would take care of the kid? It couldn't just be Mallory. He would have to help her. With what? Money? Changing diapers? What would happen when he went off to college? Would this fuck up his chances to get a scholarship?

Joey kicked himself again for making this about him. The wind picked up and now he was shivering for real. Mallory's news drained all the warmth from his body.

The burst of wind stoked the bonfire's flames, and something in the pile of burning logs and brush exploded. There was a chorus of screams as the kids circling the fire retreated. Then, an ungodly howl, as TJ burst out of the crowd running madly toward the parking lot, his jeans and hoodie on fire. Lua chased after him, but TJ was pulling away.

Joey leaped off the bale and raced toward TJ.

"He spilled lighter fluid on his pants!" Lua shouted as Joey raced passed him.

Joey unbuttoned his shirt and peeled it off as he ran down the sidewalk that flanked the parking lot. TJ was careening through the lot, running around cars, changing directions like a broken-field runner. He was faster than Joey expected. They were halfway across the parking lot before Joey pulled even with him. Joey wrapped his shirt around his hands and was about to grab TJ when he turned sharply to avoid a parked car and ran smack into Joey. TJ went down like a cornerback leveled by a pulling guard.

Joey quickly patted out the flames with his shirt. TJ's baggy ghetto jeans and his black hoodie were trashed, but they had protected him. He wasn't burned, just scared shitless. He lay on the ground whimpering, his face pressed into the asphalt.

"You're okay, Grimes. The fire's out."

TJ stopped crying and covered his head with his hands. "How bad is it, Joey? I can't look."

A ghostlike cloud of smoke hovered over TJ as if his soul had left his body. There were scorch marks on his jeans and hoodie. "Good thing you were wearing those baggy ass pants," Joey said. "With Wranglers your skinny butt would have burned for sure."

Lua ran up to them, gasping. "Nice tackle, Joey. You might make it on the kickoff team next year."

Joey gave him a look. "Kickoff team is for crazy fuckers like you." He slipped his shirt back on and brushed off his jeans.

TJ sat on the ground with his arms around his knees as he inspected his smoldering jeans and rearranged his fanny pack so it was in front instead of on his ass. "Damn. You saved my life, Joey. You should get a medal."

Lua scoffed. "This is Sheriff Joe Arpaio country. That ol' man gives medals for killing skanky drug dealers. Not saving them."

TJ's face screwed up like he was about to cry. "I ain't a—"

Another explosion from the fire. This time a fireball of debris enveloped the athletic shed next to the field. The kids who had been watching Joey run down TJ now started racing in full-bore panic mode back to their cars in the parking lot.

"Jesus Christ," Lua said. "That fire's out of control. I gotta get my fucking truck out of there. You guys better book; the law will be here soon."

Thick black smoke billowed from the shed as the tarpaper roof ignited.

TJ moaned as he got to his feet. "My hands are shaking. I can't drive like this. Can you give me a ride, Joey?"

Darville's truck was rumbling down the center of the parking lot headed for them. He stopped and Wendy jumped out. "Babe, are you okay? That was crazy brave." She hugged Joey and combed her fingers through his hair, rearranging it. "There. That's better."

"Hey, I was the one on goddamn fire," TJ whined.

Wendy stared at him with disgust. "You're a fucking idiot."

The piercing wail of a siren could be heard coming from Shea Boulevard. A firetruck rumbled into the school parking lot, bounded over the curb, and headed down the track that ran adjacent to the football field. The bonfire engulfed the shed and was closing in on the bus garage.

"Wendy! We need to get out of here!" Darville said, his cool façade cracking.

"He's right," TJ said as he dragged his smoky ass into the pickup bed. "Let's get out of here before the cops show up."

Wendy looked at Lawrence and then Joey. "Can you get in the

back with TJ to make sure he doesn't do something even more stupid?" She nuzzled his neck and ran her hands under his shirt. "Okay?" She gazed up at him. Her dark eyes mysterious and inviting. Her hands warm on his chest.

Joey felt himself grinning like a fool. He gave her ass a quick squeeze. "No problem," he said. He put his hands on the side of the pickup and vaulted cleanly into the truck bed. It was a showoff move.

Darville revved the truck engine. Two metro cop cars pulled in behind the fire truck and blocked the exit to the parking lot so Darville turned his truck around and headed across the baseball field that was just north of the football field. The powerful Tacoma rumbled across the infield, and Joey clung desperately to the sidewall to keep from being bounced out of the truck. As Darville slowed down to turn onto Thirtieth Street, Joey scrambled to the front of the truck bed and leaned back against the cab wall. He was directly behind Darville and could see Wendy in the passenger seat. Joey braced himself as the big truck fishtailed into the northbound lanes. "Fuck!" TJ yelled. He lost his grip on the sidewall and rolled across the truck bed. A handgun clattered out of his fanny pack. Joey reached over and picked it up. He looked over at TJ. "What the fuck, Grimes?"

TJ crawled over and sat next to Joey. "Protection," he said. He reached for the gun. "Fuckers are always trying to rip me off."

Joey handed him the gun. "Keep it out of sight."

"Sure thing, boss. I ain't stupid."

Darville turned on to Cholla Street. He took the ramp for Highway 51, the new Squaw Peak Parkway, heading north. The truck rode smooth as glass on the new road. He pulled into the HOV lane. The cars in the other two lanes were a blur of lights and chrome as the Tacoma rocketed past them.

"Fucking rich boy drives like a maniac," TJ said, his teeth clenched. The wind was whipping his scraggly long hair into his face.

Joey didn't respond. Darville was racing to his home in north Scottsdale. His New Year's Eve party was still on. Joey had been all hot for a sex breakthrough with Wendy, figuring that party would be a great opportunity, but now he just wanted to go home and figure out what to do about Mallory.

TJ scrunched low in the truck bed and shook his hair out of his face. "Sort of sucks, you sitting back here while that prissy, rich boy gets to sit up there with your girl."

Joey ignored him, hoping TJ would shut up, but he knew that wasn't likely.

"Of course, you being a big football hero, I guess you get pussy anytime you want. You fuck Wendy yet? I hear she's a screamer."

"Grimes?"

"What?"

"Shut the fuck up."

TJ nodded. like Joey had told him he had something in his teeth. "Sure thing. I hear ya." He raked his hands through his singed hair again. "Holy shit!" he shouted, pointing at a black Silverado that was closing fast on them.

The Silverado was inches from the Tacoma rear bumper when it swerved out of the HOV lane. The driver was wearing a straw cowboy hat and had a beefy tattooed arm. As he passed them, he shouted, "Hey faggots! Piss in your pants?"

Darville punched the truck into overdrive and closed fast on the Silverado. Joey glanced at Wendy. She was leaning forward, engaged, her face animated. This was her kind of sport. They came up fast on the Silverado, inches from their bumper, and then Darville gunned it past them on the right side.

TJ flipped off the two men in the Silverado as the Tacoma sped past them. "Piss on this, you chickenshit motherfuckers!"

Joey stared down at the truck floor, holding his head between his hands. This was stupid and dangerous. As soon as they got to Darville's house, he would call his dad and get a ride home. He didn't care what Wendy or Darville or any of their rich friends thought.

The Silverado wasn't done. As they sped past, the tattooed dude hurled his beer can at the truck. It hit the top of the cab splattering TJ and Joey. It wasn't beer, it was piss.

"Motherfucker!" TJ unzipped his fanny pack and pulled out the handgun as he slithered over to the driver's side of the truck.

"TJ! Put that gun away!" Joey screamed.

TJ pulled himself up behind the cab like he was driving a chariot. With a madman grin, he peered over the top of the cab and, holding the gun with both hands, aimed at the Silverado.

Joey grabbed TJ by his hoodie and whipped him to the truck bed. TJ lost his grip on the gun and it bounced toward the tailgate.

"You stupid fuck!" Joey slammed TJ's head into the truck bed.

The gun rattled against the tailgate, and as Joey stretched to grab it, Darville swerved the truck into the passing lane, rolling Joey into the wall of the truck bed.

The gun bounced back into the middle, and TJ grabbed it just as Darville pulled even with the Silverado. "Fuck you!" He fired wildly at the Silverado as Darville rocketed past them. The first two shots missed, but the third shot blew out the windshield. The Silverado fish-tailed, skidding into the HOV lane and then back across the highway. The driver slammed on the brakes as the truck skidded off the road, with a plume of black smoke trailing from the rear tires. The truck flattened a highway sign and did a 180, coming to a stop facing the wrong direction on the shoulder of Highway 51.

Joey wrestled TJ to the floor of the truck. He didn't resist as Joey ripped the gun from his hand. "Oh my God! What did you do?" Joey screamed as he kneeled over TJ, holding his gun. He stared down the road. A police car was closing fast, lights flashing and siren blaring.

"Throw the gun away!" Wendy had slid open the truck cab window. Her eyes were wide, frightened.

Darville slipped in behind a U-Haul van that was driving well below the speed limit.

"Jesus Christ, Joey!" Wendy screamed. "Throw it away. Now!"

Joey looked from Wendy to TJ, who remained curled up in a fetal position, and then to the police car in hot pursuit. As they crossed over the Arizona Canal, Joey flung the handgun toward the canal as if he was lobbing a grenade. He couldn't see where it landed.

Wendy slammed shut the cab window and leaned forward, her head practically resting on the dashboard as she pulled out her cell phone. Over the sound of the traffic rushing by and the growing din of the police siren Joey could hear the desperation in her voice.

"—on the Squaw Peak. Just past the canal," she said. She took a quick peek back at Joey and then continued in sort of a shout whisper. "Yes, he's here." She paused. "Okay, Daddy. I won't. I promise. Tell Tommy to hurry."

Darville brought the truck to a stop on the shoulder of the highway. The high beams on the car were blinding and the whoop-whoop-whoop of the siren deafening. Joey knelt down in the truck next to TJ, who was face down hugging the floor of the truck. He gave himself a pep talk. *Stay calm. No sudden movements. Keep your mouth shut*

The siren stopped and the loudspeaker on top of the squad car squawked. "Turn off the engine." The driver, a tall Hispanic with a weightlifter build, stepped out of the car holding a handset in one hand and a .38 police special in the other. As he ducked his head to talk to his partner who was still in the vehicle, TJ slipped over the passenger side of the truck bed, and, with surprising athleticism, scaled the chain-link fence that lined the highway and disappeared into the night.

The DPS trooper appeared not to have noticed TJ's escape. "Keep your hands on the wheel where I can see them!" he said.

Joey's heart pounded. The trooper was focused on Darville and hadn't even noticed him. Joey didn't want to raise his hands suddenly and startle him.

"Hey, you in the back," the big trooper said with a Mexican accent. "Put your hands on your head!"

His partner stepped out of the car. He was young. Blonde. Even with his Mountie hat he appeared short and unthreatening. He was tugging on his gun but it was stuck in the holster. His partner, annoyed, was about to say something when the younger trooper figured out that he needed to unsnap the flap holding the gun in place. He braced his arm on the top of the open car door and aimed his gun at Joey. His face was screwed up with concentration, lips pressed tight, as he struggled to keep the gun steady. "Facedown!" the trooper yelled, his voice breaking.

His nervousness scared Joey more than the gun. There was nothing about Joey Blade that should make a cop nervous. Joey laid facedown in the truck and interlaced his fingers behind his head, like he'd seen it done on a dozen cop shows.

"Secure him," the lead trooper said as he marched up to the driver's window.

Joey kept his face buried in the floor of the truck bed. He tried not to move a muscle. He heard the crunch of gravel as the rookie trooper approached the truck.

"Uh, Luis, how do I . . .?" The kid's voice cracked again. He wasn't tall enough to reach Joey in the middle of the truck bed. Joey thought about scootching closer so he could reach over, but decided he better not move.

"Make him sit on the edge of the truck wall. Then cuff him and take his ID."

The rookie pounded the wall of the pickup. "Sit here!" he said. He had a fake deep voice and sounded like a kid imitating an adult. "Hands behind your back."

Joey crawled on his knees and sat down. He put his hands behind his back and the trooper slipped a nylon cord over one wrist and then the other and pulled them tight.

"Anything sharp in your pants pocket?" the rookie asked.

"No sir."

He tugged Joey's wallet from his jeans pocket and removed Joey's license. He put the wallet back in Joey's shirt pocket.

"Leave him there and give me his ID. Get the girl out and curb her," the trooper named Luis said.

The boy trooper opened the passenger door. "Step down, ma'am."

"Of course," Wendy said. She jumped down from the truck, smiling. No sign of the desperation she had shown moments ago. Joey had seen that smile before. "I'm so sorry. This is all a misunderstanding. Hitchhikers, you know?"

Hitchhikers? "I'm not a hitch—"

"Keep your mouth shut." The rookie flashed Joey his I'm-in-charge look. "You talk when I tell you to." He led Wendy ten yards in front of the truck and told her to sit on the ground. Joey couldn't hear what she was saying, but she continued to talk to the boy, who was nodding his head like he understood her.

Trooper Luis asked Darville for his license and registration. He took them and the car keys and Joey's license and headed back to his squad car. Wendy was smiling and then she laughed at something the boy trooper said. It reminded Joey of how she acted when they first met.

As Joey sat on the wall of the pickup with his hands cuffed behind him, he noticed cars slowing as they passed to check out who was getting busted. Hitchhiker? Wendy must have panicked. She had to be explaining to that cop that Joey wasn't shooting at anyone.

Joey's shoulders throbbed and his back ached. He wanted to shift his position, but he didn't want to upset Wendy's new friend. The young trooper had been talking to her for at least ten minutes. She just kept smiling and giggling like she was on a date.

What was taking that cop so long? Does Darville have outstanding tickets?

Another DPS patrol car pulled up behind the first and then a black Lexus rolled slowly past and parked in front of the Silverado. A stubby, middle-aged white man in a polo shirt and dark pants got out and walked over to Wendy. He shook hands with the rookie and then he pointed to his car. Wendy, who hadn't been cuffed, strolled nonchalantly over to the Lexus and slid into the back seat.

That was a good sign. Joey got a knot in his stomach as he thought about having to call his dad to come pick him up. But at least this clusterfuck of a day would be over. This was the worst birthday of all time.

Luis was talking with the other two troopers and now they were all marching over toward Joey.

"Get him down from there," Luis said.

They each grabbed him by the arm and lifted him out of the truck.

Luis's walkie-talkie squawked. "Adam Twelve, do you copy?"

"Twelve. Copy. Go ahead."

"Adam Eight found the gun. Break . . ."

"Go ahead."

"Kick the juvies. Bring in your party. Break . . ."

"Copy that. On our way. Ten-four."

Luis addressed the other two cops. "Tell Sidney he can take off now. I'll transport Blade."

Joey wondered how they knew his name and then he remembered the license.

Luis waved to his partner. "Come on, Randy. We gotta roll." He tightened his grip on Joey's arm.

"Wait a minute. I didn't—"

"Save your breath. Big mistake shooting at a cop. They found the gun so you are fucked."

He marched Joey to the squad car and pushed him, not roughly, but not gently either, into the backseat. With his hands behind his back, it was difficult to sit.

Joey had a sinking feeling. *Those cowboys were cops?*

"I didn't shoot anyone," he said. "Ask Wendy. Or Darville. They'll tell you."

"Shut up, kid. I've heard it all before."

They pulled onto the highway with the lights flashing. Joey would not be home for his birthday.

FOUR

10:45 p.m. – Friday – December 31, 1999
Durango Jail – Phoenix, Arizona

I f you're arrested in Maricopa County for anything from public drunkenness to murder, the police—or in Joey's case the Arizona DPS—take you to the Durango jail on Fourth Avenue for intake processing. If the system is running smoothly, intake can be completed in less than two hours. On December 31, 1999, intake was not running smoothly.

Chaos reigned. It's always crazy on New Year's Eve, but on the millennium, it was a thousand times crazier. The parking lot was full, and cop cars were double-parked up and down the driveway to the station.

The DPS officer stared at Joey in the backseat like it was his fault everyone had gone crazy. "You get him processed, Randy," he said to his partner. "I'll get us coffee. Maybe it will clear up by the time I get back."

Randy escorted Joey into the station. "Won't see him for an hour," he said.

Joey felt like he'd been knocked out and was still trying to figure out what hit him. Wendy and Darville should have been able to straighten everything out. "Didn't my girlfriend tell you I didn't shoot at anybody?"

"Girlfriend? You were in the back of the truck. She said you hitched a ride." He grinned like he had made some kind of special connection to her.

Hitched a ride? Why would she say that? Joey wouldn't even have been in the truck bed if Wendy hadn't asked him. If Joey hadn't stopped TJ, the fool might have actually shot those cops. And what were those cops doing, street-racing on the Squaw Peak?

They stepped through the door and it was like waiting in the crowd for the doors to open for the Smash Mouth concert last month. Only here, half the crowd didn't really want to go in.

"Oh geez," Randy said. "Is there a line? There should be an intake officer somewhere." He craned his neck to see around the crowd.

"I think that's the end of the line," Joey said, nodding toward a big biker dude and his escort. What appeared to be a random crowd was actually a line that snaked from one end of the reception area to the other and back at least four times. It ended at a counter where a beleaguered officer was logging in a drunk who could barely stand.

"Golly, this will take forever," Randy said. He shrugged. "My shift ends in a couple hours. Guess I'll make some overtime."

"Don't I get a phone call?" Joey said. His shoulder sockets throbbed. Being handcuffed was a lot more uncomfortable than it looked on television.

Randy shook his head. "You don't get anything until you get put in the system."

An hour later they were still at least an hour away from the intake desk. Finally, another cop came out from behind the counter with a box of plastic bags and a roll of masking tape. He went down the line and handed each escort cop a plastic bag and a six-inch strip of masking tape.

"Put his personal effects in the bag, rip the tape in two pieces and put one tape on the bag and one on his wrist and write his name on the tape. Then take him over to G40."

Joey handed Randy his wallet, watch, truck keys, and high school ring. Randy wrapped the tape on Joey's wrist and then with schoolboy perfect penmanship wrote out his name: JOSEPH BLADE. He marched Joey across the room to the staircase. "G40's on the second floor," he said.

"What about my phone call?" Joey asked.

Randy's face twisted into a frown and he straightened up like he was trying to make himself taller, more in charge. "You still aren't officially processed."

A portly correctional officer who resembled the fat Elvis, but with rust-red hair was sitting on a tall stool at the door to G40 with a clipboard. "Name?" he said, barely looking up from his clipboard.

"Blade, Joseph," Randy said.

The guard wrote the name on his sheet. "Forty-three dot five nine eight. Write it on his wrist tape," he said to Randy, his voice weary. "Put that number on your O-43 so we know who we're holding."

He cut the nylon cuffs off Joey and pointed into the room. "Find a place to sit. It'll be awhile."

Joey glanced over his shoulder at Randy, but the rookie was already walking away. G40 was a rectangular room about the size of the Shadow Mountain girls' gym. When the new century arrived, Joey Blade was sitting cross-legged in the center of the room. The side walls of the room were lined with benches, but those were all occupied by Mexican and Chicano gang members. The far wall was lined with garbage cans that reeked of vomit and piss. In the front of the room, four guards leaned against the wall. They were all sloppy big – not muscle big like Luis the DPS trooper. None of them were happy to be working in G40 on New Year's Eve. Most of the room, other than the gangbangers, was occupied by drunks. Dirt-tanned, rail-thin, scraggly-haired men, like the dozens Joey saw every day panhandling on the street corners with cardboard signs asking for work.

Joey parked himself in the center of the room, equal distance from the gangs, the stink of the garbage cans, and the disinterested guards.

All of sudden, some of the gang members stood up and started shouting. "*Diez, nueve, ocho, siete, seis, cinco, cuatro, tres, dos, uno! ¡Feliz año nuevo, hijo de puta! ¡El mundo no terminó,* bitch!"

New Year's! Joey instinctively glanced at his wrist, but all that was there was his masking tape bracelet. He scanned the room. Over the door where he entered, there was an old-fashioned clock like in grade school with a white face and large black numerals. It was one minute past twelve. The world hadn't ended like some of the wack jobs had been predicting, but the new century was definitely not starting out the way he planned.

The traffic into the room slowed to a trickle. At ten minutes past the hour, a thirty-something white man in a blue blazer and a white dress shirt stumbled into the room, wide-eyed and looking like he was afraid to breathe. His head swiveled around until he saw one of the guards. He walked toward him, but the guard brandished his Billy club and pointed to the room. "Sit the fuck down, turkey. Over there!" He pointed in Joey's direction.

Joey stared down at his Nikes. *Don't come over here. Don't come over here.* This was like being a new kid in school and sitting all by yourself in the cafeteria. The last thing you want is for the school dork to come and sit down with you. *Don't come over here.*

"Mind if I sit down?" Two shiny black loafers appeared in Joey's field of vision.

Joey looked up and shrugged, which the man took as an invitation to sit down.

He extended his hand. "Name's Gordon Smith. Friends call me Smitty."

Joey didn't want to shake his hand, but his father had ingrained that habit in him. "Grip the man's hand like you mean it and look him in the eye. Tell him your name. Repeat his. That way you won't forget it."

"Joey Blade. Nice to meet you, Gordon."

"Smitty. Call me Smitty."

Smitty was nervous as a kitten and he was making Joey nervous. Joey had tried to be as invisible as possible in this room of gang-bangers, drunks, and hot rodders. Gordon's arrival was like someone flashed a spotlight on him.

"They didn't let me make a phone call," said Smitty. "Aren't they supposed to do that? Did you get to make a call? I got caught in one of them damn speed traps. Wasn't even drinking. Cop said I had outstanding tickets. Hell, that ain't no reason to run me in. What'd they get you for, Jimmy?"

"Joey. Speeding." Joey turned away and retied his shoe, hoping Smitty would get the message he didn't want to talk.

"Sorry. I'm terrible with names. Amanda—she's my wife—says it's 'cause I don't listen." He sighed, and his nervous face got even more wrinkly. "She's going to be worried about me." He started fidgeting with his gold cufflinks. Joey wanted to tell him to hide the cufflinks but he was too late.

"Hey, boss, those are pretty. Can I take a look?" One of the gang members was standing over Smitty. He was bony and missing two front teeth, and with his shaved head and jack-o-lantern grin, he could have been mistaken for a goofy kid except that the gang name "Vatos Locos" was tattooed on each arm. The Vatos Locos were a Mexican national gang with a vicious reputation.

Smitty tugged his sports jacket sleeves down to cover the links and he wrapped his arms around himself. His face screwed up tight, like his arm was being twisted.

"I just want to look at them, *jefe*. You think Fernando's a thief?"

Smitty smiled nervously. He popped the cufflink through the buttonhole and handed it to Fernando.

"Sweet. That looks like real gold. Let me see the other one."

Smitty handed him the other cufflink. "My wife gave them to me," he said, like that might make a difference.

"Tell ya what, holmes. I'll hold them for you. Keep 'em safe."

Smitty scrambled to his feet. "No thank you, Jose." He held out his hand.

"Jose? What the fuck, holmes. You think every *mojado* is named Jose?" He closed his hand into a fist, palming the cufflinks.

Every instinct in Joey's body told him to not get involved. But he had a bad habit of ignoring his instincts. He stood up next to Smitty. "Give them back," he said.

Fernando grinned. "Ooooh, Pretty Boy wants to be a hero. Bad place for a hero, holmes."

He started to slip the cufflinks into his jeans pocket, but Joey grabbed his arm and easily pried open his fist and grabbed the cufflinks.

"Big fucking mistake, *nino bonito*," Fernando said, huffing like a cartoon bull getting ready to charge. "That face won't look so pretty when I get done with it."

"I don't want any trouble," Joey said, his voice almost a whisper. He hoped Fernando wouldn't notice that his legs were shaking.

"Let him have them, Jimmy" Smitty said, his voice quavering.

Fernando smiled. "Listen to your friend, Pretty Boy."

Gang members silently surrounded Joey and Smitty.

Joey stared at Fernando, who had his hand out. "Give it up."

Joey clenched his fist and he could feel the gold jewelry pressing into the flesh of his hand. Joey knew he should just give them up—he was in enough trouble—but he was Dutch Blade's son, and the one thing he knew for certain was that he wasn't giving up those goddam cufflinks.

"Joey Blade?" A gangster with a trim goatee and an eye patch was staring at Joey like he knew him. He was lean and muscular and dressed all in black.

"Y-yeah . . . I'm Joey Blade."

"Dutch's kid, right? You're the big football hero." He turned to his gang members and said something in Spanish. And then in a harsh tone he said something to Fernando.

Fernando bowed slightly. "Sorry, man. I didn't know you were familia."

Joey stared at Fernando and then at Eyepatch, trying to figure out what was happening.

"You got balls, Joey Blade. Just like your old man. When you get out, you tell Dutch that Chico Torres had your back." He scowled at Fernando and headed back to the gang bench. Fernando and the other gang members followed him.

Smitty was staring at Joey, his mouth agape.

"Put these away," Joey said. He pressed the cufflinks into Smitty's sweaty hand.

Joey watched Fernando sitting on the bench, apart from the others. "I will tell him," Joey said softly.

FIVE

5 a.m. – Saturday, January 1, 2000
Durango Jail – Phoenix, AZ

An hour after the encounter with Chico and the Vatos Locos gang, Joey was taken to Central Intake for official processing. It wasn't like television. It took four hours for Joey to be fingerprinted, medically examined (the actual exam took less than a minute) and finally escorted by a skinny Black deputy, whose bald head gleamed with sweat, into a stuffy, windowless room in the basement of the jail.

"Sit there," he said. "Someone will be in soon to take your statement."

Joey had given up asking when he could make a phone call. He was tired, hungry and desperately thirsty. "Can I have some water?" he asked.

"Do I look like a fucking waiter? Wait for your interview." The deputy made a note on the clipboard he was carrying and then hung it on the post outside the room. "Don't mess with the furniture," he said as he pulled the door shut.

Joey tried not to think about how thirsty he was. The more he tried to ignore his thirst the more he craved water. He put his head down on the desk and took a deep breath. The desk, the whole room, had a farty smell. He made a list in his head, but he couldn't keep it straight. His mouth was dry. He couldn't spit if he wanted to. He sucked on his forearm, but it didn't help. He was dying of thirst. Finally the doorknob turned, and the door opened slowly. A middle-aged balding guy with a bad comb-over shuffled into the office studying a clipboard.

"Joseph Blade?"

Joey lifted his head off the table. He nodded. "Water." He didn't recognize his own voice. It was a guttural croak. A death rattle.

The man frowned. "Shit. They didn't get you any water?" He quick-stepped out of the room and was back in two minutes with two dixie cups. "Here. It's Phoenix tap water so it sucks, but better than nothing."

Joey gulped down both cups. "Thank you," he said.

The man settled into the chair across the table from Joey. "I'm Lieutenant Carnes. Sorry about them not giving you water. Okay. First I got to read this." He pulled out a bookmark shaped card from his shirt pocket. It was feathered like it had gone through the wash once or twice. "You have the right to remain silent. Anything you say can and will be used against you in a court of law. You have the right to an attorney. If you cannot afford an attorney, one will be provided for you. Do you understand the rights I have just read to you?"

Carnes sounded like Sipowicz on *NYPD Blue*. But he wasn't intimidating like one of those TV cops. He reminded Joey of his guidance counselor, Mr. Coots. Joey nodded his head.

"You have to answer audibly, Joseph."

"Yes. I understand."

"Good. With these rights in mind, do you wish to speak to me?"

"I want to go home," Joey said. His voice almost broke. He took another deep breath.

"Understood. If you want a lawyer, it's going to take some time.

Most lawyers are not too available on New Year's Day. And the legal aid guys are buried. It might be days before you can get one of them. Talk to me now and we might be able to get this all cleared up."

"Okay," he said.

"Joseph, do you go by Joseph?"

"Joey."

Carnes made a note on his clipboard. "Okay, Joey. You are waiving your right to counsel. Is that correct? Sorry for the legal jargon, but we have to do this by the book. You know how the bosses are."

"Yes. I am."

"Good. Just give me a minute." Carnes flipped through the pages that were tacked to the clipboard.

"Okay. What is your birthdate?"

Joey remembered how he thought his birthday had turned to shit when TJ caught fire. That was just the beginning. He should have let that shithead burn. "December 31, 1981."

Carnes made another note and then smiled ruefully. "Wait a minute. Yesterday was your birthday? You just turned eighteen?"

"Yes sir."

"So, you were out celebrating? Joyriding on the Squaw Peak?"

"Uh, no. See, there was a fire and—"

"A fire?"

"It was a bonfire at the school. Uh, Shadow Mountain . . . for the millennium."

Carnes frowned. "Where did you get your gun?"

Joey shook his head. "I don't have a gun."

Carnes scowled as he flipped through the pages of the file. "According to the statement of two undercover police officers, they were fired upon by someone riding in the back of a dark blue Toyota Tacoma. Were you riding in the back of a dark blue Toyota Tacoma on New Year's Eve on the Squaw Peak Parkway?"

"Yes, but I didn't shoot the gun."

Carnes studied the report again. "The officers are certain that the shots came from someone in the back of the truck."

Joey didn't want to be a rat, but he didn't owe TJ anything. "It was TJ who shot at the truck. It was his gun."

"Who is TJ?"

"TJ Grimes. He goes to Shadow Mountain."

Carnes frowned. "He wasn't in the truck when you were stopped. Just the two minors and you."

"He jumped out when Darville stopped the truck."

"There is no report of another person in that truck. Just the two juvies and you. The arresting officer said he saw you try to toss the gun into the canal. Unluckily for you it didn't make it to the canal. The lab will check it for fingerprints on Monday. Will they find your fingerprints on that gun?"

"Yes, but—"

Carnes held up his hand. "Okay. I've got enough." He stood and pulled a set of handcuffs from his jacket pocket. "Joseph Blade, you are under arrest for the attempted murder of a police officer. This is a class A felony, and you will be arraigned later today where you will have an opportunity to enter a plea." He cuffed Joey's hands behind his back and led him out of the cell.

Attempted murder of a police officer. Just when Joey thought things couldn't get any worse, they did.

SIX

7 a.m. – Saturday - January 1, 2000
Durango Jail – Phoenix, AZ

Carnes handed Joey over to the same Black officer who had brought him to the interrogation room. He escorted Joey to a new holding cell with bolted-down metal benches along both walls. He was told to sit down and then the officer handcuffed him to a ring in the wall. There were three other guys in the room, two sleeping drunks and to Joey's dismay, Gordon Smith, who was handcuffed to the opposite wall across from Joey.

He beamed like Joey was an old friend. "Hey Jimmy. We meet again. Didn't get a chance to thank you before. I appreciate what you did. That was a scary proposition. Good thing your old man is connected."

Joey slumped on the bench. He didn't have the energy to respond. He was so tired he couldn't even keep his eyes open. Something awful had just happened. He was being charged with a serious crime. He should be trying to make a plan, figure out what to do, but weariness permeated his body. If he hadn't been chained to the wall, he would have melted into a puddle on the floor. He just wanted to sleep, but Smitty wouldn't shut up.

"Hell of a way to start the new century, isn't it, Jimmy? Did they charge you? They're taking us all to court soon. Judge will kick us. That's what I hear. Got too many to deal with. Man, I could use a good meal."

The new century. Yesterday, before he left for the bonfire, Joey told his father about signing the letter of intent accepting U of A's football scholarship. He had never seen Dutch so happy. In less than twelve hours, Joey had gone from not having a care in the world to so many problems he didn't even know what to do next. He knew this screw up with the shooting would be cleared up soon. Wendy and Darville knew what happened. They must have seen Joey trying to stop TJ from shooting. TJ would be found one way or another. But even if it got cleared up today, the word would get out and it wouldn't be a good way to start his relationship with the Wildcats. He needed to stop fretting about that.

Think about Mallory. She can't take care of a baby all by herself. *Come up with a plan, Joey.* But every time he tried to make his brain focus on Mallory, those words of Chico kept coming back to torment him. "Tell Dutch that Chico Torres had your back." What did his father have to do with the Vatos Locos gang?

Smitty, undeterred by Joey's silence, continued talking. He didn't stop until the guard returned. He rousted the drunks and the four of them were led down the corridor to a courtroom where they joined a dozen other scruffy men on two long benches along the wall. In the front of the courtroom, there was an elevated podium for the judge, tables for the prosecutors and defense attorneys, and a desk for the court stenographer. The bailiff, a large Black man, announced that the court was in session with the Honorable Morris Crenshaw presiding.

Judge Crenshaw was a slight, owlish-looking man with wire-rimmed glasses and a horseshoe of hair on his otherwise bald head. The gallery was half-filled. Joey's chest tightened when he spotted his parents in the back row with the company attorney, Everett Blainey.

His mom, Callie, was wearing her ASU sweatshirt. She had probably been getting ready for her daily hike when they got the call. Callie was lithe and fair-skinned, and with her red hair pulled back into a tight ponytail she could have been mistaken for a college girl. She had been Miss Tucson of 1969. She had met Dutch Blade at the NAPA Auto Show where she was working a booth. Dutch had offered her a job as a customer service rep for Blade Engine, the engine rebuilding company he'd just started. Six months later, they were married. She nodded as she caught Joey's eye, her jaw set with determination.

Blainey was whispering to Dutch, who looked fierce and ready to take on the whole court. Dutch was built like a fire hydrant, and his curly black hair, even at age fifty, showed no traces of gray.

Joey swallowed hard and wiped away a tear that leaked from his right eye. It felt so good to see his folks. They would get him out of this situation and if he could convince Mallory to let him tell his parents, he was confident they would be able to help.

The bailiff called out Smitty's name. He got up from the bench and stepped over to the lectern. The clerk read the charges against him. The judge exhaled wearily and said, "I'm dismissing the charges, Mr. Smith. Pay your outstanding tickets. I don't want to see you in my courtroom again."

"Yes, Your Honor. Thank you, Your Honor." Smitty looked around and the bailiff pointed to the door. A minute later he was out of the courtroom, a free man again.

"State versus Joseph Blade. Charge is attempted murder of a police officer."

The feeling that everything would be okay was erased in an instant. *Attempted murder.* Even knowing he was totally innocent, Joey felt dirty having his name linked to that charge.

The murmuring in the defendant box ceased and the men all turned to look at Joey as he rose uncertainly. A deputy took Joey by the arm and walked him to the lectern.

Judge Crenshaw leaned forward. He was focused. The serious charge grabbed his attention. "Do you have counsel, Mr. Blade?"

Joey felt a hand on his back. "Everett Blainey, representing the defendant. I request a few moments to confer with my client."

Judge Crenshaw smiled. "Don't usually find you in my courtroom,

Everett. By all means, confer. Briefly." He waved his hand and then motioned for the bailiff.

Everett Blainey would come to Blade Engine a few times a year to advise Dutch on legal matters, mostly employee disputes and the occasional customer lawsuit. Dressed in jeans and a polo shirt, Blainey was easygoing and friendly and never let Dutch's temper ruffle him. He once told Joey that his most important job was to protect Dutch from Dutch. But today he was dressed in a black suit, and with his wavy white hair combed, he looked like Hollywood's version of a corporate attorney.

He put his arm around Joey and whispered, "We'll talk later. For now, say nothing unless I tell you to speak. Do you understand? I mean nothing." Blainey showed none of the good, old boy affability he exhibited with his father.

"Okay, Your Honor. We're ready."

"How do you plead, Mr. Blade?"

Blainey whispered to Joey, "Tell them you plead not guilty."

Joey cleared his throat. "Not guilty." He sounded croaky, but his voice didn't break.

"Bail?" The judge addressed his inquiry to the prosecutors' table.

A young man with a military crewcut—he didn't look much older than Joey—stood up as he thumbed through a manila file folder. He was trim, but his suit was too big for him, which made him look even younger than he was. "Your Honor, this is a serious offense. Attacking—"

"Excuse me, son." Judge Crenshaw peered at the prosecutor over his glasses. "Would you please identify yourself for the court?"

The attorney reddened. "Sorry, Your Honor. Lonnie Clark, Assistant District Attorney. Your Honor, attempted murder of an officer of the law is a serious offense. We request the defendant be held without bail."

Joey locked his knees to try to keep his legs from trembling.

Blainey squeezed Joey's neck. "Your Honor, my client has no record. He has strong ties to the community and is a well-known and respected scholar-athlete. He lives with his parents, who are here with him today—his father is a reputable small businessman—and it will become apparent very soon that Mr. Blade is innocent of these charges. We request he be released on his own recognizance."

"Can't try the case today, Mr. Blainey," the judge said. He looked over at the young prosecutor. "While I respect and want to protect our law enforcement officers, I think the defendant is entitled to bail. One hundred thousand dollars. Cash or bond."

Joey groaned. *A hundred thousand dollars?*

"Thank you, Your Honor," Blainey said, as though the judge had extended him a huge favor. He patted Joey on the back.

Joey looked at him, perplexed.

A deputy took Joey by the arm and Blainey lifted his arm off Joey's shoulder.

"Trust me, Joey. Your dad has the resources. We'll have you out of here in an hour. Remember what I said. Don't talk to anyone. About anything. You got that?"

"Got it," Joey said, still trying to process Blainey's words. How would Dutch come up with a hundred-thousand-dollar bail?

SEVEN

Everett Blainey was right about Dutch Blade. He did have the resources. Three hours after they took Joey back to his cell, Dutch and Blainey returned with a one hundred-thousand-dollar cashier's check. It took longer than Blainey promised because Dutch's resources were in a safe deposit box at Thunderbird Bank. Krugerrands. Hundreds of them apparently. Dutch had persuaded his banker to drive in from Scottsdale, open the branch, and then purchase 350 of Dutch's gold coins. Blainey advised Dutch to use a bail bondsman, but Dutch didn't trust those men who had billboards up and down the highway.

They were waiting in the reception area when Joey emerged. Dutch's face lit up when he spotted him, and he gave him the royal Dutch treatment—a crushing bear hug. "Joey. Joey. Joey. Joey." He pressed Joey's head to his chest, and Joey could smell the Aqua Velva. His father must have had a lifetime supply. It brought back memories of when he was a little boy and his dad would hug him when he came home from work. Even after a day working in the sweaty engine factory, Dutch always smelled like Aqua Velva.

"I'm sorry, Dad."

"Wait till you get to the car," Blainey said.

"Where's the truck?" Dutch asked.

The truck. Joey was numb from lack of sleep and food. "Darville's truck?"

"The S-10, Joey. You took it last night, right?"

Finally, his brain slipped back into gear. "It's at Shadow Mountain. I got a ride from—"

Blainey put his hand on Joey's arm. "Later."

Blainey's Fleetwood was parked in front of the jail. He and Dutch sat in the front, and Joey slipped into the back seat. It was a '97 with soft gray leather upholstery. It felt great to sit on something that was cushioned and didn't stink. On the twenty-minute drive to Shadow Mountain, Joey told them everything that happened except for the encounter with Mallory and the altercation with Fernando or Chico's cryptic comment about Dutch. He would ask his father about that in private.

As they pulled into the Shadow Mountain parking lot, the S-10 was the only car left in the lot. TJ's car was gone, so he must have retrieved it after his escape. Joey winced as he remembered the bonfire. The equipment shed was still intact but badly scorched.

"Jesus Christ," Blainey said. "That was some bonfire." A snow fence had been installed around the structure with yellow caution tape at the opening and a Keep Out sign planted in front. He tapped Dutch on the forearm. "I'll call Terry Quinn and get you an appointment. Top-notch criminal lawyer. A Brophy man. You're going to need him."

Dutch grunted. "Okay. Thanks. Come on, Joey, let's get you home. Your mom's got breakfast ready."

They rode in silence until Dutch steered the truck into their driveway. As he turned off the ignition, he looked at Joey, who was struggling to keep his eyes opened. "So that Wendy girl? Will she back your story?"

"It's not a story. I'm telling the truth."

"I don't doubt you. You ain't a storyteller like your sister. But that girlfriend of yours didn't do you any favors with the cops."

Why hadn't Wendy cleared it all up when that cop asked her? What had her father made her promise? She knew it was TJ's gun and she had to know TJ was the shooter. And why did she make that stupid comment about hitchhikers?

"I'm sure she'll tell the truth. Why wouldn't she?"

Dutch shook his head, smiling sadly. "I hope you're right," he said. And then softly like he was praying, "Goddamn, I hope you're right."

Joey just slumped in the seat, almost too tired to open the door.

Dutch gave him a friendly punch in the shoulder. "Come on. I can smell that bacon sizzling."

His mother had prepared a feast for Joey's return. Scrambled eggs, bacon, sausage, biscuits and gravy and her famous hash browns. Joey sat at their kitchen table and inhaled a full plate of eggs, six strips of bacon, and two helpings of hash browns. His mom sat across the table, studying him, her brow furrowed.

As he reached for the orange juice pitcher to refill his glass, she finally spoke.

"Tell me what happened, Joey."

Joey tried to give his mom the condensed version of his story, eliminating Wendy's pot smoking, Lua's weed transaction with TJ, and any mention of Mallory. It was what his coach would have called a tactical mistake. Callie's face flushed and her freckles seemed to glow. She had competed in beauty pageants for ten years, handled all personnel matters for the company for over two decades, and had lived with Dutch since she was nineteen. She had a very well-developed bullshit detector.

"How did the bonfire get out of control?"

"Who is this Grimes character and why did he have a gun?"

"Why were you riding in the back of the truck?"

Her interrogation was ten times tougher than Lieutenant Carnes's. In the end, Joey told her everything, except he again left Mallory out of the picture and didn't mention Chico's comments about Dutch.

"I just need some sleep and then I'll go out and find TJ and this whole thing will be cleared up," Joey said as he pushed back from the table.

Callie shook her head. "That boy's gone with the wind. You need to get your rich, Japanese friend to tell the truth."

"Wendy's Chinese, Mom."

His mother waved him off. "Chinese, Japanese. It's all the same. Her family's got money, and her daddy has a fancy reputation. Mark my words, they're going to be trouble."

Continue reading on Amazon: Dry Heat

ALSO BY LEN JOY

(WWW.LENJOYBOOKS.COM)

"Dry Heat is a page-turner with heart."

NICKOLAS BUTLER, AUTHOR OF *SHOTGUN LOVESONGS* AND *GODSPEED*

"A rousing suspenseful crime drama with memorable characters."

KIRKUS REVIEWS

"Dry Heat exposes in picturesque Phoenix a corrupt level of society, which a young man must navigate using only his own moral compass."

LOUIS P. JONES, AUTHOR *OF INNOCENCE* AND

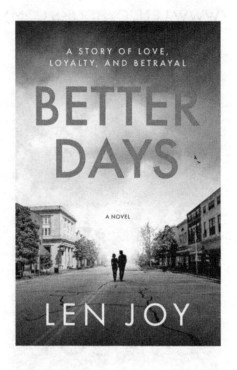

"…an attention-grabbing crime story in….a bighearted wry and tender novel that focuses on love and loyalty."

FOREWORD REVIEWS

"Joy's storytelling prowess is exceptional…. his ability to tell a story so well is what makes it memorable."

US REVIEWS

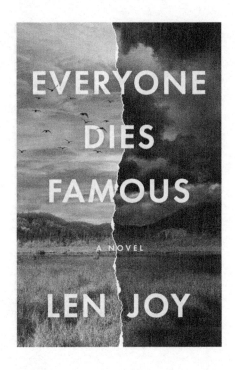

"A clear-eyed examination of how we live in an uncertain world."

KEVIN WILSON, NY TIMES BESTSELLING AUTHOR
OF *NOTHING TO SEE HERE*

"A striking depiction of small-town American at the dawn of the 21st century."

KIRKUS REVIEWS

1st Place Top Shelf Book Awards Fiction

Gold Medal Winner - Readers' Favorite

Finalist - Beverly Hills Book Awards

"Darkly nostalgic story of an American family through good
times and bad. A well-crafted novel that will appeal to sports and
history aficionados."

"...a timeless classic."

ABOUT THE AUTHOR

Len Joy has published four novels and two story collections, all with small presses.

He is an All-American triathlete and competes internationally, representing the United States as part of TEAM USA.

He lives with his wife, Suzanne, in Evanston, Illinois.